WHITE GOLD

MICHEAL E. JIMERSON

WHITE GOLD

A NOVEL

atmosphere press

This novel is dedicated to all those who for thirty years extended to me the awesome privilege of partnering with them in the pursuit of justice. Your commitment honors your lost loved ones and serves as the bedrock to the greatest system of justice this side of heaven.

CHAPTER ONE

THE BULLET MADE A HOLLOW THUD, COUPLED WITH THE high-pitched whinnying noise of sheet metal shearing and rolling back along the left rear quarter panel. The crashing calliope ended abruptly against the interior of the steel back bumper. E.J. felt the sharp bite of a flake of chrome break off close to his forehead. His ears were ringing like a handbell banging out a Christmas carol. He reached to his forehead, half expecting a torrent of blood, only to discover the bright leafy metal shard.

He yelled upwards, above his head toward where the bullet originated, "Mr. Copeland, I need you to put the gun down so we can talk about this before someone gets hurt."

"My land. Always been my peoples' land. I got to pass it to my sons the way I found it. Not 'bout to have no store-bought lawman from some oil company tell me they get to go in and out at all hours of the night shaking the foundation of my house. Never ends. Man can't even hear his-self think."

Just wait until they drill, thought E.J. He barely had a moment's sarcastic chuckle when the big diver's side mirror, specially made for trailer hauling, splintered into an infinite number of pieces. He felt the percussion of the round whiz above and instinctively jerked his head back from the edge of the rear bumper.

E.J. appreciated the danger in his current tactical position. When he first saw old man Copeland on the porch with the rifle, E.J. stopped his three-quarter-ton truck in the driveway and took cover, figuring the old man would have to fire through the engine block and the length of the truck to hit him.

The wisdom of the decision now seemed suspect. Penned down behind the corner of his pickup, Copeland could outflank him in either direction without leaving the big sweeping porch of his home. Worse, E.J. hadn't had time to reach for his own rifle. A forty-five caliber 1911 pistol made a poor choice at seventy-five yards, even in the hands of a marksman.

E.J. chided himself for being so stupid. In thirty years of law enforcement, had he equaled this level of ignorance? His mind spun with images landing like a marble on a roulette wheel with the image of a young officer killed on his watch. For a moment, E.J. thought he could smell the lavender perfume the boy's mother wore at the funeral.

He broke away from the image, finding no consolation in the litany of appalling errors in judgment committed over the course of his career, nor did he settle on a strategy to improve his position. In fact, he surmised his tactical situation was hopeless. The glassless side mirror revealed an enormous hole through the center of its chrome housing, bearing witness to the debacle.

A dog's muffled howl emanated from the cab of the truck. E.J. had forgotten Yak amidst the excitement of the firefight. "Hit my dog and I'll kill you."

A loud, raspy tone projected from the house. "Not aiming at no dog."

The truth of the statement chilled E.J.'s shoulders, then ran down his spine. This guy hit exactly where he aimed. Shooting the mirror was an attention-getter. The earlier round, which came to rest against the bumper, was likely intentionally fired above E.J.'s head.

The coldness had permeated E.J.'s entire body. He wiped his forehead with his hand, then pressed on his head in a vain effort to stop the ringing in his ears. Copeland could kill him anytime the old-timer chose. The only option was to establish a rapport, come to some common ground. Copeland was letting him live for a reason. He quickly reviewed his mental file on Copeland. The man was a widower, a retired lineman from the electric cooperative. He was a cowman with two sons.

E.J. hollered across the recently mowed pasture separating him from the white frame house with the sweeping porches. "What you shooting. Cannon you rolled out on wheels?"

Copeland yelled back in the same scratchy, deep sound. "444 Marlin. Hot, ain't they? My hand loads."

E.J. lifted and turned his head, spitting out sandy loam, gravel, and the Redland dirt native to East Texas. His back ached, tired of lying flat, and beyond the point of trying to make a smaller target to a shooter of Copeland's obvious skill. Shooters load their own ammunition to achieve maximum consistency. Some developed an affinity for odd calibers, even if they had to endure powerful recoil like his own 45.70.

The grit slid deeper between his gums and teeth when he spoke. "I knew it was some kind of buffalo cartridge. Impressive for open sights on a lever action. Where'd you learn to shoot?"

"Camp Pendleton, California, but I got my advanced certification in Vietnam, City of Hue." Despite a limp, the old man appeared to straighten, and his chest bulged under a weather-beaten face.

"I appreciate your service. Never served myself, but my son was a marine."

Copeland had taken a rest against one of the porch posts. He lowered the big carbine, keeping it close to his shoulder. "Semper Fidelis, marine's a marine, can't be 'was a marine'."

"My boy would have agreed with you. He was so proud. Came back from Afghanistan in a coffin." E.J.'s voice crackled and snapped like expensive china crashing across a tile floor.

"Then I appreciate your sacrifice. Can't imagine. I got two boys, both meth junkies. Neither one has enough teeth left to gnaw grits. Already dreading the phone call I know will come, maybe today, maybe tomorrow," Copland said.

"I thought you had to leave this place to your sons the same way your folks left to you."

"Yeah, they can't even hold jobs, much less give me a grandchild. After Effie died, this place is sort of my family." The distance made Copeland's loud words sound even more tragic, ringing across his ancestral home. He lowered the rifle further and stepped off the porch, walking toward his former target.

E.J. lifted his body, rising to his knees. "Lawyers say the mineral estate is the dominant estate. Don't make much sense, so I explain it this way." He walked along the driveway as he continued speaking. "You took the company's money, promising they could drill. Of course, the company was using other people's money, right? Company promising those folks to bring in a gas well. Then before we can get the drill site made, you dump roofing tacks on it and threaten our contractors with guns."

Copeland lowered his head as E.J. approached.

E.J. added, "Those dirt men are just trying to make a living, and you got them changing high dollar tires on equipment the bank owns. You're not hurting the company. The company will pay nothing. They'll hire some other old boy who owes the bank for his dozers and finish building the site."

Stepping off the gravel drive, E.J. walked across a bright green field toward the house. He marveled at the vivid green grass. Spring rains had made keeping up with the Bahia grass near impossible. The split open seed head made an endless sea of swaying peace signs. Copeland was closing the distance with his face and the rifle pointed at a downward angle.

Behind Copeland and his home, E.J. saw dark clouds far in the distance, keeping vigil over the pines. To the right of the house were the cattle pens, and a barn roofed by rusty tin. The barn's lumber walls were bleached grey from the sun.

As he walked toward Copeland, E.J. stepped back in time and place. His fingers slid through the tall grass, dislodging the tiny seeds like he had done so many times running across his family's home place. Absently his head turned, looking toward the big oak to see if his mother was ringing the dinner triangle.

The armed man before E.J. crushed the illusion. When their eyes met, Copeland barked, "You're the big ranger the deputies told me about. Bought and paid for law."

"Fair enough. Calling me bought. I took their money, but you took their money too. We a pair, brother."

"You think I went to Paris and seen the Eiffel Tower on their dime. I used it to pay for doctors, experimental treatment in Houston. What the VA couldn't handle. I had prostate cancer. None of it worked. I didn't want to fight. Effie insisted, claimed she didn't put fifty years training me to let me go dying when her hard work might pay off." Copeland laughed while his eyes watered at the corners.

E.J. saw that the old man's mocking laughter served to fight back tears. "Then I lived, and she up and died on me. Right next to me. Same bedroom where we slept for fifty-two years."

He turned the butt of the rifle toward E.J., offering the gun to him. "Hear you folks got cable TV and medical care up there. You might as well feed me. I got nothing here anyway."

E.J. looked away. The dark horizon capping the white house nestled in a pasture made almost neon by the bloom of spring. He caught the faint sight of some White Dutch Clover almost lost amongst the sea of emerald green. He rarely saw clover like that anymore, and for a moment, the absurdity consumed him. Why was he thinking about clover with an armed man in front of him?

After the long silence, E.J. turned back to Copeland.

"Mr. Copeland, I will get the company to move the drill site back another five hundred feet. You are going to go out there and get every one of those tacks picked up, unarmed, and apologize to those construction hands. You're gonna tell them you've seen Jesus and won't be sinin' no more."

Copeland looked bewildered, then released the tension in his face with a subtle grin.

E.J. pushed the butt of the rifle back to Copeland. "Put your gun up and move your hands. I'm not gonna cuff you."

"Appreciate it."

"Well, I appreciate you not shooting me. You got a glass of tea or a cup of coffee. I got a mouth full of this dirt you're so proud of out here."

"I got tea, coke," Copeland smiled, "maybe some stronger if you'll drink with a man who nearly killed you. Come in the house." The old man extended his hand.

E.J. took it. "You wanted me dead. I wouldn't be breathing. I'll settle for the porch and some tea. I got my dog in the cab. Better check on him, likely scared to death."

The tea tasted stout. Ice and sugar couldn't cut the bite. He swished it across his tongue, satisfied the brew had sat far too long. Couldn't the same be said of Copeland? His weathered rail frame made him look every inch the wore-out cowboy.

The two passed the time talking about rain, heat, drought, gardens, and cattle prices. E.J. had driven his truck the rest of the way to Copeland's house. He assessed the damage to the pickup. Cosmetic, though, he had enjoyed the view from the large fancy motorized mirrors. Well, it had probably made Copeland feel considerably better shooting the mirrors, more oil company's property.

Maybe hitting them had part way dispelled the man's anger and saved E.J.'s life.

The distant familiar noise of EJ's cell phone caught his attention. He was grateful he had left the device in the truck. After a few more moments he rose, shook hands with Copeland again, and walked to this pickup.

The sweet smell of moisture rolled over E.J. as he watched the clouds slowly grow darker, springing thick with water vapor. He cranked the truck and closed the door to call the office.

E.J. spent the entire afternoon on the phone with corporate. Everyone knew company founder and president Rex Ashe had hired him. E.J.'s edicts had carried the weight of an ancient pharaoh; so let it be written, so let it be done. Such prior transactions had spoiled him.

Normally, E.J. downplayed his friendship with Rex Ashe. However, frustration overcame him, and he played his hole card. "This is E.J. Kane, head of corporate security. I report directly to CEO Rex Ashe, and he has approved the following...."

The line went quiet for a long time. Then another voice came over the speaker. The person questioned E.J.'s authority before beginning a series of transfers to executives, refusing to acknowledge they worked for Rex Ashe. Finally, someone identified only as the acting CFO spoke. She spoke curtly yet agreed to fulfill the promises E.J. had made to Copeland.

Grateful to achieve success, E.J. didn't ask her name, nor did he carry the conversation further. The CFO's high-pitched voice went to great lengths to pronounce each syllable. E.J. surmised the perfect pronunciation hid an eastern accent, New York, Boston, perhaps New Jersey.

Stepping from the truck, E.J.'s boots felt heavy, like being mired in quicksand. Arguing with fools can make a man more tired than working. Copeland's eyes were closed, mouth open, and his head leaned back against the chair. No point in waking the old man.

E.J. turned to walk off the porch, followed by a bluish-black and white dog. He whispered, "Load up, Yak."

Copeland opened his eyes, looking up from the tall oak framed wicker rocker. "You're a good man."

E.J. stopped with his back to Copeland.

Despite not facing him, Copeland continued. "I mean, people say you're so crooked, when you die they'll have to screw you in the ground. More cross than the devil on Sunday. Ain't none of it true. You treated me decent."

E.J. stepped into the rain toward his truck. He yelled above the squall without ever looking back. "Don't you go telling nobody Copeland or I'll come back and finish our little gunfight."

Copeland snickered a gravelly chuckle.

E.J.'s cell phone rang through the radio in his truck. E.J. understood mechanical contrivances, yet Bluetooth technology eluded him. Every so often, for reasons unknown to E.J., the phone and radio seemed to come off the rails, and his company's technology department had to pair the device again.

He pushed a button on the steering wheel, and his daughter's voice was in stereo. "Daddy, are you home?"

"No, working."

"Making the planet an environmental wasteland for Devekon and Rex Ashe's greed. You know the polar bears don't have a home anymore because of you."

"That's right, princess, I'm literally wrecking polar

11

bear houses as we speak. Melting them big ice cubes with a hair dryer. Did you just call to give me grief, or you going to visit your pop sometime?"

There was a pause, then she sighed, "Dad, I need some money."

Her soft voice was almost inaudible over the rain. Was it the sound system, or was his hearing weakening? E.J. didn't need to hear. It seemed like all she called about was money these days. "How much?"

"Seven hundred dollars. My computer got fried with my entire term paper, and it's due Monday." Her voice had taken on a whiny quality.

"What did your mother say?"

"You know I can't talk to her about anything real. You know how she has been since Konner's death. She's ready to bite everyone's head off. She checks my grades online and chews me out every day. I'm nineteen years old. She's moody and rude to my friends, and I'm tired of it."

"Calm down, breathe, come home tonight. I even bought the stuff to make you a bean sprout sandwich. Sunshine misses you something awful."

"I don't have time," said Sharla.

E.J. didn't want to play his hole card, though he did. "I'll get you the money."

CHAPTER TWO

E.J. PULLED INTO HIS YARD NEXT TO HIS DAUGHTER'S
Prius. A mechanical voice reported a phone call. The
display recited a Houston number he didn't recognize. E.J.
touched the screen to ignore the call.

Oddly, Sharla hadn't gone into the house to wait for
him. She sat in her car, playing on her phone. "You lose
your key?"

"I can't stay. There are finals and papers. Nothing has
gone right since my computer got stolen." Sharla stepped
out of the car, though she didn't approach him. She
sported an oversized tee-shirt and messy hair.

Before college, more before Konner's death, Sharla had
taken after her mother. Both prided themselves on being
meticulous in dress and hygiene. E.J. smelled the faint
odor of urine. "Load up; we'll go to Wal Mart and get a
laptop right now," said E.J.

"No, can't you understand? I don't have time." Sharla
moved her hands upwards.

"Com'on, let's visit Sunshine. He misses you."

"I'm not a little girl. Not here to see the horse. Really, I need to do my work," said Sharla.

"Why you need money?"

Sharla smirked, tilting her head and putting her hand on her hips. "My computer is fried. You need hearing aids."

"Tell the truth and you never have to remember what you said. Earlier, you claimed someone stole it," said E.J.

Sharla rocked her head before E.J. could finish. "You need hearing aids. Mother told you. I told you. If you want me to fail, say so," said Sharla.

E.J. looked past her across the pasture. After Konner's death, one of E.J.'s patrol officer contacts providing security at a club had called E.J. to tell him Sharla flashed a fake ID to enter a bar. When confronted, E.J. had witnessed the same head tilt and vigorous denial. "I want you to ask for help."

"Here we go again, over the joint. One joint and my jack-booted thug daddy wants to lock me up in rehab."

E.J.'s phone rang, and he slid across the screen, rejecting the call. Rejecting the call agitated a tense situation. He wanted to turn off the ringer, yet wasn't familiar enough with this model phone. "You're lying to my face for money. Don't care how you look. Your grades stink. I'm not stupid. You need help."

"I'm lying. You're the one lying like always. Lure me out here to play Daddy because you killed your golden child with your backward view of God and country." She drew a deep breath and shook her hand at him. "Maybe if you hadn't got your cop friends killed, you wouldn't have to take charity from your drunkard enviro killer buddy—"

E.J.'s phone rang again. Irritation made him fumble the device between his hands. He knew she only repeated her mother's insults, yet they pierced his heart.

Sharla yelled, "Just take it."

E.J. rejected the call again. "I'm sorry. I don't want this. I love you. You're all I got in this world."

"Then give me the money like you promised—"

The ringer chimed out. E.J. hit the screen. "E.J. Kane. What is it?"

A shrill scream bellowed, "Terrorist blew up a storage tank, and they think a man is dead."

E.J. had been intent on yelling at the caller and throwing the phone. This news pushed him off balance. Trapped between the two crises, he literally wobbled for a second. He looked to Sharla in time to see her crank the vehicle and punch the throttle.

Should he chase her because he wanted to fall to his knees crying? He had messed up again. Why didn't he get some counselor to tell him how to broach the subject? No, he bulled through, crushing everything like glass, catching her in a lie. He wasn't working on a case. This was his daughter, his baby girl, his whole life.

He watched Sharla swing onto the road from the driveway. She was gone. Had he overreacted? Was his work experience clouding his judgment? He had always strived to insulate his family from the evil he investigated. She couldn't really be a drug addict, or somebody would have noticed other than him.

Chasing her would likely cause a wreck. He needed professional advice on how to bring up rehab, and maybe he was overreacting. E.J. turned his mind to the emergency thrown at him through the cell phone.

It took a moment to calm the Devekon Energy dispatcher. In fact, he wasn't a dispatcher or an employee at all. The person worked for an answering service in Houston. For years, the answering service had answered a number posted on lease signs to call in case of fire. The service enjoyed the income since answering services were no longer in demand. Devekon was a great customer because the company paid on time, and there had never been a call.

This call had come from the landowner, an avid jogger. He went out for an evening run after work when he came across an object which, at first, he didn't recognize. Then he realized it looked as if someone used a can opener and peeled off the top of a huge metal storage tank. A far more gruesome sight awaited him.

A few feet past the storage tank appeared a foot sheared above the ankle and still in a sock. Jogger looks around for a body or a shoe, and that's when he sees the flame. The well is on fire.

The dispatcher took another hurried breath before adding to the obvious. "It scared the man."

It occurred to E.J. the dispatcher couldn't appreciate how excited and distraught he sounded. Even listening to a recap of the events had scared this person. E.J. continued to parse the information. "How do we know it was a bombing?"

"What?"

"You said someone blew the tank up. How do we know that?"

"Top got blown off, and the well caught fire, didn't you hear me, he said like a can opener? The caller and I both think it has to be a terrorist." The dispatcher's voice exuded excitement.

"Thunderstorms with lightning are far more common. Usually, there's a tank for salt water, the other for condensate. Even when grounded and well-ventilated, lightning doesn't have to hit directly to set the condensate off." From the location provided, about thirty miles remained between E.J. and the well site. He couldn't drive too fast in heavy rain.

Days were still fairly short. E.J. surmised his estimated time of arrival was dark thirty. Terrorism seemed implausible, though he had long thought well sites seemed easy targets. Fear might cripple markets, sending the price of oil and gas skyrocketing, not to mention the environmental fallout and lack of security.

If he could educate the dispatcher, perhaps some formerly obscure fact would jump out at him. He also asked the answering service employee to overnight the recorded call. Then felt stupid when the employee pointed out he could email it.

The rain subsided, leaving only a mist. It had rained long enough to soak the deputies and firefighters already on scene. In times past, E.J. had endured it, soaking wet despite rain gear, with no time to go home and get dry. He had been on many a crime scene battling the elements from bone-chilling rain to the steamy Texas heat, which made the putrid odors of death all the more rancid.

Even the remote possibility of terrorism meant the Federal Bureau of Investigation and the corresponding State of Texas investigations unit, the Texas Rangers, assigning agents. It might take some time to get a special agent from Tyler or Shreveport. E.J. chuckled to himself, thinking there was plenty of time given Sheriff Benjamin

Berryhill's checkered history working with other agencies.

E.J. followed the directives of his global position system along a myriad of county roads. He was somewhere near the Louisiana border, hoping he wasn't in Berryhill's county. As he drew closer, he realized despite his delusive hopes, he remained in Sheriff B.B.'s jurisdiction. The sheriff's department logo on the side of a Ford Explorer confirmed his dread when he turned off the oil top road onto a gravel lease road.

A young deputy built like a football player and dressed in a clear plastic rain poncho motioned for E.J. to stop his truck at the cattle guard marking the entrance to what signs denoted as the Martin number three gas well location. The deputy wore a straw hat sporting a wide brick crease and a five-inch brim.

E.J. partially rolled down his window.

"Sir, don't you see the yellow tape? This is a crime scene; you're not allowed to enter. Exit the vehicle." The deputy bent a little at the knees, placing his hand on top of his holstered pistol.

Yak growled from the passenger floorboard. E.J. waved the dog quiet, then lifted his hat off the dash. He stepped from the truck, raising the dark beaver hat onto his head. The rain cooled off an otherwise warm spring day.

"Hands on the vehicle, sir. Now." The deputy drew a black polymer pistol from his hip, pointing it at E.J.

E.J. looked at the gun then back to the deputy. E.J. carefully reached into his pocket to display a leather billfold. On one side was his company identification card, and the other was his driver's license. "My name is E.J. Kane, Chief of Security for Devekon Energy. This here is our lease. You can't exclude me. Now get me your crime scene log, so I can sign it and open your tape."

The deputy smiled, then pointed to a small black box on his chest. "Don't use logs anymore, old-timer, all digital now."

E.J. saw the little red light and realized he was being recorded, a fact he should have assumed previously. Still, hadn't even the transparent poncho blurred the recording in the misting rain? He thought about advising the young man to keep a pen and small notebook in his pocket under the poncho; then he remembered this was Berryhill's department, Berryhill's county.

Noticing the deputy's gear brought E.J.'s attention to the young man's duty rig under the transparent poncho. He recognized the thick leather hand-tooled belt and holster as a ranger's style sold through the Texas Department of Corrections and made by inmates, far too expensive for most young deputies. The deputy still hadn't holstered the weapon.

"Sir, I don't care if you're the Dalai Lama, you ain't coming through here."

E.J. smiled. He didn't need to examine the deputy's sidearm to know it probably held three times the number of shells the old Colt Police revolver he wore in his early years or the current Sig 938 secreted in his own pocket. The deputy's tone turned harsher, his demeanor stern, plus the Dalai Lama line was a pleasant touch. A big dumb looking lug using words like Dalai Lama.

Had he been so ridiculous as a young deputy? When he was the deputy's age, he would never have known such a term as Dalai Lama and probably still couldn't spell it today.

"Before I was an old-timer, pride wouldn't have let me draw on an old man. Old Sheriff Wharton would have had my badge for a coward." E.J. thought better of the remark as soon as it passed his lips. The petulant officer had tapped into a pet peeve. The boy's attitude and demeanor were the perfect example of what he lambasted many times over coffee with retired officers.

E.J. remembered a time when law enforcement wasn't criminal justice in a college catalog. Once upon a time, someone had pinned a badge on a big lug because he looked intimidating and told him he was a peace officer. If such a young man were resilient enough to grey in the profession, then he pinned a badge on the next big fellow.

Officers weren't as well educated, professional, egalitarian, diverse, or as inclusive as the modern era, yet the 'old-timers' kept the peace in a time when the public wasn't willing to pay for such niceties as training and education. As a commissioned law enforcement instructor, he knew modern was better; still, he couldn't help but admire his mentors.

For the old-timers, riot gear, body armor, and urban assault vehicles had all amounted to a police or trooper model revolver accompanied by a tin star thrown across a desk. He spanned both eras, having started as a big lug of a deputy himself before later graduating from the Texas Department of Public Safety Academy. He chuckled, realizing his mind still wandered aimlessly; this was the second time someone had pointed a gun at him today.

"You aren't hearing me, Pops." The young deputy appeared beyond annoyed.

There was no Tazer, no pepper spray, nothing less than lethal on the deputy's duty rig. Snapped back to the moment, E.J. began searching for what was now being taught in the profession as de-escalation techniques when a familiar voice sliced through the tension—

"Ranger Kane, God Bless America if it's not a bona fide real-life oil company tycoon." The dark complected man moved from the shadows between E.J. and the deputy. The gold FBI letters on his windbreaker and cap caught the light from E.J.'s headlights. He added while extending his hand, "Forgive the excessive patriotism. Got saved and gave up cussing."

E.J. extended a hand to his old friend, Hall Oglethorpe. "Not enough Jesus to save you. Won't be no grace left for the rest of us poor sinners."

The young deputy slid his weapon back in the holster. "This is Ranger Kane?"

"Son, this is him." Hall lifted the crime scene tape. "I imagine if he doesn't qualify to pass this tape, none of the rest of us do." He turned back to E.J. "Grace is in infinite measure. It's the sinner's mind that's limited." With his back to the deputy, Hall gave a quick nod, telling E.J. he needed to move. The two were stepping down the lease road, leaving the deputy at the entrance.

About a quarter mile ahead of them were several large portable banks of lights extending to the top of three poles anchored by their generators. Hall spoke under his breath. "We got to move quick. Eventually, he will call his dear old daddy. When B.B. shows up, you let me do the talking. He hates the Bureau, but he hates you more."

"I can handle B.B. Been doing it since we were kids. So that's 'Son'." E.J. referenced the nickname denoting Sheriff Berryhill's son, recalling a child dragged around in his father's shadow. The kid had never had a chance of being known by any moniker other than what his father always called him, 'Son'.

"Still, let me do the talking when B.B. gets here."

"No offense, but B.B. won't respect a black man in authority."

Hall stopped whispering. "God Bless America, I saved your sweet land of liberty butt back there. You didn't know I could speak 'cracker' when I needed to."

E.J. nodded, chuckling a little under his breath. "So, Son made a man?"

"Depends on how you measure a man. A little jumpy. The kid is no coward. I saw him walk through a hail of bullets and clean out a meth cook. Like a Sunday picnic mixing Kool-Aid." Hall smiled. "That part reminds me of you. Shoots like you, too."

"Fast."

"Faster than you. Where's your gun, anyway?"

E.J. decided there was no point in giving Hall information the man might have to deny later. Even trying to tell himself he was more accommodating his limited armament than lying to an old friend didn't sit well, so he tried to sidestep the question. "Between the FBI and the DAs, I have about decided it's a bad idea to carry one. Shoot an outlaw so mean, his momma can't love him, and I get grilled for four hours by federal agents. Then I still have to go to a grand jury. After some shyster lawyer signs momma up, telling her I could have kicked the gun out of her baby's hand like Walker Texas Ranger."

Both men knew the back story behind the detailed example and turned to walk in silence. The night air cooled, following the rain. The moon made a yellow crescent hanging far away in a black sky. Every quick-paced step crunched the gravel under their boots until Hall asked what E.J. already knew.

After E.J. relayed the facts provided by the answering service employee, Hall began his narrative. "Chicago people by way of Houston. Man is an engineer at the new natural gas-powered electric plant. The woman is some kind of counselor, substance abuse, or kids or something. Man is the jogger, alternates between pasture and county road near every night."

"I take it he was running through pasture tonight."

Hall swung his arm past the direction they had walked, and E.J. saw the tiniest lights, which he took to be a house through distant woods. "So, he is running from the house, and then he crosses near the road we were just walking before he steps over the lid to one of those big tanks and a foot."

"A foot?" E.J. asked.

"A foot," Hall repeated.

"Where is it?"

"We got more. Over by the dehy is an arm and the torso and head are back near his truck. I expect his legs flew out in the pasture."

They passed a motte of trees nearing the well site, and E.J. could make out the shapes of a typical gas well location. Two large tanks were to the left. Something peeled off the top of one tank, twisting the remainder of the vessel. Along the back stood the dehydrator or dehy, while to the right was the wellhead or Christmas tree. E.J. saw the outline of the tanker truck past the tanks. "Who?"

Hall opened the gate over the second cattle guard. "Who?"

"Fellow who belonged to the foot?"

They descended the short distance from the cattle guard to where the fenced perimeter of the well site made a square. From this vantage point, the generator and tall light station illuminated the entire square of gravel and gas production equipment.

Hall answered, "Truck has WelCo Salt Water written on the door and a phone number. I called the number. The Martin number three wasn't on their list for today, but they got a driver who didn't check in, one Chester Arnold."

"Searched the truck yet?" asked E.J.

"No, I'm hoping to talk B.B. into letting me call the crime scene unit from a bigger department or let your rangers do it with their mobile unit."

"Not my rangers anymore. Where is Cooper?" asked E.J.

"Still about twenty miles away. Daughter playing volleyball."

"No reason to rush her. B.B. will likely run us all off, anyway. Is that torso and head you mentioned attached?" asked E.J.

Hall pointed toward the back of the well, leading the way. They reached a large diameter pipe rising from the dirt about three feet, running parallel to the ground before returning. There, trapped by the pipe, was the eerie-looking human trunk with the head hanging on top of the pipe.

Hall touched E.J.'s arm. E.J. stopped and kneeled, studying the corpse. A tattoo on the upper right chest read nineteenth and displayed something like a warrior with a spear and maybe a lightning bolt under a crescent moon. "Prison Ink?"

Hall kneeled prior to answering. "Probably not, but

he's been in on a burglary."

"You run him, NCIC?" asked E.J.

"I got some identifiers from this WelCo. He got released over a decade ago, nothing since, bunch of drugs and thefts in the day," said Hall.

"Aryan Ink?"

Hall smiled. "You know I teach the class in sovereign citizens."

"I thought it was some offshoot of AC or AB because of the lightning bolt," said E.J.

"Nephilim, like in the Bible. Lightning and the line is a marker for a mile." Hall pointed toward the mark, which was slightly taller than the warrior figure depicted.

"Nephilim? Not in the Baptist Bible," E.J. said.

"In all of them, right at the start. They're some giants; some think the offspring between angels and mortals. Racist plenty all right and buy into the whole illegal annexation like the Republic of Texas and invalid confederate surrender, but their primary thing is God. Law of God types like God's champions," said Hall.

"True sovereign power. Guess every cracker wants to be a cookie." E.J. mirrored Hall's grin. "You know we need to get into that truck."

"Let the experts do it," said Hall.

"Do Son and his buddies qualify as experts? Because we both know B.B. is not letting anyone else do it," said E.J.

They turned over their shoulders in unison, blinded by bright lights. A new black Tahoe sped toward them, stopping hard only feet away. The door swung open, besides the general badge like the other units, this one denoted Sheriff Benjamin Berryhill. An athletic man stepped around the door and fender.

Hall rose while E.J. turned back to the tattoo. He saw better in the additional light cast by the headlamps. E.J. could make out the figure was wearing armor with the familiar lone star flag pattern across the chest.

"Bless my soul, it's the old pretender and Mr. Yankee affirmative action done graced my little crime scene," said Sheriff B.B.

CHAPTER THREE

"SHERIFF B.B., YOU KNOW THE FBI INVESTIGATES ALLE-gations of domestic terrorism. I'm only here to observe until I show terrorism is probable. It's your show, sheriff." Hall raised his hands, feigning surrender.

B.B. closed the distance between the two men until his lips near touched Hall's face. "Lightning ain't terror. Besides, folks didn't elect you, Mr. Affirmative Action, to protect them. They elected me. So, take your federolly ass back to Dallas and stop mucking up my scene."

"Sheriff, may God praise our great nation and pour his blessing out on you and your family. I need to call my superior." Hall stepped back yet still stared at B.B. until B.B. made a little motion with his fingers, communicating his intent for Hall to run along. Hall turned and stepped away while placing his phone to his ear.

E.J. didn't plan on rising. Sheriff B.B. failed to appreciate personal space and mouthwash. E.J. yelled from his still crouched position. "This is Devekon property, at least the well site. You'll have to get Rex Ashe to run me off. I know you got the number. You call him every four years begging for a dollar bill."

"You can't bully me, pretender, the way you did my son." Sheriff B.B. closed the distance to E.J.

E.J. rose, still trying to avoid confronting Sheriff B.B. "The opposite, I tried to teach him a peace officer can back a bully down by using his head."

Sheriff B.B. stepped even closer. "Stay away from my son. You won't betray him to the cartel like you did your own outfit, pretender."

E.J.'s index finger slid along the steel frame of the pistol in his pocket. The cool feel comforted him. He stepped back, distancing himself from B.B.

There had been a time when his view of manhood wouldn't permit him to step back. Rather, he would have inventoried his options. Maybe consider if the fool would have gone for his gun on him and whether he could draw. Better yet, could he lift his thigh, thumb down the safety, and hit the trigger without removing the pistol from his pocket. Be a stout powder burn, wouldn't it?

The passenger door of the Tahoe flew open. A well-dressed woman stepped out and slammed the door. Both men turned, but Sheriff B.B. spoke.

"Widow, you can wait in the car. I'll have this trespasser off the property straight away."

"I see that." The corner of her mouth turned up as Sheriff B.B. looked back at E.J.

E.J. produced his cell phone, pushing buttons until a ringing noise came over the speakerphone.

"Who you calling?" asked Sheriff B.B.

"Rex Ashe, let you explain to him how I got run off his

well site."

Sheriff B.B. grabbed the phone and canceled the call before handing it back to E.J. "You stay out of the way, or I'll arrest you for interfering with an investigation and impersonating real police."

Sheriff B.B. walked toward the tanker truck. E.J. hoped Hall was watching what would likely be an amateur search of the cab. He wasn't. From the faces he was making, it was clear Hall was arguing over the cell phone with someone.

E.J. stepped toward the woman and then took another series of steps, mindlessly taking in the thick fragrance of vanilla and fresh flowers. She extended her hand for a handshake.

"Ruth Welchel, but everyone calls me Widow Welchel."

"WelCo?" E.J. pointed toward the logo on the tanker truck door.

"Didn't expect a woman in the oilfield?" Widow Welchel asked.

"Nothing of the kind, ma'am. I figured you wouldn't want to see the body." He couldn't tell her the truth. There were plenty of women in the oilfield, but none smelled like lilacs and looked like her. There probably weren't many women who looked like her outside of Hollywood.

She stepped around E.J. "Not much left, is there?"

"I'm sorry," said E.J.

"Why? You didn't do it, did you, mister—"

It occurred to him he hadn't identified himself despite shaking her hand. How silly to get sidetracked by a pretty face? "E.J. Kane, chief of security for Devekon. Did you know him?"

"We called him 'Troll'. He preferred nights. Speed

freak, I heard. The few times I spoke with him, he was tweaking," she said.

"You don't drug test?" asked E.J.

"Sure, but I don't do equipment checks, so I don't know if it's junk or a whizinator. We need drivers." She looked down at Troll's head slung unnaturally across the pipe. "Tweaker probably blew himself up."

E.J.'s shoulders twisted, rotating his neck. If Hall had said the same thing, then E.J. wouldn't have looked up. The thought was sexist, and there was no place for it anymore. He wanted to look away, yet the shade of blue drew him. They must be contact lens. No one's eyes could be so blue.

"Am I a little cold for your taste?" she asked.

"Not at all. Appreciate you telling it like it is, ma'am."

"Then this ma'am business needs to end. We're about the same age," said Widow Welchel.

"I'm fifty-five," E.J. said.

"I'm not. Call me Widow like everybody else."

During the conversation, E.J. kept stealing glances at B.B. searching the truck, hoping to see what he recovered. So far, he noted the only item B.B. removed was a shotgun.

"Suppose big Devekon is going to want me to pay to repair the tank and whatever else, or I lose my contract?" Widow said.

"Likely an act of God anyway, lightning and all," said E.J.

"Arnold's family will probably sue us all, act of God or not." Her voice turned terse. "I'll get somebody to notify the family."

E.J. stepped closer. "Can you help me figure something out? What was Arnold doing here if this well wasn't on the route for salt water removal tonight?"

"How about you take care of Devekon, and I'll handle WelCo? I thought you were going to ask for my phone number." Her tense posture eased.

E.J. likewise relaxed. "I've never been the swiftest runner in the race."

She smirked at the comment and excused herself to make phone calls while E.J. continued to study the truck. E.J. thought the truck should have been connected to the salt water tank. If he hauls off salt water, then why wasn't the truck connected to the tank.

Could Arnold have been tweaking and blown himself up? E.J. heard kids hanging out and smoking on top of the tanks had ignited vapors off the condensate tank. He walked all around the tanks. They were in a poor state, and he didn't have enough expertise to know what was distinguishable from lightning versus man-made causes.

Sheriff B.B. stepped aside, returning to his Tahoe. E.J. suspected Cooper had arrived. Cooper was too professional and smart to take on Sheriff B.B. in a confrontation. A ranger learned how to work with all sheriffs. She knew which ones to talk about hunting and which sheriff to discuss kid's baseball. It was like Cooper to be waiting at the gate for Sheriff B.B. to show her around. Let Sheriff B.B. be the big man while Cooper worked the case.

This meant if he moved quickly, E.J. could get a peek in the truck. He did his best nonchalant beeline for the cab. These drivers spend their entire shift in the cab, so he expected it to be a mess.

The interior surprised him. Everything neatly stowed. Arnold probably never even ate or drank in it. An empty cradle made E.J. conclude Arnold's cell phone had been removed, whether by him or someone else.

E.J. scoured the cab for a logbook. He decided he had done what Cooper called his twentieth-century thinking again. He had been too far behind the times. Arnold must have had everything on his phone, or there had been a laptop, and Sheriff B.B. had taken it. Then he saw the corner of a grey notebook under the seat.

When he pulled the notebook, a black leather-bound Bible slid from behind it. He pushed the Bible back under the seat.

He opened the grey notebook. An old school log book notating dates, times, and well numbers. The listings looked complete for the past several months. E.J. found no listing for the Martin number three. Why? Was Arnold doing something he wanted to be kept off the books, or had this been an unexpected change in an otherwise meticulous itinerary?

E.J. felt someone on the truck steps behind him. Startled, he jumped straight up, hitting his head on the roof of the cab. Raucous laughter erupted behind him.

"You jumped out of your skin. Must have thought your prayers had been answered. Old B.B. was goosin' you." Cooper came off the truck step, continuing her laughter.

A red-faced E.J. popped back, "You gave me a start is all. You being so unnaturally ugly and all." The quip referenced an inside joke. E.J. had mentored the young female trooper. The jabs were his way of bonding with her and encouraging their colleagues to ignore her attractiveness. She later told him she appreciated the backward way of drowning out the sexist comments of others.

No one had been prouder when she made ranger, prouder when she informed him; she had earned his old spot. Even the taint of his reduced circumstance didn't dampen his excitement.

Cooper answered the unasked question in E.J.'s mind. "Sheriff B.B. ran to town to get burgers for the deputies out here. You know it's always an election year."

"Where's he sending the body?" asked E.J.

"Nacogdoches," said Cooper.

"The fellow cutting before he got licensed?" To E.J., the name denoted the city, the laboratory, and the pathologist.

"They got rid of him a while back. Not saying it's good, but it's cheap and better than it was. You know I can't make Sheriff B.B. use Dallas or Fort Worth," Cooper said.

E.J. tried to remember the name of the case where he first met 'Nacogdoches'. Originally, the doctor impressed him by fixing the time of death to the minute and the last meal in its entirety. His opinion had changed when he witnessed the pathologist cross-examined or, more aptly, described as crucified. The torture ended with the doctor confessing he couldn't tell the jury anything.

"All a water haul anyway, don't you figure?" Cooper stepped back, taking stock of the entire well site.

"Where's Hall?" asked E.J.

"Sheriff B.B. run him off. Feds don't want to fight over jurisdiction to a lightning strike," said Cooper.

E.J.'s phone buzzed. It occurred to him he should take pictures of the logbook. First, he read the text message. "Mr. Ashe will call in approx. 30 min. to discuss future changes."

"Something important?" Cooper asked.

"I guess I wait a half hour to find out if I still have a job," said E.J.

"You even want to keep working for Devekon?" Cooper's question alluded to one of their many discussions where E.J. had confessed he would as soon draw his pension and stay on the farm.

E.J. paused before answering. He couldn't tell her he wanted what he had lost, all of it. She would feel guilty for taking his position. However, the career was the least of what he wanted back.

He wanted his son alive, marriage with Rebecca, a real relationship with his daughter, Sharla. Besides, it was too much to dream, too much to want. He lied. "I don't know what I want, Cooper."

CHAPTER FOUR

"YOU'RE BECOMING HARDER TO GET AN AUDIENCE WITH than the pope," said E.J.

"Pope, don't need your services. He's right with Jesus. I, however—"

"However," said E.J.

"It's the however that has me calling you. I got a little careless with the books and dropped a fortune in an offshore play that's not coming online anytime soon," said Rex Ashe.

"But it's your company. Can't you do whatever?" E.J. asked.

"Didn't they teach y'all about derivative suits at Texas A&M?"

"I'm sure they did, but my Agribusiness degree is heavy on Agri and light on business," E.J. said.

"Between my kids, creditors, and shareholders, I'm lucky they still let me drive," Rex Ashe said.

E.J. erupted in laughter at the thought of Rex Ashe

answering to anyone. Even in old age, the scrappy little man had always seemed vastly larger. The old phrase about stout as a bull ox came to mind.

Rex Ashe ignored the laughter. "I hear about this man, Arnold, dying on a Devekon well site."

"Definitely no fault of your company. You know how it is, we don't know what we don't know right now." For a moment, E.J. pondered how absurd such an assertion must seem. One of those thoughts which sounded better in his head than spoken.

"You go to the family. I know he wasn't really one of ours, but that's the way I run this business. Give them my sympathies, make sure there's money to bury him. You know what to do."

"I do." E.J. expected the call to end. Rex had earned loyalty in business by stepping up when his employees needed him. Likely this had to be the reason Rex Ashe called.

E.J. didn't always approve of the man's lifestyle. Over the years, E.J. had located and paid off women and discredited false heirs from Rex's many indiscretions.

Yet on other occasions, Rex Ashe possessed a powerful moral compass. He had held onto a code from his youth. Here, the code demanded the highest respect shown to the decedent's family.

"There is a new Chief Financial Officer, Clara Brandis. I told her you would be in her office tomorrow, early," Rex Ashe said.

"In Houston?"

"I'm trying to save your job. You'll kiss her backside. It won't be easy. She's young and rude." Rex Ashe trailed off, and E.J. offered no comment.

After the long pause, Rex Ashe added. "The mess is mine. Still, I always felt bad for you because you got poor cards as long as I've known you. You've kept the bodies from floating up for Devekon. Show up and keep your mouth shut. Clara Brandis wants my company. She's smart enough to pay you off."

"I don't want money," said E.J.

"You saved me and this company many times over, so keep your mouth shut and your hand out." Rex Ashe shouted the admonishment. After another awkward silence, he added, "Besides, when I get settled, you are going to sneak some scotch in, and I don't drink cheap stuff. This time you're going to have a drink with me too."

E.J. made the only plausible response. "Yes, sir."

The call ended. That was Rex. When he finished talking, he hung up. The man didn't subscribe to pleasantries.

Yak barked.

"You think he owes us something more. I expect he's doing all he can."

The bark turned to a howl, and the diluted dark spots of the dog's coat bristled. Rex Ashe had given the animal to E.J. years ago. A quick search of the internet revealed the coat coloring and light eyes made the Louisiana hunting dog unique.

Experience taught E.J. it was best to let Yak succumb to his high-strung nature. E.J. swung the door open, so Yak could chase whatever had agitated him.

Yak might not be back until morning, sometimes worse for wear from tangling with feral hogs. E.J. had at one point taken steps to keep Yak from such risky behavior. He had tried ideas like keeping the dog in an electric fence, placing it on a run when outside, even building a large kennel.

Yak's pedigree overcame every attempt. On each occasion, the canine had hunted action. Hence the name E.J. settled on Devil Yak, after the famous Texas lawman, Jack Coffee Hays. Like a crack of lightning, the dog creased the darkness out of sight.

About four-thirty in the morning, Yak whined outside the door. E.J. greeted Yak, trying to explain why he couldn't take his primary companion in the truck. It took three hours to reach Houston. However, there was no accounting for traffic when he arrived and nowhere to put Yak in downtown. E.J. appreciated the absurdity of apologizing to a dog, yet he did so.

The tall pine trees and landscaped lawns made him want to pull into Stephen F. Austin University and wake his daughter. He wanted to take her for breakfast. Then a thought froze him.

What if she wasn't alone? What if there was some near-do-well boyfriend shacked up in a love-nest while he paid the bills?

Sharla had been a straight-A student before her brother's death and the divorce. Now she always needed money, and E.J. tried to ignore a lifetime of law enforcement intuition gnawing through his gut.

He couldn't even share his fears with his ex-wife. Trying to have a conversation with Rebecca was impossible. She would only mock him like when he found marijuana in Sharla's car.

'User amount', a term he deemed essential to the lexicon of legalization. His fear then was his fear now. A terror gripping his heart, honed by years of talking to junky informants.

It was true there were some people who used marijuana and never graduated to methamphetamine and cocaine. However, virtually everyone addicted to meth or other hard drugs started with marijuana.

He decided he would call her after meeting with this Clara Brandis. Maybe they could have a late lunch when he came back by the campus.

In contrast to him, Rebecca liked anything urban. E.J. expected she would leave East Texas when Sharla graduated college, if Sharla ever graduated. Rebecca could practice anywhere. E.J. envisioned the glossy photos from Super Lawyers magazine.

The Devekon corporate offices encompassed the entire top floor of a bank building in downtown. Parking a F250 pickup in a high-rise parking garage amounted to threading a needle with a rope. E.J. winced as the antenna scraped the top of the roof. The screeching continued until he reached the top floor and open sky.

If Clara Brandis expected him, no one informed her assistant.

"I told you no E.J. Kane on her calendar. Do I have to call security?" The man was a third of E.J.'s size and dressed in a cashmere sweater.

It might be spring outside, yet a chill gripped the office suite. "I am security. It's what I need to talk to her about. Rex Ashe told me she was expecting me. Can't you just ring her?"

"No, No, Nooo."

E.J. studied the man for a moment. "Yes."

"No. If I call for you, then I have to call for everyone. How can she get anything done if I am calling her? What if I call for you and not the Asian or African American?" Said the petite man.

"I am the only person here," said E.J. He surveyed the empty waiting room. Gone were Rex Ashe's big framed photos of derricks, replaced by impressionist art. Traffic chairs replaced green leather loungers.

The man pursed his lips. "I must be consistent."

An overwhelming odor of potpourri churned E.J.'s stomach. After another thirty minutes and several passing thoughts about jumping from the thirty-second floor, E.J. gleaned Clara Brandis wasn't there, and this gentleman was the assistant to the assistant. The assistant, once removed, showed E.J. to an office.

A degree on the wall drew E.J.'s attention. Clara Brandis had earned a law degree from Yale. Modern furnishings filled a vast office, combined with a conference room and work space.

He had googled Clara Brandis on his phone. He found only a two-sentence curriculum vitae under a picture of a young stern-looking woman in business attire.

A poster-sized photo in a black-trimmed frame caught his attention. Two women holding an infant between them. Clara Brandis and her family. Well, what did he expect? No one needed his approval to live their life.

The other woman was familiar. He couldn't place her. Her looks were striking, with an all-American blond, blue-eyed appearance. Was Clara Brandis plain, or did the other woman make her mousy by comparison?

The door swung open. "Mr. Kane, I have been looking forward to meeting the person who thinks he can command this entire company." A booming voice from so slight a frame momentarily shocked E.J.

E.J. recovered. "The man is Rex Ashe, not me."

She sat a leather satchel on her desk. "Are you going to test me, Mr. Kane?"

"No, ma'am," said E.J.

She frowned, then gestured to E.J. to take a seat. "What do you do, Mr. Kane?"

"Security." E.J. waited until Clara Brandis sat in her white leather chair.

"No, we have contractors. I can't figure out what you do except indulge Rex Ashe's eccentricities. For example, does Devekon really own a dozen Longhorn cattle on your farm, an expensive hunting dog, and an antique cotton gin?

"Yes, ma'am, everything is there, but the dog's a gift."

Clara Brandis leaned forward. "I hate 'ma'am'. Look at you, boots, hat in hand, you wait to sit until I'm seated. You reek of chauvinism and backward hick masculinity."

E.J. looked past her at the view of downtown behind her for fear she would take eye contact as offensive at this point.

"You're on administrative leave. I will prepare an accounting of all Devekon property, and it all better be there, Mr. Kane." Clara Brandis raised her hand to catch his attention.

E.J. rose. "Why did I drive to Houston? You made your mind up before I ever arrived."

Clara Brandis smirked. "Oh, I wanted to fire you, then prosecute you for taking Devekon property. Suspended with pay made a more valuable chip in a bigger game. As long as you stay in your lane, you're useful. I knew dealing with a neanderthal like you I had to look you in the eye."

E.J. turned and walked to the door. She deliberately

goaded him. She wanted him to explode.

He wouldn't give her the satisfaction. E.J. stopped, holding the knob. "You're contracted with Mike Stapleton, Stapleton Security. Retired military police contractor, bank prefers him. Fourteen personnel at any one time, four in the parking garage, and six at entrance armed with Sig Sauer P365s. Panic buttons on all floors. This room, it's in the upper right-hand desk drawer. I could walk you through the protocols for different contingencies, but I'm suspended."

"Be grateful you're driving home in a Devekon truck instead of wearing a barrel, Mr. Kane," she said.

E.J. ignored the assistant once removed when he told him to have a nice day. A considerable task, given E.J. wanted to throw the man out of one of the large glass panes around the room.

E.J. couldn't stop the self-pity exacerbated by the recollections of all the disgruntled employees and vendors whom he had caught stealing from the company. The gall of this person to call him a thief.

Wham, he lurched forward. E.J. looked around, thinking, please don't be the concrete pylon. He got out, making himself walk back toward the cement column.

The truth proved nearly as good. His trailer hitch had slammed into the concrete and broken a small piece of the pillar onto the ground, otherwise all was fine.

He tore out of the parking lot and through a red light. Soon, his mind cleared. Thoughts of seeing Sharla on the drive home buoyed him.

It had been a long time. Sharla had spent little time with him or her horse, Sunshine. He had given her the paint quarter horse on her eleventh birthday. Her face beamed, and her eyes were wide with excitement. A smile exploded across her face before her much smaller frame near lifted him in a bear hug. It was many years before the news of her brother's death.

E.J. cherished the special memory. She hadn't saddled Sunshine in over a year. He couldn't remember the last time Sharla had spoken to him without calling him a Nazi or accused him of perpetrating climate change.

"Call Sharla." In a moment, he heard the ringtone through the truck's audio system. No one answered. He was about to end the call.

"Yo, Taint."

"What?" E.J. asked.

"It's Taint, baby."

"Taint what?" E.J. asked.

"Taint Right, dawg." The voice laughed.

E.J. looked at the display 'Sharla'. He asked, "Where is Sharla Kane?"

"Indisposed."

"What does that mean? Get her on the phone. This is her father."

"Daddy law dawg. Hey, black lives matter, law dawg." His tone came across loud and harsh.

"Get Sharla on this phone," commanded E.J.

"Say her name, law dawg."

"Sharla." E.J. heard what he thought was a curse word as the phone cut off. He tried calling back, but there was no answer, so he left a message.

He would have to do what he desperately wanted to avoid. Calling Rebecca always ended in an argument. So far, he had never won an argument with Rebecca. He knew when they were dating, she thought quicker. E.J. gave himself a pass because she made her living in a courtroom.

"Call Rebecca Johnson." The very name reminded him of one of their first arguments.

In a moment, her voice rang through the truck in her sharp business tone. "What is it?"

"I called Sharla, and some guy calling himself Taint Right answers."

"Her boyfriend, Big E." Years ago, a captain had referred to E.J. as Big E. and she knew he hated it.

"When did this start, and who calls themselves Taint Right?" E.J. asked.

"Black guy too much for you?" Rebecca asked.

"I didn't know he was black, but I suspected when he started asking me Black Lives Matter questions," said E.J.

"White people support Black Lives Matter too."

"Well, I'm sure they do." Rebecca had sidetracked him again. His suspicions were really the main issue, so he changed the conversation. "She needed money again?"

"Stop giving it to her, and she will stop asking," said Rebecca.

"Rebecca."

"What do you expect? You never really talk to her. Do you know what she asked me? She asked me how Konner really died?" Rebecca asked.

"Are you going to tell me that's why you sued the Defense Department?" E.J. said.

Rebecca exhaled, and through the truck audio, it sounded like a wind storm. "We have a right to know the truth."

E.J. fumed because, "right to know the truth," referenced to their past fights. "They told us, but you and Sharla want to believe it's some grand conspiracy. Konner loved the service. You're disgracing his memory."

"And you're the reason he's dead. All he ever saw or heard was duty, badges, uniforms. How else was he going to turn out? He had to live up to his high and mighty father. So, he volunteers to become cannon fodder—"

E.J. lifted his thumb from the disconnect button on the steering wheel. He knew he had made a mistake calling Rebecca.

He wasn't a racist any more than he was a Nazi or a global warmer. Sharla and Rebecca pushed his buttons. Sharla couldn't keep weight on. Once an outstanding student, she had become a poor one. She always needed money and seemed to have an endless number of new boyfriends. The once avid rider took no interest in her horse or really anything from her old life.

One could explain each fact in the abstract, especially when he added Konner's death and his divorce from Rebecca to the equation. There were many ways to explain all the changes in the abstract. He couldn't compartment-alize and explain away the individual signs any longer. Sharla had a drug problem. He could no longer ignore the truth.

CHAPTER FIVE

SUNSHINE TROTTED AN IRREGULAR PATH TOWARD THE
barn. The early morning darkness near shrouded the big
gelding. E.J. slung the feed bucket over the wood fence of
his corral. The fresh smell of left-over barn stored hay
elicited a calming breath.

Sharla hadn't been at her apartment. Likewise, Taint
Right had left, leaving behind enough clothes and personal
effects to show he lived there too.

Sharla's roommate, Shasta, folded like any teenager in
the presence of a thirty-year interrogator who remained
close friends with her father. She confirmed E.J.'s worst
fears, although Shasta knew little detail. Taint Right sold
drugs, not any actual weight, but enough to make him a
hero to Sharla. Sharla had followed a predictable path of
experimentation from marijuana to mollies to crystal
meth.

Beige coloring doused large patches of the white coat
on the big horse. Sunshine placed his bleached-looking

head in the feed bucket. E.J. had thought the horse too big, too athletic for Sharla, yet the skewbald coloring captured her. Later, the horse's playful personality won both their hearts. Age had robbed the mount of his former power.

"I reported her missing. She hasn't been in class in days. I drove everywhere Shasta thought she could be." E.J. stepped one foot onto the bottom board of the corral.

Sunshine lifted his head for a moment before returning to the sweet feed. "I'm doing all I can do. There's no point in calling Rebecca. You know how she is."

"Gonna catch the ranger and some troopers this morning, then I'll say something to the deputies and PD at shift changes to get them to drive by these places Shasta suggested. Yes, they're mostly drug houses."

E.J. continued, despite Sunshine expressing no interest in the whereabouts of his owner. "True Taint is the supplier, and I never knew a user who wouldn't break a bump for a ten or a twenty. Users deal and dealers use; it's why you can't break the dealers."

E.J. brushed the horse, and Sunshine turned his head in quick fashion. "I also told Shasta to put out the word I had money to buy Sharla a laptop. Might draw her in. I got to stay busy, or I'll go crazy. Maybe talk to horses, huh? Wouldn't Clara Brandis love that?"

He threw open the tack room door and placed the brush on a nail. While walking to the truck, Clara Brandis went through his mind. Wouldn't she love to fire him for going crazy?

He pulled into the parking lot at the Department of Public Safety. After greeting everyone, including several old-timers who had been retired most of his career, he helped himself to a cup of coffee and took a seat.

"Was you wondering what the poor folks was doin' this morning?" asked Cooper.

"I've got to have help," said E.J.

A highway patrol sergeant E.J. remembered teaching at the academy, said, "What do we do?"

E.J. walked to the coffee maker, lifting the paper and tape in his hand. "My daughter, Sharla, may be at one of these addresses." He taped a picture of her next to the list, then looked at his feet. "She has a drug problem."

Cooper opened her mouth to speak but made no sound. Her shoulders went limp as she looked at E.J.

A sergeant raised his phone and photographed the wall, followed by the other active troopers. "We'll circulate it. I can get it to the lieutenants at PD and SO."

They walked out, leaving Cooper, E.J., and a pair of retirees. One of the retirees, Captain Weber, said, "You should go home, try to rest. It doesn't look like you slept."

"I searched all night. Haven't done any good. I can't sleep or do nothing," said E.J.

Cooper asked, "Thought about pinging her phone."

"She left it in the apartment," said E.J.

Captain Weber stepped closer. "Probably good news. She's coming back soon."

"No, looks like she took her makeup and an overnight bag, which tells me she doesn't want to be found," E.J. said.

Cooper gave Captain Weber a look like nodding toward the door.

Captain Weber rose and gave Cooper a good-natured sneer. "I only come here for the coffee. I get my conversation and company from my cows and horses. Come on, Charlie, they're going to talk ranger business, probably do their secret handshake and all."

Cooper squared up to E.J. with a stern look. "You can't look for Sharla. Let me. This is how you got drummed out, remember." She paused. "You were too close, and you lost your cool."

"I got cleared," E.J. snapped.

"Only after you had to resign, and Hall went to the mat for you with the feds. You work on this truck driver, Arnold, for me." She raised a hand to stop him from arguing. "Arnold is bigger than you think it is. I'll work on Sharla. I promise to treat her like my own. You know I will."

E.J. looked down. Cooper made sense, irrefutable sense, yet he wanted to argue. After a pause produced no way to cast doubt on her plan, he asked, "What's going on with Arnold?"

"Good," Cooper said.

E.J. felt like a dog retrieving a frisbee for the first time. "Maybe it'll keep me from going crazy. I spoke to the horse this morning."

"Well, I don't know if Arnold was an accident, suicide, or murder. Widow Welchel won't talk to me, and an autopsy isn't much use until we can get toxicology," Cooper said.

"Sure, you don't want to add terrorism? You got everything else on the list," said E.J.

Cooper laughed. "No terrorism, but there is more here than you know. A lot more."

E.J. stared at her, curious, waiting for the rest of the story.

"Did you ever hear talk about condensate or maybe casinghead gas?" asked Cooper.

"Like off oil wells?" E.J. said.

"More thinking of gas wells," Cooper said.

"My grandpa used to joke someone was running drip gas because their motor knocked." E.J. raised and lowered his shoulders, a sign he couldn't understand the import of Cooper's question.

"Yeah, drip gas, raw gas, wet gas, white gas, and my favorite white gold are all names for a condensate that is like refined gasoline. It's valuable because you can mix it to dilute really viscous crude. Something about the way the atoms connect makes it useful," explained Cooper.

"Wasted," said E.J.

"What?" Cooper asked.

"An academic mind like yours wasted rangering," quipped E.J.

She retorted, using the same sarcasm with E.J. he had used speaking to her so many times. "Listen, grasshopper, what if salt water haulers aren't really hauling salt water from the well; instead, they load this condensate? So instead of a negative value product that has to be transported to an injection well, they got something more valuable than crude oil?"

E.J. looked down then asked, "Aren't there records on how much condensate production?"

"Not at the wellhead and usually not until measured in the tank or taken off the tank, so no, no meter, no paper trail. Anybody suspicious in the companies gets bribed," answered Cooper.

"But you can't sell it on the street, can you?" E.J. asked.

"You've seen the little refinery over the Louisiana line in Greenville?"

"They're buying this stuff?"

Cooper gestured up with the palms of her hands. "Not

legally. Little outfits mostly take junk oil from oil changes and try to refine, sort of clean it so they can recycle it. So, a little light, clean stuff might be worth a lot to them, plus it sort of washes it into the system."

"Did Arnold stumble onto it, or was he in on it?" E.J. asked.

Cooper leaned back. "Don't know. Can't even tell you if it is really going on."

"How do you know what you've told me?" asked E.J.

"About a year ago, this trucker, salt water hauler, gets stopped on fifty-nine. Trooper's Daddy had owned a salt water injection outfit, so he picks up on some little oddities and calls for a canine. Bunch of old-school compartments everywhere, big weight ice. Pharmaceutical-grade meth, like the cartels, made in labs in Mexico. So, you know what DPS and DEA are thinking, right?"

"Try a controlled delivery," said E.J.

"Right, but the truck driver knew nothing. He was following a rental car which didn't turn around to check on the salt water hauler, so no controlled delivery. Bad record, member of a security threat group, so he's going to spend the rest of his life in Ad Seg at Huntsville unless—"

"Unless?" E.J. interrupted.

"He tells them he knows something else, something big, which is when I get a call," said Cooper.

E.J.'s scowls. "All you got? Some meth-head trying to avoid hard time?"

"Nope, meth-head gets out on bond, big bond, his gang post for him. About two weeks later, he gets stabbed to death in a bar."

"Suspicious, but it could have been over the drugs by the cartel," said E.J.

"Gets better. Bar is a topless joint, a headquarters for a gang. Odd name for the gang, want to guess it?" Cooper flashed a grin.

"Nephilim, like Arnold," said E.J.

"Better yet, a woman in this topless joint says he made unwelcome advances."

"Took offense, did she?" E.J. asked.

"Low rent joint. You know she's trafficked, probably drugged up and beat down so bad the only complainant her pimp allows her is about his money," Cooper said.

"Nephilim, let you talk to her?" E.J. asked.

"Gave a statement to the locals before I got there and supposedly gone ever since, though I think she's still there."

"Where is this bar?" E.J. asked.

"Don't make me say it. Doesn't matter; we both know a dozen places where these outfits pay off duty local departments for security, and everyone looks the other way. So, I tried undercover," Cooper said.

Shock overcame E.J., Women shouldn't go in such places. "You went to this nudey joint?" Immediately, he felt the sting of his antiquated attitude. He knew he would be reproached about female officers being able to do anything a male officer could do. "I mean, not that, that's not okay."

"'Not that, that's not okay'? I sent a C.I. Did you go stupid?" There was a sarcastic snark in her voice, cutting the air.

"Somebody called me a neanderthal for not being modern enough," explained E.J.

"Blowing off mandatory diversity training is not funny, now is it?" She nodded, though E.J. didn't acknowledge the quip. "Why you got hip, young people like me. I'll tell you when you're being a neanderthal, and you're not, but you get stupid sometimes."

"Thank you." E.J. decided there wasn't any other response.

"Anyway, I didn't put any credence in this mule either until I counted maybe two murders. For what?" Cooper asked.

"And you been sitting on this a year?" E.J. said.

"I interviewed the guy who owns the oil reclamation outfit. He lawyered up when I pressed him." Cooper paused. "What am I supposed to do? Get an eighteen-wheeler load of white gold and drive it to a low-end refinery. I guess you forgot we don't have those, plus I don't have a C.I. stupid enough to risk getting murdered."

"You need a stupid neanderthal who can get his hands on a tanker truck of condensate," E.J. said.

Cooper nodded. "You're no neanderthal, not if you can pull this operation off, anyway."

"You've been planning this little undertaking since you saw me at the Martin number three." E.J. turned on the way out the door. "Okay, I might know a guy."

"Figured you did," said Cooper.

"Bet you also figured afterwards, this lonely neanderthal could go lookin' for love in all the wrong places," said E.J.

"No urban cowboy. I got something classier in mind," said Cooper.

CHAPTER SIX

A SUDDEN PULL YANKED THROUGH THE SEAT OF E.J.'S
pants. He swung over seventy thousand pounds into the
left lane to avoid a collision. Looking through the mirror
after the fact, he realized he had cut off a tractor-trailer on
Interstate twenty.

He cussed Earl. Last night, he had praised Earl as a gift
from God, bringing light to a dark world. Earl broadcast
the secrets of truck driving on YouTube. Further, Earl
would train anyone at Earl's driving academy.

Not only would Earl provide these services, but he
would also use his influence to place drivers with
companies for a small percentage of their earnings. The
universe owed its gratitude for the efficient delivery of
goods to Earl. Now in E.J.'s mind, Earl's legitimate
paternity was sorely in issue.

E.J. couldn't tell the supervisor at the Devekon yard in
Marshall that he didn't have a commercial driver's license,
nor only the most cursory education from Earl and the

internet on truck driving. Thirty years in the Department of Public Safety, a lifetime of driving farm equipment, and hauling some good-sized trailer loads behind his pickups had seemed more than satisfactory in E.J.'s mind.

Reality gripped him like the chill in the bottom of his belly, telling him it wasn't enough. Pulling onto the interstate, he had swung around the nineties model Chevrolet pickup. E.J. had made a waving gesture in his mirror to explain a tanker truck doesn't stop on a dime. Wasn't a wave the international symbol for I'm sorry?

The driver of the older blue truck returned the gesture with the international symbol for wishing a non-merry Christmas. For the next fifteen miles, E.J. endured harrowing adventures.

This blue vehicle would climb so close to the back of the tanker trailer E.J. could barely see it in the mirrors, then slingshot past him, only to apply the brakes. Such caused E.J. to take evasive action. He could hear the plaintiff's lawyer in a prospective lawsuit against Devekon, former highway patrolman and Texas ranger driving recklessly without a commercial license causes multi-car pileup on the interstate. A vision of his ex-wife accompanied by a long line of neck braced litigants walking into a courtroom past him.

What an ignominious and ridiculous end to his career. To get caught doing something stupid because he didn't want to secure the truck for an undercover officer. He needed to be active.

He needed his mind to stop punishing him for not seeing the early signs with Sharla, for not having the courage to confront her. Would she have hated him forever, like her mother? Would she have reminded him

Konner's death was his fault?

E.J. wanted to stop, to pull onto the shoulder. It was too late. There he was, mister blue pickup becoming larger in the mirror, swinging into the blind spot behind the big rig. E.J. continued downshifting, trying to slow the enormous weight behind him. Was the truck on his bumper or moving into the blind spot in the other lane?

There was the one-finger salute held high in the wind. The pickup bobbed in the breeze like a toy compared to the tractor-trailer. The brake lights consumed his vision, and electric fear ran up E.J.'s spine, shooting out the tips of his fingers, which were pressing between the cold dark steering wheel and the white tips of his nails.

E.J. hit the brakes. He flipped all three positions on the Jake brake. A process Earl promised would rob the cylinder heads of power and slow the truck quicker.

A force lifted him as if he had taken flight. He hadn't felt the sensation so naked, so powerful since driving exercises in the academy. Either the back end would soon swing around in a jackknife or would fly.

"Panic is death. Gradual into the skid." The old sergeant's words erupted in his brain. E.J. turned the wheel cautiously to the right. He fought the urge to pull on the wheel, knowing as counter-intuitive as it seemed such could only rob him of what little semblance of control he had. He had tens of thousands of highly combustible tons behind him.

He crossed the entire inner lane, feeling another yank through his gut as the big trailer tires bounced on the rough shoulder before he regained the handle. Sweet Jesus, he would live. E.J. looked down, then back up the road. The tiny blue vehicle gave him a final salute before disappearing over the horizon.

E.J. took a deep breath before commencing again. Moving through the H pattern of the transmission, he realized his hands weren't cool and dry. The experience took a toll on him.

A drawing of a white pelican looking over a lily in royal blue letters against a light green background read, 'Green Earth Reclamation'. The sign stood in stark contrast to the silver-colored forest of pipes, tanks, cylinders, and smoky stacks.

E.J. followed arrow signs to the metal building designated as the office. After parking, he gave himself a quick pep talk, trying to calm down from the wild ride. A few deep breaths, and he was ready.

He imitated a cooperating individual who had made a lot of cases before a heart condition, the C.I. Self-medicating with methamphetamine ended the man. A brief narration to the button camera on his shirt provided the date, time, and location.

E.J. twisted the cool metal doorknob and opened the door, revealing an older lady sitting at a desk. She didn't look up. A pair of flat-screen monitors shared space with neat stacks of paper, framed pictures, and a nameplate.

"Now there, sugar, got you a truck of—" E.J. looked around, and in a quieter tone, said, "Wet gas."

She looked up over her bifocals and held out a palm, "Paperwork?"

E.J. reached for her hand and bent forward like he was going to kiss it.

She jerked her hand back. "What's wrong with you, fool? You know paperwork, your railroad commission form or our forms, but I can tell somebody as ignorant as you got to be Texan. Always trouble."

E.J. looked down. Though in character, he knew he had earned the rebuke. He had to keep himself from grinning while he spied the nameplate, 'Vanessa'. "Sug, I ain't got none. I'm new and Arnold. Well, Arnold said I could make some quick money. Y'all do the paperwork. Said 'Nissa' would do it."

"You mean, Nessa," she said.

She hit a button on a blue tooth headset. "Mr. Blake. There is a gentleman here to see you." Her eyes met E.J.'s.

Had the nickname been enough to sell it, or was she onto him? How could she be onto him? Her eyes gave no hint. If he were ever a gambling man, he wouldn't play cards with this woman.

"No sir, he doesn't have an appointment, and I don't know his name?"

E.J. blurted, "Ed Jackson." Her nose scrunched ever so slightly. There it was, the sign he had sold her. She revealed her irritation, and why shouldn't she? He had been rude and uncouth like the real cooperating individual, Jeremy something or other.

"Yes, sir. He can wait." She tapped the keyboard, and E.J. figured the headset connected to the keyboard, too. "Go wait outside."

"I can't wait for him in here?" E.J. asked.

"No." Her stern tone increased in volume.

E.J. took two steps toward the door. As he opened it, he said, "I was gonna ask for your number but I ain't gonna do it now."

Her face downcast, she said, "Don't make me shoot ya."

E.J. shut the door, making a production of stepping

quick. He looked to the cloudy sky. The old-timers would say it smelt like rain. Perhaps he had played this boorish character a little too over the top. He wanted Vanessa sidetracked by the idea he was a loser trying to hit on her.

However, he hadn't intended to condemn himself to the possibility of standing in the rain. Besides, after Earl's YouTube Trucking school, he had perused LinkedIn. Artimus Blake held the title of President and CEO of Green Earth Reclamation and Blake Environmental L.L.C. He assumed this was the owner Cooper mentioned lawyered up when she interviewed him.

The picture depicted a stout, baby-faced man who was active in the local chamber of commerce, rotary club, and regularly attended charity events. Pictures from a toy drive, boys and girls club gala, and a skeet shoot convinced E.J. the man's wife was an attractive woman named Carmen. From all appearances, a young successful power couple climbing the social and economic ladder in an affluent suburb of Shreveport.

If it did rain, did this video camera work? How much battery did he have? He had purchased the button video recorder for Devekon, still he couldn't remember. E.J. tried to picture the writing on the box. He had thrown the instructions away when he opened the packaging over a year ago. He chided himself for being stupid. Why wouldn't you look to see how long the thing recorded on a charge?

Artimus Blake looked taller, less rotund, and more pleasant in his picture. "You need to see me?"

"Sure do, sir. I need some help with paperwork, ain't got none," E.J. made the remark with his best snicker.

"No," said Artimus Blake.

"Fella said you could help me out," said E.J.

"What 'fellow'? Who does he work for?" Artimus Blake spoke in a quick, smooth cadence.

"Arnold drove for Widow Welchel."

"You work for Widow?" Artimus Blake asked.

E.J. shook his head and winked. "No, I'm talking about the down-low, *comprende*?" The ruse wasn't working, or the mule lied to Cooper, or Artimus Blake pegged him as law enforcement. Which one?

"Stay here." Artimus Blake turned and walked inside.

This wasn't going well at all. Was Blake calling law enforcement? The business executive might be as good as his profile looked. E.J. had made a mistake letting himself get pulled into Cooper's wild theories, complete with white gold. Might as well tell him a buried treasure story.

In the alternative, what if Artimus Blake wasn't squeaky clean? What if Artimus Blake was the ring leader of a sophisticated criminal enterprise? What if he had ordered the snitch truck driver and the trafficking victim killed?

CHAPTER SEVEN

A DOPER TRUCK DRIVER AND A STRIPPER WERE THE people no one really missed. He had pretended to be a similar person. E.J. put his hand on the pistol in his pocket. The door startled E.J., and he near drew the gun.

Artimus Blake carried some papers in his left hand, jutting them toward E.J. A clipboard of documents filled his right hand. "Here is a copy of what you should have, and this is a set I'll help you with this one time." He wrote as he spoke.

"'Preciate it, brother," said E.J.

"I'm going to need the well name, the operator number, your company." Artimus Blake handed E.J. the pen.

E.J. gave him a confused look. He returned the pen. "Com'on, man."

"So, you can't read or write." Artimus Blake stared at E.J.

E.J. returned the look. "Right, appreciate you filling it

out for me." He watched Artimus Blake completing the form. The name of the company, the lease number, and the well name he recognized, 'Martin number three'.

Between east Texas, southern Arkansas, and western Louisiana, there were thousands of wells. Why the same well where Arnold's body was discovered? Devekon operated the well.

Wouldn't Devekon have filed something with the regulating authority, the Texas Railroad Commission, about the well damage? Did he know? Was this some kind of test?

No, he didn't know. E.J. recalled Devekon encompassed many companies, one of which was B.H. production. B.H. production was the operator Artimus Blake listed.

Artimus Blake looked up. "Shame about Chez."

"Who?"

"Chez."

E.J. thought he had to be referencing Arnold. Was this happening? Same well, and now he admitted he knew Arnold. Ignorance might be the best play. The best way to get Artimus Blake to turn on the light was to stand in darkness. "All I knew was Arnold. Something happen?"

"You hadn't heard?"

"No, what happened?" E.J. asked.

"Chez got himself blown up," said Artimus Blake

"What? How?" E.J. asked.

Artimus Blake shrugged his shoulders. "Lightning hit a tank. I heard you could bury him in a shoebox. I don't even know where it happened." Artimus Blake shook his head while he pulled a pair of work gloves from his back pocket.

E.J. watched Artimus Blake produce a cigarette

wearing the work gloves. It had to be some kind of violation to smoke anywhere in a refinery, but why the gloves? Maybe Mrs. Carmen Blake didn't tolerate smoke. Old boy would probably put on a rain coat next.

"You're going to keep driving around to the back. You'll see where to unload. Mr. Jackson, if you ever come here again without paperwork. You won't be driving to the back, *comprende*?"

E.J. nodded.

"How did you know Chez?" Artimus Blake asked.

How could one person be so stupid? E.J. had put himself here without a sufficient cover story. Crossing paths as truck drivers wasn't enough. There had to be a plausible reason for Arnold to take him into his confidence and share his criminal activity.

The Nephilim held oddball religious beliefs. E.J. gave voice to what crossed his mind. "We both listened to Barry Cross' Holy Smoke Wagon. So, we struck up a conversation down at the Hilltop Cafe one time."

Artimus Blake looked up at E.J. "The cowboy church preacher who does the archeology."

E.J. gave thanks that he still favored the old a.m. talk radio stations instead of satellite radio. "Yeah, pretty 'mazing, man. I mean, he got a genuine relic from the ark."

"Chez and you ever go to any religious meetings?"

"Kept inviting me to something. I was always tied up." E.J. pointed like it was all coming to him. "Wait a minute, are y'all in like the same Bible study or something?"

"You might say we were in the same benevolent organization like the Rotary club or the Lions or Elks. All same things. We got a meeting this week. Give me your number, and I'll drop you a pin later. A good way to remember Chez," said Artimus Blake.

E.J. had been wise enough to get a burner phone.

Artimus Blake turned and re-entered the office without further comment. E.J. exhaled. Adrenalin coursed through his veins.

He wanted to tell himself he had done well. E.J. knew he had near blown the operation twice. His investigative career had been spent interviewing witnesses, assembling records, cultivating informants, and managing the cooperating individuals who went undercover. Rarely had E.J. performed undercover. In fact, he couldn't remember the last time.

Chiding himself occupied him so much he startled when a sharp aroma burned his nostrils. A stout chemical smell comparable to the fresh tar of a road working crew, yet more pungent.

He thought he understood enough from his crash course to unload the condensate. However, E.J. stepped aside without complaint when a scruffy young man in what at one time had been a blue uniform shirt took charge. A patch on the oversized uniform denoted 'Geoffrey'. It didn't suit him because he looked more like a Jeffie or Jeff.

E.J. knew he hadn't got enough on Artimus Blake. His results were the worst possible. Hadn't E.J. made it clear the load amounted to stolen goods, what old-timers called 'hot oil'. Other questions had arisen. Why did Artimus Blake join this strange gang, the Nephilim?

For the moment, there was only one issue looming before him. Did Geoffrey know anything, and could he turn him? After several pleasantries and several attempts to get the correct last name so he could run a criminal history and other reports later.

At first, Geoffrey wouldn't be baited into anything over two words.

E.J. grumbled, "I couldn't get my paperwork right. Glad Mr. Blake got me straight. Could've been bad, couldn't it?"

Geoffrey made no response other than a brief nod. Blood stained his fingertips. The stains drew E.J.'s attention to sores on Geoffrey's arms and face. Mostly they were healing, which made them less noticeable. The young man, or more likely someone who cared for him, tried to doctor him.

Undeterred, E.J. threw the bait and lure back into the water. "Never would have thought to use the Martin number three for the well after what happened and all."

Geoffrey's face turned surprised. "What happened?"

"Blew up, that there's what it was. Pieces of some old boy spread out over a football field." E.J. chuckled without laughing.

"Who?"

"Don't know, feller worked for the Widow woman. You know, WelCo." E.J. set the hook, letting the news pour over a deflating Geoffrey. Then added, "Hey, how 'bout that. No wonder Martin number three struck a bell with me. You think your boss knows something, or maybe he's tellin' me something?"

"Chez." Geoffery more mouthed the word than spoke it.

"Chez?"

"His name, Chez Arnold?" Geoffrey asked.

"Oh, know him?" E.J. moved closer to appear concerned. "I shouldn't run my mouth. I'm always doin', just like that right there. Kinfolks?"

Geoffrey looked down. "Got me out of a jam."

"What kind of jam?" E.J. asked.

"You're unloaded, mister."

E.J. pressed the issue. "Tell me why Martin number three and if the boss man knew what happened to your friend."

Geoffrey shook his head. "You ask too many questions."

E.J. stepped back, moving toward the cab. "Hey man, passin' time that there's all I'm doing." He drove out the gate, hoping he hadn't gone too far. This kid knew more, a lot more.

For the first time in days, he had not thought about Sharla for some period. E.J. believed she would appear when she needed money, although he feared for her safety.

He had to compare this reprieve to the first time he had had a few hours of peace after Konner died. Too often, his mind tortured him with the worst potential outcomes, and a litany of all the opportunities he squandered to avoid the tragic events of recent years. E.J. convinced himself the introspective habit made him an excellent investigator. His mind whirled as he made an otherwise uneventful return to the Devekon yard in Marshall.

E.J. had pre-arranged a meet with Cooper at DPS headquarters, intending to move into step two of her plan to investigate what Cooper believed amounted to a sophisticated crime syndicate. She met him at the door, and after the initial pleasantries, E.J. discussed the next task.

"Likely, many gang members can identify me from the

refinery. If this bar is their hangout, then it looks a little hinky. I mean me claiming to be listening to evangelical radio and talking God with Chez Arnold," said E.J.

"Got one of the DEA task force guys to work on your ugly mug," said Cooper.

"Not wearing make-up."

Cooper laughed. "No, I'm thinking beard. Maybe something makes you look like a toupée-wearing loser."

"Yeah," said E.J.

Cooper stepped toward him with what looked like a tanned squirrel hide. "You know so many fat cat lawyers because of Rebecca. Can't you play one?"

"I'm wishing I'd have watched all of that Tarantino movie about vampire strippers," said E.J.

"*From Dusk Till Dawn,* never figured you for a Tarantino fan," said Cooper.

"Tried to be cool and watch it with Konner. Figure it's same seedy, dark, and dirty prostitute cribs." E.J. took the dead squirrel-looking wig.

"I thought all men had been to bachelor parties at these joints," said Cooper.

E.J. shrugged. "Never been invited."

Cooper shook her head, chuckling. "Bet you hadn't. Figure you gave your fellow troopers field sobriety test."

E.J.'s attention turned to a rough-looking character who had clipped his credentials to his shirt, Drug Enforcement Administration. After nodding to Cooper and making his introductions to E.J., the federal agent went to work on the hairpiece and beard. Cooper reminded E.J. the goal was for it to look like a bad toupée, though the well-kept goatee conveyed authenticity.

The transformation impressed E.J., though he cringed

because the disguise reminded him of Rebecca's boyfriend. Specifically, the loafers looked more akin to slippers forcing him to channel his inner Stuart. E.J. practiced stabbing his words the way Stuart enunciated every syllable, displaying a hint of a lisp. Despite his best efforts, E.J. failed, resulting in a harsh, piercing tone and a more rapid cadence.

Cooper handed E.J. an ankle holster with a small Ruger polymer pistol.

E.J. tapped the suit pants pocket. "Got mine."

"Big boy, you might want to rethink the whole gun in your pocket...." Cooper said.

E.J. frowned, knowing she had a point. Yet E.J. loathed to give up his trusted Sig for an untested chunk of plastic. "I always carry it. Figure if it ever comes to it. I can depress the safety and jab the trigger over the pants."

The DEA agent chuckled. "Whoo, I bet it'll burn your thigh up. She is right, I'd wear an ankle. New guy throwing money around. They're gonna be checking you out."

"Money?" asked E.J.

"You know the department. Devekon'll spot you," said Cooper.

E.J. took the gun and ankle holster. A grin pried at the corners of E.J.'s mouth, thinking how much Rex Ashe would love this assignment, spend money, and act a fool over women.

"I checked a corolla out from forfeitures. We want the successful grandpa easy mark look," said Cooper.

E.J. pointed at a wallet Cooper held. "Tell it."

"Weldon Harris, lawyer from Mansfield, Texas, going to Shreveport on business. You've been talking to Georgia, which brought you into the Lion's Den," said Cooper.

E.J. chuckled, "The Lion's Den?"

"Yes," said Cooper.

"Georgia, is she the one who killed the informant?"

Cooper nodded and showed him a photo on her phone.

"What do I do when the killer doesn't remember talking to me?" asked E.J.

"They're all prostitutes talking guys up. She won't remember any one man over another."

E.J. looked at her. Cooper had made the statement in her matter-of-fact tone. The reasoning made sense. Yet was it the kind of deduction he would bet his life on? "Ever tell you about the Cajun noodler my dad worked with?"

"No," said Cooper.

"You know, grabbing catfish out of stumps under water in nasty old bayous. So, Daddy asks him, isn't he afraid a cottonmouth will bite him reaching in them holes?" E.J. let the story linger.

"Okay, you got me. Why won't the snake bite?" asked Cooper.

"This webbed footer tells Daddy snake won't bite you underwater, can't breathe. He'll drown. Point is my dad thought there was no way a man with any sense would risk his life on an old wives' tale whether or not it made sense."

Cooper asked, "The point?"

"This Georgia will figure out in two minutes how I've never talked to her on the phone," said E.J.

The DEA agent interjected. "She's not paying attention to these losers. They're all pathetic. Either big mouth liars or sad-sack losers going through a divorce after losing their only gal. You can't mess it up."

"You're an expert; you should do this," offered E.J.

"Not my rodeo, man. Just promised Cooper I would get you ready," said the fed.

Cooper raised her hands in a pleading motion. "Worst happens, she makes you as police and clams up."

"Wire? Maybe a button camera?" asked E.J.

"Too dangerous. You're walking in their headquarters. They may sweep it. One thing for her to get suspicious, much worse to get caught wired up," said Cooper.

E.J. didn't like any of it, yet he could see Cooper wanted the operation. She had bought into the theft ring theory and had probably been kicking this hair-brained plan around for a while. He needed her to try even half-brained ideas to find Sharla, so how could he say no. "Sure, Cooper."

The doubts nagged him all the way to Silver City. E.J. expected to find the Lion's Den in the middle of nowhere. Visions of confederate flags hanging in the rafters of a sawdust floor barn soured by the smell of rotgut whiskey danced in his head. Likely, darkness would shield his view of meth queens missing most of their teeth and making meager attempts at dance motions, moving their naked bodies branded by ink denoting knuckle-dragging Aryan boyfriends.

He didn't stop when he saw a well-landscaped single-story brick building with a commercially made sign, 'The Lion's Den'. E.J. turned the sedan around and pulled into the parking lot. He found no thirty-year-old farm trucks with gun racks across the back glass.

Instead, the parking lot held the status symbols of the young and upwardly mobile in this part of the world. Porsches, Lexus', and cowboy Cadillacs like his Devekon work truck dotted the asphalt.

E.J. stepped through a heavy door to see a young woman seated behind thick plexiglass. She requested his identification and twenty dollars.

"Thank you, Mr. Harris. I hope you enjoy yourself." She could have passed for a model until she handed his driver's license back through a hole in the plexiglass. He saw the makeup caked covering a sore on her arm. A casual observer wouldn't have noticed, especially given the scarcity of her garment.

She buzzed him through an inner door. Once inside, his preconceptions based upon *Dusk till Dawn* and biker-style dive bars shattered for good. The furniture wasn't mismatched style, nor were there broken and dilapidated foosball and pool tables. Eighties hair bands didn't fill the air; rather, modern pop music blared.

Recessed fisheye fixtures lit the room. A large center stage with two side pull-outs further away caught his attention. The traditional long narrow bar had been superseded by two pocket corner stations. Likely something far better than the forty-rod whiskey poured into clean glasses. Stamped concrete made the floor look like expensive tile.

A handful of men sat around the room in twos and threes. E.J. figured his chances of meeting Georgia improved if he sat alone. Prior to finding a seat, he studied the room for security and exits; what tactical instructors called situational awareness.

Nothing resembling guards appeared anywhere. Even high-end dance clubs employed bouncers. E.J. deduced either hidden cameras reviewed the establishment in some secure room or, more likely, most of the patrons were Nephilim. They all served as security in their own clubhouse.

He looked for something distinctive about the men or the room, like colors or patches for a club. Over his shoulder, he viewed a long line of portraits. Figured they were a gallery of club presidents, E.J. focused on the last one. The image stood out by sheer girth, highlighting a bulbous nose.

E.J. took a seat about half distance from the pictures to the stage, trying to keep his back to the wall. A strong, overwhelmingly sweet odor overtook him while a snip of a woman materialized in a bikini, asking him something. An Imagine Dragons song made communication challenging when E.J. realized another stranger had pulled onto his other side.

"Your drink order," yelled the newcomer, dressed in a sky-blue camisole. Her long brunette hair had swung across E.J.'s shoulder. Despite their attractiveness, both women invading his space unnerved him.

E.J. reached his hand to his thigh, attempting to touch the Sig in his pocket, and its absence echoed through his gut like an enormous, hammered gong. He remembered the Ruger strapped to his ankle and took some small comfort in the knowledge.

"Minimum two drinks or thirty dollars for newbies," she said.

"Maybe, I'm a regular."

"No, you're not." She turned to the server, "Two whiskey sours."

E.J. felt relieved when the smaller woman stepped away. He turned to the other, "Maybe, I wanted a coke."

"No, you don't. You want to take me to the champagne room."

"I am a newbie. On Lion's Den dot com is an ad for Sassy swingers dot com, and I been talking to somebody there," said E.J.

She put her hand over his hand. "Who?"

"Georgia."

"Georgia." She laughed, slapping his shoulder with her hand before settling her nails into his bicep.

E.J. looked at her, pondering whether she was high when the server placed drinks before them.

She near snorted before she contained herself. "I'm Georgia. Don't you recognize me?"

E.J. thought back, trying to envision the driver's license picture Cooper had shown him of Martha Wilmington, a woman who used Georgia for her stage name. She was a blond. Perhaps she dyed her hair.

He had told Cooper this Georgia would out him. She could be lying. A prostitute pretends she is what's requested, right? A dose of honesty presented the only option. "You look different in person."

Georgia reached up and swung off the long mane of brunette hair, revealing dishwater short blond hair like the photo. They both chuckled.

"It's me, you silly bear. Finish your drink, then we'll go to the champagne room, like we talked about," said Georgia.

"Right." E.J. rose while Georgia remained. He caught on quicker this time. "How much for the champagne room?"

"One hundred then fifty dollars a song. But drink your whiskey." She moved quickly when he produced his wallet.

Cooper had warned him about the expense. She led E.J.

to a curtain divider at the end of the room. He had erroneously assumed the curtain was on the wall during his earlier assessment. More curtains and a magnum of champagne on a table next to a chair appeared inside.

She poured two glasses, presenting one to E.J. before wrapping her arm inside his, urging him to drink. E.J. let the liquid touch his lips without consuming it, then watched her do the same before both placed the glass on the table.

"Ketamine, something else?" asked E.J., "You got some muscle behind the curtain to help roll me?"

"Pretty smart for a newbie." She sat on his lap, using both her hands to swing his right wrist backwards and over. Extreme pain crunched E.J. in a vise of agony.

She eased the pressure a small amount, and E.J. drew a deep breath. "Men come here to be touched. Not you, so what do you really want?"

E.J. looked into her eyes, and before he could speak, she reapplied the pressure, and he gurgled, stifling a yell.

"Military Police. Much more, and I'll make you left-handed."

This gig had ended. E.J. came clean. "Gibson, remember him, the fellow you stabbed—"

"I didn't stab anybody," said Georgia.

"I don't care. Who did he work for? Who wanted him killed?"

She looked up. E.J. raised his leg, lifted his boot, and stabbed the heel through the open toe of her shoe, near severing her toe. Georgia shrieked, releasing his hand and jumping into the air onto the other foot. E.J. shook his arm, trying to regain some feeling.

The curtain was flung open. Something solid and

metallic hammered E.J.'s jaw, swinging him onto the floor.

An awareness came to E.J. that an overweight man slammed Georgia to the ground, yet he couldn't be sure what was occurring. The world spun around him as his head bounced off the floor.

The heavy man yelled, "Only brotherhood. Everybody else out." He swung open the curtain.

E.J. tried wobbling forward, hoping to rise.

"Stay down." Turning the other way, the heavy man yelled, "Get my bottle."

Leaning up from his waste E.J. saw the enormous silver gun aimed at Georgia's head. The man cursed her and demanded she tell him what she said. He seemed unconvinced by her assurances she had said nothing. Evidently, he hadn't been behind the curtain the whole time, or he would have known she revealed nothing. The heavy man kicked Georgia in the teeth, and blood poured from her mouth, making the unmistakable combined scent of blood and alcohol.

Another server brought a liquor bottle and set it up with glasses on a table provided by two men who stepped back afterward.

The heavy man poured from the bottle with his free hand before motioning for E.J. to take. Georgia slammed the shot back. E.J. didn't move, prompting the man to turn up the bottle and drink from it. "See, there's nothing in it except the nectar of the gods."

E.J. stared at him.

He swung the gun to where E.J. looked up at the massive barrel. "Drink, sweetie."

E.J. said, "I don't drink."

The heavy man smiled and poured Georgia another.

She consumed it as quickly as the first, and the man pointed to her. "She knows. We gonna play the feud, sweetie."

He opened the enormous cylinder on the revolver, flipped it up, and dropped some bullets into the gun with his free hand. "No use lying; Karen heard Gibson's name, so what did you tell him?"

Georgia's face melted in tears, slobber, mascara, and foundation all pouring down dirty cheeks. "I swear, I swear."

He placed the barrel on her forehead. E.J. heard the hammer snap, and his own belly turned over and forced a sharp, nauseous feeling.

"Stop, she said nothing," yelled E.J.

"Not your turn, sweetie." He turned the hand cannon on E.J. "Gibson, talk!"

E.J. stared into the man's pale grey eyes.

Air and powder exploded down the barrel, scorching the side of E.J.'s head in hot air. The world collapsed in noise followed by ear-ringing silence while his head swung and fell to the floor as if it wasn't connected to his torso. E.J. questioned whether he lived. The round probably missed by less than an inch.

"Wrong answer. Mr. Weldon Sweetie Harris. Wrong answer for Nephilim purposes." The heavy man made an odd smirk standing over E.J.

Immediately following the realization, he would die. Visions of Sharla flooded E.J.'s mind. Even if Rebecca and Cooper found her, they were incapable or unwilling to do what it took to get her home. In his mind, she lay in a filthy prostitute's crib covered in meth sores shooting dope. He had to reach the ankle holster.

Georgia lurched backward, shrieking at the sight of the barrel. "Your turn," yelled the heavy man. For him, whether a primer ignited the powder charge remained a mystery. However, Georgia could see the hollow copper points of the rounds in the chambers, and experience had taught her which way the revolver turned.

She clinched her eyes, unwilling to see the massive bullet enter and blow out the back of her head like a melon on a target stick. Silence reigned as her limp trunk fell over.

E.J. swung his hand while lifting his leg to release the Ruger LCP. Small and supple, the tiny pistol moved into his palm, and his hand extended until the barrel jammed into the side of the big man's skull.

The heavy man spoke in a slower, more purposeful cadence. "You'll never get out of here alive."

Out of his periphery, E.J. saw a room covered with firearms pointed in his direction. As he feared, the members served as security for the hideout.

"Chief Reid, I believe sweetie wants to report a crime." The heavy man continued to mock E.J. and disparaged the murdered dancer. "Com'on, Chief. Look at Sweetie's little gun."

E.J.'s eye fell on someone clad in tactical pants and shirt, in the general direction of the heavy man's gaze. A lifetime of commitment to duty welled in his soul and extended throughout E.J's body, contracting his index finger. In an instant, E.J. fired a projectile through the chief's knee and returned the gun to the heavy man's cranium.

Chief Reid buckled forward. His face bounced off the hard flooring. "I didn't do nothing."

E.J. announced, "I'm walking out of here with your grand poohbah. Move, he dies. Open the door after I close it, he dies." Trying to walk backwards while guiding or half dragging an overweight man paled compared to finding the knob without looking.

E.J. couldn't resist looking up at the distant stars. He kept walking backwards, fighting back the desire to stare into their intoxicating freedom. Involuntarily, he further stabbed the gun into the heavy man's head.

Drawing and pressing the keys meant E.J. had to take his hand from the man's neck. E.J. pressed the fob; then, the big man's elbow hammered E.J.'s ribs. Wind escaped his lungs, and E.J. fought to maintain his balance while holding the keys and weapon.

The heavy man dropped and rolled under a parked truck. E.J. didn't dare stop or try to get a shot at the man. A nasty army of white supremacists and sovereign citizens were armed far better than the .380 caliber pea shooter E.J. held.

The sedan Cooper had chosen fish-tailed onto the road. The police chief's officers would likely give pursuit. However, the more important question, would they put out a bulletin for him? They couldn't risk him telling another agency about the crime scene until they disposed of Georgia's body.

He thought Cooper could have picked something better than a family ride as he pegged the vehicle. He couldn't suppress the thought of Georgia. Wasn't it a horrible waste?

How does someone become so intertwined with the sex industry she doesn't want out? At some point, Georgia had been capable of more, or she wouldn't have been police in the Army. Somebody, probably lots of somebodies, lost a loved one, a daughter, a sister, a granddaughter in a moment of grand moronic bloodlust.

He had to report it, yet all the technology and modernism of the greatest democracy in history couldn't break the fiefdom of a small-town police chief. No one could help. Assuming E.J. could get a team of rangers or federal agents moving into Chief Reid's little empire. Chief Reid's small-town officers joined by a host of ex-cons could clean and bleach a crime scene to the point no one could confirm the slaughter nor that anyone called Georgia had ever stepped foot in the club.

He should have killed her murderer, even if it meant his death. He had sworn an oath to do so. He might lose Sharla like Georgia had been lost, and he would want someone to avenge her murder.

A moment later, his mind turned to Chief Reid. What would E.J. tell Cooper? Chief Reid would never tell the truth about what happened. Telling the truth would force him to admit he frequented what amounted to a known brothel and criminal gang headquarters.

Cooper couldn't understand shooting a man except as justified by the Texas Penal Code. Only an imminent physical threat justified deadly force used in self-defense. Unfortunately, a threat to humanity's dignity hadn't rated capital punishment since civility had overtaken honor in the criminal justice system.

No doubt, for the rest of his life, Chief Reid would walk with a limp. E.J. hoped every painful step Chief Reid took reminded him of how he failed Georgia and who knows how many others.

Still, E.J. chided himself because only now, well down

the road, did he admit he had almost killed Chief Reid. He recalled the sight-picture of the man's head past the front post of the pistol. The smell of burning powder filled his nostrils again. At the last second, he had pulled away and fired, blowing out the cartilage and ligaments of the knee.

No benefit came in reporting any of it. Rather than determine how to parse his words with Cooper, E.J. elected to call her and attempt a cursory summary in hopes she would want to get home to her own family. Every detective knows questioning someone about an event when the interviewer is privy to little information eventually proves unproductive.

She insisted on meeting to debrief. Wasn't that Cooper? She did things by the book. He wouldn't lie to her, and he couldn't tell her he shot the police chief. A visceral pain burned through E.J. thinking about the coward watching an innocent die while wearing a badge promising to protect and serve.

He shot Chief Reid in the knee, and the man didn't draw to defend himself. Even if someone had the drop on you, wasn't it better to make a play than rely on the mercy of someone who already shot you through the kneecap?

Chief Reid didn't reach for his gun, likely sensing any threatening movement would end his life. Instead, the mouse clinched his eyelids. Chief Reid snapped his eyes shut forcefully. A pair of words came to E.J.'s mind, solving the entire dilemma. He knew what he would tell Cooper.

What old-timer had first assembled the words coiling his thoughts and recollections into a steel spring ready to explode around the facts? Whoever constructed the phrase crafted a paradigm of grey where policies and written codes failed.

Cooper caught him in the parking lot. She insisted on a moment-by-moment account. In short order, E.J. walked her through the last minutes of Georgia's life. Repeating the story enhanced the parallels between Georgia and Sharla, already plaguing him.

E.J. next turned the conversation to the maiming of Chief Reid. The phrase he employed had no practical definition. "Police chief made a furtive movement after I drew my gun on the killer."

"Furtive movement, huh?" She shook her head. "Didn't think he had it in him," said Cooper.

"You knew his entire department did security for the nudey joint as a way to launder bribes, right?" E.J. looked away.

"You kill him?" Cooper's tone heightened.

"No. No. Drag his leg a little, maybe," said E.J.

Cooper raised her head, looking upward. She turned back to E.J. before forcing eye contact. "He'll never admit the truth."

"What I figured," said E.J.

Cooper stared through him. "You report what happened, and there is nothing to corroborate you. No one will find DNA. Probably no one will find your fingerprints in the topless bar."

"Figure so." E.J. nodded.

"Chief Reid will come up with another story, likely at another location. He'll say you attacked him and present an army of witnesses," said Cooper.

E.J. grimaced. "A swearing match."

Cooper shook her head.

She needed to say nothing, E.J. knew. A police chief validated by witnesses versus the disgraced rogue officer who got his people killed. "So, the old saying is true, not only can you not rape a prostitute, you can't murder one either?" asked E.J.

"No. My report includes Georgia's murder. I'll alert DPS intelligence and the FBI. We'll start constricting the Nephilim. I bet they already have this heavy man on the radar," said Cooper.

"In some ways, you remind me of old Sheriff Wharton. Always said it's a marathon, not a sprint. More of a sprinter myself," said E.J.

"Yeah." Cooper turned for the building and left E.J. in the darkness.

Exhausted, E.J. drove home, trying to remove the thoughts of a busy day. Years ago, he would have forced himself to push the day out of his mind with more pleasant thoughts. Since Konner's death, there had been no pleasant thoughts.

Even now, his son, Konner, crossed his mind daily, sometimes many times a day. There were moments in the quiet of the evenings at the farm when it was too much. Whether this was one of those evenings or whether Sharla's disappearance, compounded by the constant fighting with Rebecca and the harrowing encounter with the Nephilim, were too much, he couldn't determine.

He stepped out of the luxury work truck. The moon had risen, providing a view of the longhorn cattle past a fence Konner had repaired. He didn't need daylight to see the fence. Konner never wrapped wire like his father taught him. Instead, he made a loop, then looped the other wire and bent it back on itself. E.J. worked his jaw to hold the river of emotion behind him. Touching the coolness of the barbed wire threatened to release the dam of emotion.

He stepped forward into the security light, walking toward the smaller barn, then opened the bin storing Sunshine's feed. Rusty tin gave the structure an ancient look. Like his father and farmers everywhere, he salvaged building materials wherever he could. Konner and Sharla had helped him roof it.

He recalled the boy, a high school junior, complaining about the lack of broadband access while Sharla sneaked away to call Sunshine. E.J. needed to crush the image from his mind, or he couldn't function. The air grew sour and short, forcing him to gasp harder for dwindling oxygen to fill his lungs. Then his knees buckled like they never intended to hold him.

The sparse contents of E.J.'s stomach emptied into the emerald grass. A coolness rising to his face from the ground made him feel better. He rotated his head, studying the edge of the pasture closest to him under the yellow moon. Some volunteer clover might break through. The sprouting seed heads adorned their distinctive red.

At one time, he had planted the entire bull lot in crimson clover. Konner had asked so many questions about inoculating the seed, fertilizer, when to plant, and so forth. E.J. had taken pride in knowing his son would make a farmer, a builder, a grower. The good earth spilled between his fingers.

The world needed growers. There were plenty willing to harvest. A scream rang out from deep within him toward the heavens, "Cheated." Why had God seen fit to take his son? He knew if he were in a more rational state, he might find answers based on theology that made sense, but in a less emotional state, he would never have permitted himself the question.

E.J. finished feeding the animals. Yak lay on the living room floor while E.J. moved toward the answering machine. He pushed the button, and Rebecca's voice boomed over the recording.

"Sharla is right. You are an absolute dinosaur. Who still has their landline and answering machine? She's never been gone this long without calling. I called the campus police, and they told me you made a report. I'm sure you have been searching all this time, and I thought it was just like you not to tell me you found her...."

Two more messages played before the shower drowned out Rebecca's voice. The scorching water calmed him. His mind cleared. E.J. assembled a turkey, lettuce, and spicy mustard sandwich.

He scrolled Facebook on his phone, looking to see if Sharla had updated anything. She considered Facebook geriatric; however, she occasionally posted or used messenger, and it was about the only platform E.J. knew how to navigate.

The phone revealed Sharla had sent him a video on messenger. Excitement gripped E.J. She probably needs money. He would drive to her, promising her anything to arrange a meet. Then grab her and force her into a rehab tonight. Rebecca could find out after he got Sharla evaluated by a counselor.

He slid a finger across a screen. The phone exploded into music and video. The video depicted Sharla from the shoulder and above, implying she may have been nude. She did not shield her body. Her long red hair hung in greasy, matted strings bobbing out of time with the music. The motion exacerbated how bugged out her eyes appeared. Experience told E.J. she was tweaking, as methamphetamine addicts referred to it.

The music stopped. A male voice from off-camera yelled, "Make Walker Texas Ranger lay off, or I'll call T."

In abbreviated, fast-paced words, Sharla began explaining she was safe, interrupted by occasional indecipherable gibberish.

E.J.'s back tensed while his shoulders tightened as he yelled questions at the image of Sharla on the phone. Then the realization it wasn't a live call. He knew it was a video. Why was he yelling like an idiot? Because there was nothing else to do at the moment. He drew the nine-millimeter from his pocket, feeling its heft. Who to shoot? How to get her home?

CHAPTER EIGHT

"I WAS UP ALL NIGHT. I SAW NO REASON TO TEAR YOU apart too, and I'm not sending you the video. I gave it to Cooper. She will pass it to the campus chief and those who should see it." E.J. exhaled, regretting having answered the phone. About a half hour ago, E.J. had phoned Rebecca to share the news of the Facebook message. The earlier conversa-tion hadn't gone well either.

"Why haven't you found her?" Yelled Rebecca through the phone.

"Because she wants to stay gone. I have to leave it to people more detached. There's a real chance I would shoot Mr. Taint Right where he stands if I saw him."

She sighed. "His actual name is Nathaniel Raney. He's really not a bad kid."

"I told you she was high in the video. You hear this guy yell about telling T if she doesn't comply. T must be Taint. An investigator will assume Taint has traded sex with Sharla for drugs."

The phone went silent for a long pause. E.J. thought perhaps he had been too blunt. However cruel Rebecca was, no mother deserved that. Yet it was true, and he faced it. She shouldn't have made excuses for Sharla.

Rebecca inhaled a deep breath and then spoke. "You can't look for her."

"You called, jumping on me for not finding her already," E.J. said.

The sharpness in Rebecca's tone softened before rising again. "I know what I said, but you got too close last time. How much worse with your own daughter? You're a walking violation of the Bill of Rights in the best of times."

"That's a cheap shot," said E.J.

"Get Cooper to find Sharla," Rebecca said.

"Already decided, but I'm helping. I hunted for Taint. He is missing too. Did you know Mr. Nathaniel Raney is no longer an enrolled student? He flunked out before Christmas." E.J. collapsed into his dining room chair. Rebecca tired him even under pleasant circumstances.

"I know you hate me." She paused.

E.J. wanted to object. He couldn't form the words before she started again.

"And I hate you too, but we have to call each other every time we hear something, no matter what."

He couldn't dispute her. He should have called her last night, even if waking and upsetting her. His thoughts turned back to how to object to the hate remark. A chill pulled up his shoulders when he realized the truth wasn't as objectionable as hearing it out loud. She wasn't offering him an olive branch now, only a practical concession he couldn't oppose.

"I'm sorry," said E.J.

"Don't let it happen again," Rebecca's voice made his spine straighten.

E.J. admired Rebecca's authoritative tone. One of the many qualities making her a powerhouse trial lawyer. Talk of the video had crushed her, and yet she wouldn't give any quarter, at least not in front of him.

He looked at his phone, though he didn't need to. He knew she had ended the call.

E.J. brewed a fresh pot of coffee. Sleep wasn't an option. It was best to stay busy.

He walked from the house, intending to repair the roof on his barn. Over the winter, he had ripped the rusty tin with the tractor front-end loader, trying to get stacked bales out. He couldn't put his weight on the old tin, making repair attempts which expanded the hole.

Sharla flew through every moment, followed by reminders of Konner. What could he have done? Didn't matter because she would never have turned to drugs had her brother not died.

The tin popped, casting off rusty debris as the hammer flew through the roof. Having thrown the hammer, there was no use in keeping the tin, so he pushed the short sheet over the top.

He wanted to call Cooper. How many times had crime victims' loved ones sidetracked him, costing precious investigation time by meaningless phone calls? He decided visiting with the pathologist was a better use of time for both of them.

Besides, the sheriff's office had released the body so he could stop by the funeral home for visitation this evening and pay respects on behalf of Devekon, as Rex Ashe had directed. The plan had the additional benefit of putting him in Nacogdoches all afternoon, in case there were any developments with Sharla.

On the way to Nacogdoches, his phone rang. The truck's display read, "Rex Ashe." It wasn't Rex Ashe.

Even though E.J. only met Clara Brandis' assistant once, E.J. recognized the nasal quality of the man's voice, "Please hold." E.J. pushed the button on his steering wheel, ending the call.

The assistant called back. "We must have been disconnected."

"No."

"No?"

"No. I hung up on you," said E.J.

The snarky, nasal voice reached a higher pitch. "You hung up on me?"

E.J. couldn't resist pressing the button to disconnect the call. He settled on the nickname of Mr. Snarky for the assistant.

Twenty minutes expired before Mr. Snarky called back. This time Mr. Snarky spoke quickly, well aware his time was limited. "Mr. Kane, please provide your availables for a Zoom meeting with Clara Brandis."

"Do you really want to keep playing this game, Mr. Snarky?"

"I don't appreciate name-calling, Mr. Kane. I will inform Ms. Brandis of your attitude. Thank you." This time Mr. Snarky hung up on him. E.J. decided that worked equally well.

The new pathologist, Dr. Meecum, made a strong impression. The young man spoke in a thick accent with a European quality. He explained he was African. However, the good doctor studied in Nashville and Memphis. "Go,

Vols," never sounded so odd.

E.J. already liked him better than the last pathologist. The conversation danced around E.J.'s current law enforcement role. E.J. tried to avoid admitting he had held no real law enforcement status in years without explaining why.

Dr. Meecum handed E.J. the file. The action surprised E.J., who expected to spend another five minutes making his unofficial status sound more official.

E.J. suspected surprise showed on his face because Dr. Meecum said, "Cooper told me you were the ranger who Chuck Norris patterned his character after. We had Walker Texas Ranger in Ghana."

Cooper, she told the lie to everyone. He debated setting the record straight. It made the doctor more cooperative and pleased the doctor to be connected to Chuck Norris in a fictitious second degree of seven degrees of Kevin Bacon kind of way.

E.J. studied the file. Law enforcement loaded the bodies as they found them with as little movement as possible. Arnold had carried an Alcoholics Anonymous medallion and wore a wedding ring; otherwise, there were no objects on his person.

Wasn't it curious how these items were so valuable to a felony convict gang member? E.J. had expected a baggie of meth, a crack rock, a glass pipe, or gang-related crime trophies like a shell casing or bullet.

"I'd like to see the AA chip."

Dr. Meecum shook his head. "The sheriff took them, and I already released the body back to the funeral home. You have the photos."

"Right, thank you again. I assume you're still waiting

on the toxicology?" E.J. asked.

"Cooper said to tell you the lab is not any quicker," said Dr. Meecum

Doctor Meecum's report recorded height, weight, and all pertinent details down to the number of grams Arnold's liver weighed. A markings and scars section memorialized the tattoo. "The tattoo? After you cleaned him up, you were certain it was a man hurling a lightning bolt under a crescent moon and stars?"

"Yes, I assume white supremacist because of the lightning bolt," said Dr. Meecum.

"I've been told yes, but not run-of-the-mill Aryan. Have you ever seen it before?" E.J. asked.

Doctor Meecum paused, looking down. "No, not even heard about it at seminars or peer reviews."

"Me either. Nephilim, they tell me," said E.J.

"Like the giants who walked the Earth and took humans for wives?"

E.J. looked at Doctor Meecum. Is that what Genesis said? He should have googled it.

"We have Bibles in Ghana," said Doctor Meecum. The doctor smiled.

"I didn't mean to imply you didn't. Of course, you're Christian or, or Muslim, it's really your choice." E.J.'s inartful attempt to pull his foot out of his mouth trailed off as he looked at the floor, and the doctor chuckled. He decided the good doctor had intended the Bible in Ghana remark as a joke. A joke at E.J.'s expense requiring a dry wit to appreciate. Rebecca would have loved it.

"I couldn't do my work if I did not believe I examine empty vessels," said Dr. Meecum.

"Thought you people of science were all atheists," E.J.

said.

"For me, that's impossible. *To be absent from the body is to be present with God*. Is far more pertinent than Nephilim." Dr. Meecum gestured his hand to E.J. like he was displaying something.

"What we tell people." E.J. looked around the room, noticing for the first time family pictures, many taken in or in front of a church. The doctor posed with a wife and four kids. He couldn't help kicking himself. Perhaps his keen powers of observation were not what they had once been. "Doc, your report notes eggshell fractures at the anterior cranium."

"Yes,"

"I've read a lot of reports, and they always explain the positioning, but I never get the vocabulary; anterior, posterior, premortem, perimortem. Can you lower it all a couple of degree levels?"

Doctor Meecum chuckled, "Yes."

"I didn't see any injuries to his head that night," said E.J.

"You wouldn't have seen it. You might have felt it running your hand along his head. We peeled the skin and tissue back to examine the skull." Doctor Meecum pointed to a picture in the file.

"See, I would have said the top back right of his head had a bunch of hairline fractures. Of course, he had other injuries."

Doctor Meecum nodded. "Horrendous injuries. Literally blown apart. I have seen nothing like it, except in textbooks documenting war wounds."

"Still this injury to his head you describe as perimortem meaning while he was dying, right?"

"At or near the time of death."

"How near? I mean, did he suffer this injury before or after the other injuries?"

"There is no way to know the order or whether they all happened at one time or if some were anterior to the other artifacts by a small amount of time."

"Doc?" E.J. shook his head, admonishing the doctor.

"I mean, we will never know if some were after the others by as much as several minutes or if they were simultaneous."

"What caused the damage to the skull?" E.J. asked.

"Blunt force trauma."

The answer perturbed E.J. Doctor talk, E.J. thought, speaking without saying anything. "With what doc? Did he hit something, or something hit him?"

"Impossible to say. There are no pattern marks, like some shape imprinted on the skull. From history, I would say it is possible the force of the explosion sent him into a pipe or tank or anything solid," answered Dr. Meecum.

"Most likely, but it is possible somebody hit him and then took him to the scene."

"Possible, between you and me, it's not likely," said Dr. Meecum.

"When a doctor says 'between you and me', then I perk up because I'm going to hear some real backwoods CSI stuff. Why is it possible but not likely?"

"No sign the body formed an immune response to the injury, so the trauma occurred all about the same time. Probably not enough time to move him, plus the skull injury alone would have been fatal."

"I've heard without pattern injuries, there is no way to be certain if there was one point of impact or many.

Usually, only on CSI do they know if it was one blunt force trauma or a number, and if a number, which one killed him?" asked E.J.

"I'd phrase it differently. However, I see your point, which is why I am trained to answer only what is possible in the courtroom," said Dr. Meecum.

"As opposed to what actually happened. You will send me the tox when you get it?" asked E.J.

Dr. Meecum raised his hands. "Chuck Norris' autograph?"

"You know the saying, 'I might know a guy', Doc." E.J. couldn't think of a better way to extricate himself. Go figure, *Walker, Texas Ranger*, possessed some kind of universal appeal.

E.J. didn't recognize the name of the funeral home. He stated the address for the navigation system and followed the directions.

E.J. stepped through a pair of ornate wooden doors, finding a splendid room filled by African-Americans. He suspected someone at Devekon pulled a good prank. Maybe Mr. Snarky gave the wrong address to whoever emailed it to him.

A well-dressed man asked him whether he was here for Chester Arnold. E.J. introduced himself, extending his hand.

"Lexon Howard, I'm one of the funeral directors. We put the Arnold family in the parlor. Straight, then follow the hall to the right."

E.J. shook his head. "No. I'm looking for Chest-er Arnold."

Lexon Howard leaned forward and bent toward E.J. Then he raised his arm, pointing toward the hall at the end of the great room. "A-l-l the way for-ward then to the ri-gh-t."

What was wrong with this Lexon Howard? He realized, looking into Lexon Howard's dark eyes, that the man feared E.J. suffered some affliction. E.J. nodded and followed the instructions.

Walking toward the parlor and stepping into line, E.J. asked himself, how does a white supremacist end up in a black funeral home?

Pews lined each wall, leaving narrow walkways stacked with people. At the end of the aisle wasn't a casket, rather a table of photos under a flat-screen television. The television displayed images of Chester Arnold and a large, dark woman. Among the photos were Christmas pictures depicting the couple surrounded by handsome children of mixed race.

The odd tattoo with the lightning bolt broadcast through E.J.'s mind like it was the next slide in the presentation. He shook his head. This Arnold fellow had to be the oddest white supremacist ever, or a miserable failure at racism.

When he reached the front of the room, the line intersected with the family's receiving line, the wife from the pictures looked up at E.J. The air conditioning kicked on, and their attention was drawn to the vent above them.

He fumbled with the wide-brimmed Resistol hat in his hands. "Ma'am, I'm E.J. Kane, head of security for Rex Ashe and Devekon. It was our well site. Mr. Ashe wants me to make sure and express his condolences. He wants me to figure out exactly what happened."

"Thank you."

"Ma'am, can I ask something? I only ask because I

think it might help us figure out what happened."

"It's about the tattoo, isn't it?" She smiled and took E.J.'s extended hand. After the surprise settled over him, she responded to the additional unasked question. "You want to know how I knew?"

E.J. nodded.

"Lexon Howard thinks you're special, like short bus special, so he whispered to me and pointed to you, 'the white man dressed like a sheriff'. So, I figured you're a detective, and the tattoo has you curious. It was our little joke anyhow."

· "Pretty good detective work ciphering all that out," E.J. said.

She smiled at the compliment. "He still went to some gatherings. Said he had to go, but he hadn't been serious since he quit drinking and drugging back when we met."

"Did you know any of them?"

"No. Chez didn't bring friends around, and he didn't do technology, so no Facebook or Instagram."Her brow raised, and worry replaced her smile. "You think it was an accident, don't you?"

"Yes, ma'am, I used to be a ranger, and we check every box. Can I talk with you some other time when we can talk more about Chez?"

She nodded. E.J. turned, walking past the other family members who were being inundated by people expressing their sympathies. He felt the gaze of Lexon Howard before the man reached in front of E.J. and opened the door.

"You have a go-od night."

Should he explain? Might Lexon Howard attribute racist thoughts to the politically incorrect confusion? E.J. decided better to be retarded than a racist. His mind issued an involuntary correction, intellectually disabled. He hadn't really blown off the mandatory cultural diversity class.

He walked through the door, only nodding at Lexon Howard. After stepping into the truck, E.J. stared at the steering column. He would rather take a beating than see Rebecca.

His phone buzzed. Campus security found a body.

CHAPTER NINE

THE FIRETRUCK'S EMERGENCY LIGHTS STROBED IN THE
center of the road. A civilian, likely a volunteer firefighter,
yelled something. E.J. ran, despite his bad knee.

Each step drove a hundred needles through the joint.
He looked forward, pushing the pain out of his mind. In
the distance, he could see a bank of lights on and around a
concrete bridge. Then he saw deputies, the campus police
chief, and more civilians. E.J. recognized a Justice of the
Peace.

Cooper rose from under the bridge. She moved
quickly, throwing her arms around E.J. Despite his size
advantage, she subdued him. "I told them not to call you.
I'm virtually certain it's not her," yelled Cooper.

E.J.'s entire body clinched, tingling along his spine.
"Virtually—"

"I don't have a positive ID, but she's a different hair
color, and I expect her normal height is shorter," said
Cooper.

E.J. felt Cooper's hold. She had him positioned to roll him backward. Cooper had done well. "Normal height?"

She released him, and in the same moment, he passed her, moving to where Cooper had entered the roadway. The heel of his boot slid when he saw the body suspended from the concrete pylon.

E.J. tumbled backward, looking up at a young woman in a T-shirt and shorts. Her neck stretched a distance further than a human neck should extend, alive or dead. Her skin showed a macabre blue in the bright spotlights.

He paused, trying to look into the girl's eyes. Birds or something had pecked at her eyes. Still, he knew. She wasn't Sharla. He lay on his back coated in foul-smelling ditch muck.

"I tried calling the new doc before I moved the body. I need to roll her thumb to compare with the known you put on file, but I'm pretty sure." Cooper extended her hand to help E.J. up.

"It's not her." At the moment he said the words, his lungs exhaled with the force of an explosion. His body lost all the tension. Then guilt overtook him as he gazed at her pecked eyes. Somebody's baby girl hung before him.

"Looks like she made the noose out of a bathrobe and then climbed under the cement guardrail. You see, the claw marks around her neck. Must have changed her mind. Never will understand people hanging themselves." Cooper shook her head.

E.J. needed to help her, to get her down. You never touch bodies until it's time to load them. Yet he needed to lift her. He needed to hold her because a family somewhere loved her.

A drop of hot, tart-tasting water touched E.J.'s lip. He

stiffened, realizing it was a tear. After touching his cheek, he looked at his muddy hand. A physical reminder of why he shouldn't work the case.

His gaze drifted to the deputies' uniforms. Thankfully, Sheriff B.B.'s jurisdiction didn't extend this far west and south. Sharla's potential death produced an anxiousness and fear only partially relieved by the news the body belonged to another parent's daughter. He didn't want an argument with Sheriff B.B., nor could he explain his newfound sentimentality.

Cooper directed deputies to set an interior perimeter. E.J. figured she intended to keep them away and give him a moment. Gratitude spilled over his full heart. When did he become an emotional wreck? How many bodies had he stood over or cleaned off the roadway in pieces?

"Let me turn this over to the campus chief, and I'll take you home," said Cooper.

E.J. shook his head, then looked into Cooper's brown eyes. "No. This girl's family deserves the best. There shouldn't be any doubt about her death." He began the long walk back to the firetruck blocking the road.

E.J. sat in his pickup, watching the lights in the distance. How had he done it all those years?

He had collected evidence of wickedness with a detached eye like an accountant zeroing columns, complaining about the late hour or the weather, discussing sports or local politics, and always looking to crack a joke. In hindsight, he had done so to avoid genuine emotion.

His mind raced all the way home. Why suicide? What drove her? Where was Sharla? Did she battle the same demons? Pulling into his driveway, E.J. looked twice, seeing a silver Mercedes Roadster shimmering in his headlights.

The sports car's sleek lines gave the illusion of movement while standing still. Were he to buy a two-seater, this vehicle presented the logical choice. How would he pull a cattle trailer? Then the more pertinent question, whose car?

Rex Ashe could afford one, but it wasn't his style. When Clara Brandis implied she was going to make an inventory of Devekon property, she meant she had people to do so. No, it had to be Rebecca.

As he came to a stop, the Mercedes doors opened, revealing E.J. had erred. Far worse than Rebecca, this was Rebecca and Stuart Jackson. Rebecca bounded out of the sports car in her typical formal attire. Despite summer still being some time away, Stuart wore his trademark seersucker suit. E.J. expected he probably wore it even in winter.

For a moment, he considered putting the transmission in reverse, then he slid the truck into park and opened the door. Odd how in their twenty-year marriage, she never uttered a curse word in his presence, and now it was her standard greeting for him. After the opening salvo, he raised his head back up.

She ended the shower of crude language. "What happened to I'll meet you at your office after the funeral home?"

"I said, 'I'd try'. There was nothing definitive. I got tied up," said E.J.

"Not at the funeral home. You made quite the impression. They can't imagine you can take nourishment by yourself, much less drive," said Rebecca.

"Calm down, Rebecca. We'll go in and talk about this—"

Rebecca cut him off, wagging a finger in his face. "You don't tell me to calm down when my baby is missing. You can't even be bothered to meet with me."

Stuart chimed in as well. "Let's not lose sight of what's important, finding Sharla."

Stuart's voice grated on E.J. In an instant, his cowering from Rebecca ended, and hatred of Stuart moved to the fore. E.J.'s irritation at himself contributed to his ire. He knew better than to tell Rebecca to 'calm down'. Enough rage swept through E.J. his chest rose. "What's your boyfriend doing here?"

"He is my friend. Here to witness your verbal abuse."

"Our life coach suggested I support Rebecca during your interactions," Stuart added.

E.J. winced. "Life coach. Life coach, tell me, Stuart, what does the life coach say about you diddling my wife." The sharp sting of Rebecca's fingers slung across E.J.'s cheek, catching him by surprise.

"Don't reduce yourself to violence," said Stuart.

E.J. stepped toward Stuart. Stuart back-peddled into the car.

Even in the dim beam extending from his barn floodlight, E.J. saw enough of the expression on Rebecca's face to know she regretted the slap. "Wait in the car, Stuart."

In her eyes, he saw the look when they heard the news about Konner. Those green pools held more than sadness. Somewhere submerged was the hint of the look when she put Sharla in his arms and when she stood before him at the altar.

His muscles eased, and his tone softened. "Rebecca, the campus police called, but it wasn't her. It wasn't

Sharla."

"They thought they had her body, and you didn't tell me?" Rebecca asked.

"It wasn't her."

"You don't decide what to tell me. You're not my husband, but Sharla is my daughter," said Rebecca.

E.J. acquiesced. "You're right. I should have called."

Rebecca yelled, "You will call next time."

"Yes. Tell Stuart I'm the one out of line." E.J.'s apology drew down the tension. He knew he had messed up. Sharla, both his kids, ran to Rebecca when hurt or in need. Lawyers and judges called parents like her primary. She had every right.

"Yes, very much out of line. I apologize for slapping you. You make me so mad sometimes."

"You and Stuart want to come in. Have a glass of tea, or I can make coffee," said E.J.

"Just promise me you will call when you hear anything."

E.J. raised his hand like taking an oath, "I promise." Memories flooded over him as Rebecca walked to the Mercedes. As they drove away, Stuart gave him an ugly look.

E.J. mocked Stuart's line, 'Don't reduce yourself to violence'. Somehow, there was an insult directed at him in the remark.

He dwarfed the smaller Stuart. The man wore slippers, not wingtips, not boots, not loafers, not even tennis shoes. How do you lose the love of your life to a man in slippers?

E.J. swung open his door. He missed lunch without a thought, but now hunger consumed him. After opening a can of chunky soup and placing a bowl in the microwave, he looked at his cellphone.

Normally he didn't check voicemail except for his antiquated landline. He pressed speaker as the microwave dinged.

"Ruth Welchel, Widow Welchel. I originally called to discuss coordinating a defense to the unfortunate employee's claims. When I couldn't get you, I called Cooper. I'm terribly sorry about your daughter. I've got a big number of drivers over Texas and Louisiana. Send me her picture, and I'll circulate it. The more eyes and ears, the better the chances."

He sat the bowl aside, then pressed the call button. Maybe he could get a picture out to her dispatchers tonight. They could broadcast it to every driver's cell phone and laptop.

"Thank you for calling me back," said Widow Welchel.

"Thank you for your generous offer," responded E.J.

"I have a daughter myself, and I can't imagine what you're going through."

"She's fine. We just need her to call." Why did he feel the need to lie? The soup smelled good, and his stomach turned. He hadn't been hungry in a long time.

"Of course, but text me her picture, and I will get it to all our drivers."

"I'll do that, and thank you," said E.J.

"How are you holding up, Mr. Kane?" Widow Welchel asked.

"Well." E.J. didn't see any reason to confide his difficulties to anyone at this point. Nothing would help.

"I suspect you're not, well, are you? I suspect you're sitting down to a sandwich or a can of chunky soup," said Widow Welchel.

He looked at the contents of his bowl, startled. "Soup. How did you know that?"

"It's not rocket science. I know men, Mr. Kane. Meet me for lunch tomorrow at Keller's steakhouse. I think I've come across a little heartless, and it makes me feel better knowing you have a good meal," said Widow Welchel.

E.J. turned over a spoon of the beef medallion and a chunk of potatoes. Keller's sounded good. A thick ribeye with a baked sweet potato.

He ended the conversation and sent her two pictures of Sharla. What he would have called a good picture. Then he caught himself. A screenshot from the video Sharla sent likely captured her current likeness much better.

Widow Welchel, was she coming onto him? No, a smart, attractive businesswoman had a lot better options than a broken-down old lawman. She must feel sorry for him, or she seems super motivated to protect a dollar from a possible impending Arnold family suit.

E.J. sat the bowl on the TV tray next to his recliner before collapsing into an exhausted sleep. He woke early, fighting the urge to call Cooper. He had no ideas, no leads. Anything he occupied her with would only take her out of the investigation.

His first cup of coffee tasted strong. E.J. recalled all the ribbing he had taken over the years for coffee many claimed curled their stomachs from the smell. Coffee was a nectar best brewed strong for full aroma and flavor. In his opinion, anything less cheated the experience.

A pink and orange glow from the sunrise broke over a spring green field, illuminating Sunshine's movements. White patches on the paint mixed with shadows, giving the impression light poured down from heaven over the powerful gelding.

The autopsy doctor's faith filled his mind. Somehow, a learned product of education and reason expressing a belief in a Savior seemed incongruent. The modern world displaced so much of what E.J. had never thought to question. He had assumed the good Lord didn't fit in the new era, either.

"God, you've not listened to me in a long time, so I don't know why I'm asking." The strength seemed to pour from his body. He leaned against a fence post. "Send me Sharla. Send me Sharla. You can call in all my markers; just get my baby girl home."

Keller's steak house looked out of place, like a big barn in the middle of the small old-style downtown. E.J. stared at his phone. She had texted him when the pictures were disseminated, and she would text him were there any sightings.

Should he call Widow Welchel? Why didn't he ask what she drove? Maybe she was already inside. Should he go in?

Why were his nerves worse than a nerdy boy on his first date? The answer came to him. They were about the same age. Yet if life were a rodeo, he'd ridden too many broncs while Ruth Welchel remained the queen of the grand entrance. He recalled the image of her light blue eyes piercing the clouds, creating a perfect sky.

He looked in his rear-view mirror. Widow Welchel arrived behind the wheel of a red corvette. Stepping out of the truck, he looked toward the entrance. Widow Welchel remained in her seat. Was she all right?

Then a thought overcame him. Perhaps the modern era hadn't dawned on her. He walked to the door of the corvette and opened it.

A fresh green salad with a tart house dressing began a conversation about gardening. E.J. had half finished his steak when guilt overtook him. What must Sharla be suffering now?

Widow Welchel shook her hand in front of his face. "Worried?"

"Sorry, I must be poor company," said E.J.

"I can't imagine what you're going through. I've got a daughter a little older than Sharla."

E.J. looked down at the red table cloth.

"I have feelers out everywhere. We will find her, I promise," Widow Welchel said.

E.J. looked back into the pale blue saucers. "Tell me about your daughter."

"Not much to tell. She's all grown up. Graduated from Yale a few years ago and has her own family in Houston. I think God punished me for trying too hard to make her like me. She rebelled and I'm still coming to terms with it." Widow Welchel paused, rolling her eyes upward.

"Sounds like she's doing well. Sharla and I were so close. Now, I look back, and I can't remember the last time she wasn't gaming me for money."

"Her mother can't get through to her?" Widow Welchel asked.

E.J. noticed the woman staring at his wedding ring. He had forgotten he wore it. His right hand slid over the ring and removed it. "We don't talk."

"You didn't want the divorce, did you?" Widow Welchel leaned across the table and touched the light impression where the ring belonged.

"How do you know? I might be a rake." E.J. tried to

cast his most mischievous look.

"Congratulations, you are the first one to use the term 'rake' in the twenty-first century." She laughed. "I can tell you're no quitter, and you're no rake."

E.J. lifted his thumb to take her hand. "Seen a lot of them, have you?"

"Like it's four a.m., and the drunks are lining up at Whataburger," said Widow Welchel.

E.J. laughed. "Are you sure you don't want me to call you Ruth?"

"Widow's been my name since seventeen. Child bride."

"What happened? That may be too personal," said E.J.

"It's all right. If I were still in El Dorado, Arkansas, you would have heard the story. I shot him. Thirty ought six. Could have driven a truck through his chest."

"I'm sorry."

"I promised my grandma no man would hit me. Course I got caught, but jury agreed he needed killin'," said Widow Welchel.

"Everybody started calling you widow?" E.J. asked.

"After the next one."

"Next one?" E.J. choked a little on the phrase.

"Hunting accident." Widow Welchel's tone remained flat.

"So, you're twice widowed."

"Well, David died in the oilfield, and Bergram had a heart attack," said Widow Welchel.

"Wow." E.J. looked down at the table covering again. "I'm sorry."

"It's part of life," said Widow Welchel.

"Got to put a crimp in your social life."

"Darlin', don't be. They still line up around the

corner." She giggled.

E.J. joined her in laughter. He leaned forward, still grasping her hand. "Stupid, aren't we?"

Widow Welchel licked her lips. "No. Predictable, yes. Stupid, no. Why, I can't even fathom not being attracted to men. It's the kind of afternoon where I almost wish you were a rake."

His phone went off with a loud, treble tone, startling both of them. He didn't apologize; rather, E.J. jumped from the table to take the call. He stepped away, then returned after saying a few words.

"News on Sharla?" Widow Welchel asked.

"No, something else I got to go do right now. Might have a guy who knows who killed your employee," said E.J.

"Not an accident?" Widow Welchel asked.

"I'll tell you the next time we talk." He rose to leave.

"Promise me."

"Promise. I really enjoyed your company." He turned to the door.

"I'll call you." She said in a louder tone. "Darlin', I don't wait on a phone call anymore. I'll call you."

E.J. didn't have red and blue wig wags anymore. The best Devekon could do was some sort of yellow led transport lights under the grill. The four hundred fifty horsepower diesel ate up Interstate Twenty.

He pulled off the interstate as the phone rang. Rex Ashe's voice rang through his speakers.

"Why are you going a hundred miles an hour?" Rex Ashe asked.

"How do you know that?" E.J. couldn't help but look around him, confirming there was no one there.

"Company truck and phone. Got an app," said Rex

Ashe.

"A friend of mine caught a little fish, and I want to use him for bait." E.J. shrugged his shoulders.

"Playing a hunch, huh?" Rex Ashe asked.

"Maybe. How can I help you?" E.J. asked.

"Can't. I wanted to call before they took the phone. Got me in a nursing home, some kind of senility unit," Rex Ashe said.

"You're not senile."

"The kids and my board all testified, I'm certified," said Rex Ashe.

"Why didn't you tell me?" E.J. spoke before he could filter the irritation from his voice.

"You got Sharla to worry about, and you're doing what you do best, finding the stitch to unwind the whole dirty flag."

"I could have testified—" E.J. parked in front of the police station in Waskom, Texas.

"It was saucered and blown. Banks called in my markers too many wild gambles. It's not just my family and the board. Bankers own the big law firms, the judges. Nobody can stand up to them," said Rex Ashe.

"Rex, you hold on. I got you a lawyer. Let me work this lead, and I'll call her."

"Not gonna help. The devil his-self is an amateur against these wicked SOBs," said Rex Ashe.

"They'll beg Lucifer to take 'em home after this woman gets a piece of them." E.J. took the phone, pressing a button, and shut the truck door.

Rex Ashe's pitch faltered. "I called to apologize. You saved my little girl all those years ago. If I could—"

E.J. jumped in, hoping to spare the old man. "I know.

Cooper will find her. I know she will. Take care, Rex."

A young officer jumped out of his chair as E.J. stepped through the door.

"Yeah, he's locked in the holding cell, but the chief is going to get wind of it any minute."

Walking past him, E.J. knew the holding cell doubled as the bathroom. He opened the door and took the handcuffed prisoner by the arm, leading him to the desk. The young officer's uniform denoted him as a canine handler. "I got to go anyway."

E.J. shook his hand and thanked him. A puzzled Geoffrey looked on from the other side of the desk.

"I got locked in a filthy stank can for a half hour with no phone call, no rights read, and no lawyer."

E.J. pulled out the chair across from him. "Took me an hour to get here."

"Yeah, I sat out here for the first thirty minutes while Johnny Fuzz tore the toilet up. Then he put me in it. That ain't humane," Geoffery yelled across the table.

E.J. choked back laughter. "Look, you don't have to talk to me. Three grams is some pretty good weight. I can get Johnny Fuzz as you call him back here, and he can take you to the county lock up."

"I'll listen to you, big man. What you coming down on me for?" asked Geoffrey.

"You made me at Green Earth Reclamation. Did you tell your boss, Artimus Blake?" asked E.J.

The kid shook his head. "No. I didn't know for sure, more like I smelt pig."

"Police and outlaws can make each other quick. I knew you were a meth-head, and Geoffrey's kind of an unusual name." E.J. leaned back in the chair. "See Geoffrey, you fill out credit card applications, enter a contest, complete employment, and rental applications. Did you ever wonder who gets access to the information?"

Geoffrey's eyes were red. E.J. surmised probably from crying, despite the tough talk and old school punisher logo tee shirt. "Don't explain how you got Johnny Fuzz to do an illegal stop."

"So, I know you live here in Waskom and drive back and forth to Greenville, Louisiana. Narcotics guys, especially canine officers, deal in information, right? Johnny Fuzz, as you call him, volunteers to knock you down. Meaning follow you until you violate a traffic law."

"Right pig, thirty-seven in a thirty-five. Like you don't drive way over the limit." Spittle flew from Geoffrey's mouth while he spoke. "Yeah, I didn't have three grams in my console. I gave a guy—"

"A ride, and he must have left it in there." E.J. finished the sentence for him.

"Why hassle me?" Geoffrey asked.

"That's the hunch part. Ever play a hunch." E.J. stared into the boy's dark eyes and escalated his tone. "I could tell you knew Chez, probably unloaded his truck many times. It surprised me how Chez Arnold turned out to be the real deal. If you overlook a little oilfield theft. Tried to help you, didn't he? Because you took the man's death hard? You know something, or you think you do, right?"

The boy looked away, staring at the blue walled office with a black line along the wall. "I don't know. I just think."

"What do you think?" Whispered E.J.

"I think Artimus Blake killed him."

"Why?" E.J. asked.

"I don't know. I just think it."

"Why?" E.J. repeated the question.

"They're both in some quirky Bible crap together. Chez thought Blake cheated him. Cheated him a lot," said Geoffrey.

"Did Atrimus Blake ever say anything in front of you?"

"No. He wouldn't," said Geoffrey.

"So, how do you know he killed Chez?" E.J. asked.

"Man, I told you. I'm guessing."

E.J. nodded. He couldn't lose the kid at this point. "I promise I'll ask what you know. Did you know Chez moved unaccounted for condensate? What amounts to hot oil?"

"Yeah, a lot of them did."

"Drivers for WelCo?" asked E.J.

"Probably a dozen drivers for all kinds of companies, usually salt water haulers, but not always. I don't know for sure and didn't want to know. Seemed hinky."

"Were they all in what you call the 'quirky Bible crap'?" asked E.J.

The kid shrugged. "Nah, I don't know. Are you going to cut me loose or what?"

E.J. uncuffed Geoffrey. "You can go. Promise me to keep your ears open for Chez."

"You were right about him trying to help me. He preached to me all the time. I finally told him I was getting straight to get him to shut up. You know what he told me?" asked Geoffrey.

"No." E.J. smiled and handed Geoffrey his car keys.

"He told me lying about getting clean was the first step." The kid lingered

"Anything more?"

"Just I pump a few wells too, part-time work for a real pumper. There are dry holes making and good wells barely pumping on paper and nobody watches. The Railroad Commission just wants a form. They don't need it right," Geoffrey said.

"You're telling me I can't ever get to the bottom of it?"

"I'm telling you it's like Chez dying; nobody who matters cares." The kid walked out the door.

When E.J. got home, he found he'd left a gate open. He caught Sunshine playing rodeo with Rex Ashe's longhorn cattle. Ordinarily, the horse ran to him, yet this time the gelding hesitated, unwilling to give up the game.

There was no good way to heat cold steak without cooking it, so he opted for another can of chunky soup followed by ranch-style beans. The TV tray didn't appeal to him, so he sat on the porch watching the last light flicker away.

Should he call Cooper? Could she ever find Sharla as long as Sharla chose not to be found? The incident with the girl hanging from the bridge convinced him his love for Sharla compromised his effectiveness to a huge degree. He couldn't be professional, not about Sharla.

Geoffrey upset him, too. Maybe the boy reminded him of Sharla? "Nobody who matters cares." The report from the internet service listed the boy's parents and some of their information. They seemed middle class, even average.

This wasn't supposed to happen. Good kids like Geoffrey and Sharla don't drug out and become so depressed they believe, 'Nobody who matters cares'. He looked out into the darkness, unsure how long he had sat there.

The cell phone rang. Widow Welchel's number appeared on the smartphone next to an empty blue circle where a photo might have populated the display.

The conversation amounted to pleasantries, an update on the Arnold investigation, and no news about Sharla.

"Do you want me to come over?" The question creased the darkness like a gunshot.

"Yes," said E.J.

CHAPTER TEN

"HELLO, E.J. KANE'S RESIDENCE."

"Who am I speaking with?" Rebecca asked.

"Ruth Welchel, but honey, everybody calls me Widow."

"Ms. Welchel, I'm not, honey."

"Sorry honey, there I go again. How can I help you?" Widow Welchel said.

"You can put Mr. Kane on the line," said Rebecca

"May I tell him who's calling?" asked Widow Welchel.

"His wife—"

"Ex-wife, honey, and he's in the shower, anyway. I'm not a maid taking messages. I'm the woman in the house, but if it's about Sharla—"

"You know Sharla?" asked Rebecca.

"I know she's missing. I own an oilfield service company, and I have my employees looking," said Widow Welchel.

"No word?"

"Sorry, honey," Widow Welchel said. The sound of

Rebecca's teeth grinding broadcast over the signal.

"You can tell my husband that when he asked me to help Rex out, he forgot to tell me the judge had set a jury trial months ago for this Monday," said Rebecca.

"Well, I'm sure E.J. can find someone competent to handle it," quipped Widow Welchel.

"I'm handling it. Going crazy sitting around the house. You just tell him, Ms. woman of the house, or leave a note for the next woman of the house to tell him."

"Honey, I'm gonna be around as long as I want to be around." Widow Welchel finished the sentence, though she suspected Rebecca had ended the connection.

"Who called?" E.J. walked into the room wearing a towel, watching Widow Welchel place the phone back in its cradle.

"One of those auto warranty extension services. I get five a week trying to sell me. I'm sure they're a scam. Repeat performance, cowboy?" Widow Welchel asked.

"I'd love to—"

"That's the 'I'd love to, but', tone of voice if I ever heard it." Widow Welchel placed a hand on her hip, closed her eyes, and pursed her lips in an over-accentuated pout.

E.J. took two quick steps to give her a kiss. Widow Welchel's light sapphire eyes popped open. She returned the kiss and pulled away the towel.

"Hey, I really got to get. Going to swing by headquarters and try to get an update without bothering Cooper, then I may check on my new friend Geoffrey," said E.J.

Widow Welchel asked for directions to the coffee. E.J. offered to make it on the condition he dressed. She declined his terms and began filling the carafe.

E.J. dressed in blue jeans and a pearl snap shirt. "You can leave the house unlocked, and if Rebecca should call, don't talk to her. Tell her to call me on the cell."

"Don't worry, I speak heifer," Widow Welchel said.

As he walked out the door, E.J. yelled over his shoulder. "That's why I worry."

Cooper shared all she knew. Neither Sharla nor Taint had contacted anyone. Informants told campus police the two owed their drug dealer a considerable amount. However, no one seemed to know the drug dealer's name. The same word on the street speculated Taint had Sharla working off the debt.

Despite the federal government shutting down the back-page years ago, there were dozens of prostitution websites on the web. Some masqueraded as legitimate dating sites while others offered escorts, nude modeling, strippers.

E.J. appreciated what Cooper didn't want to tell him. Since Sharla knew her father searched for her, she likely didn't use her name or even her own image. Someone could respond to an ad now for a 'date' with Sharla. E.J.'s stomach turned at the prospect, and bile bubbled up in the back of his throat.

"I got cyber crimes searching." Cooper's words rang hollow.

"Still nothing on phones or vehicles?" E.J. asked.

"You know it's burners. We tried to ping the number that sent you the video. It's likely at the bottom of the Angelina River. Sharla's car is still at the university lot. Taint's got an old-school whoopdie. No hiding it. Troopers stopped his cousin in it. Kid claimed Taint told him to use the car. Taint left town for the week."

"You got a heaping pile of nothing." E.J. swiped his arm across his body in disappointment.

"I promise you I work on leads every day. Campus PD has interviewed about a third of the school. We're quietly jamming up every dealer who doesn't signal within four hundred feet of a turn. I promise you something will shake loose," Cooper said.

Cooper's phone rang. "Cooper. Yes, aha, text me the address."

E.J. stared at her, trying to read whether the call concerned Sharla.

"You won't be talking to Geoffrey again. One of Sheriff B.B.'s deputies saw a parked truck sitting on a well location. Thought it might be theft. Found Geoffrey dead. Says accidental."

"Too many oilfield accidents, don't you think?" E.J. asked.

"'Me no Alamo'. Your informant, your case, for me, it's another accident until proven otherwise. I promised to spend my time looking for Sharla. You're better at fighting with Sheriff B.B. anyway."

E.J. looked at his feet. "I need to be looking for Sharla."

Cooper punched him in the shoulder. "Knocking in heads, trying to prove your old boss right. Because you know that's what'll happen. The thought of her out there makes you sick like it would any parent. Leave it to me. I promised I'd work it like she's mine, but because she's not mine, I keep my edge."

E.J. looked up, and their eyes locked. He felt the sincerity of her gaze.

"You know, if you'd have listened to me, you'd still be DPS," said Cooper.

"What happened to not lording it over me?" E.J. asked.

"Only do it when you're stupid."

"Thanks, Cooper." E.J. brushed her shoulder with his hand. The gesture expressed trust, gratitude, an acknowledgment she was right. His version of a hug.

Near noon, E.J. pulled his truck behind the deputy's patrol car in front of the cattle guard and gate.

"Son, what are the odds. I not only get to see my old friend B.B. again, but you're on the gate," E.J. said.

"You're not allowed, Mr. Kane. Devekon doesn't own this well. And please call me Deputy Berryhill." The young officer looked down at his chest where a light on a small box denoted the body camera recorded.

E.J. pulled his hat off. "Deputy Berryhill, we got off on the wrong foot, and I apologize. My confidential informant is somewhere lying dead up there. I'm already a little frazzled because my daughter's been missing for days, and I'm probably unemployed. Let me pass, and I'll follow all your father's rules."

"No."

"No?" asked E.J.

"No."

Hall Oglethorpe would not appear in his FBI windbreaker and run interference for E.J. "Would you call your father and ask him?"

Son laughed. "All right, Mr. Kane, I'll call Daddy, but you won't like it."

After about ten minutes, a cloud of dust enveloped a Tahoe, stopping at the gate. Sheriff B.B. stepped out. The broad grin on his face told the story.

E.J. wouldn't get access. Sheriff B.B. wanted to enjoy telling him in person. Sheriff B.B. walked toward him, and

E.J. stepped back.

Sheriff B.B. continued approaching until E.J. felt the grill of his truck pressing into his back. "Pretender, wannabe ranger, what you pretending to do out here?"

"You got my C.I. up there. I want to see him or his body," E.J. said.

Sheriff B.B. snickered, "Aww, he's not doin' any pretending. 'Graveyard dead', old Jerry Clower would say."

"He's dead too," said E.J.

"Who?" asked Sheriff B.B.

"Old Jerry Clower, nobody tells Jerry Clower jokes anymore."

Sheriff B.B.'s eyebrows raised, and his hand moved, extending a finger toward E.J.'s chest. "Get, pretender."

E.J. whispered through gritted teeth, "I'm having a bad day B.B. Don't make me whop you in front of your boy."

The loud clatter of a diesel motor turned both their heads to see a one-ton ram pickup with WelCo stenciled on the door. Widow Welchel swung her door open, effectively pausing the testosterone-fueled contest between the men.

E.J. watched as Sheriff B.B.'s face moved from agitated to a big smile. He made a mental note to ask Widow Welchel how close she was to Sheriff B.B. Then he conquered the jealously welling in his belly.

One night of passion didn't pass for vows. Neither of them made demands on the other, and she hadn't misled him.

E.J. said, "Boy wasn't one of your drivers—"

"He pumped this well on the side, worked for Blake over in Greenwood," Sheriff B.B. said.

"No, he wasn't mine, but we service this well. A driver

told me, and I got curious. Figured since I know the sheriff." She trailed off and winked.

"Yeah, you know the sheriff, don't you?" E.J. said.

"Then you boys show me around," said Widow Welchel

Sheriff B.B. looked at E.J. "What am I taking him for?"

"Because I asked, B.B." She walked to the passenger door on the Tahoe, and B.B. ran to it. Son beat him to it. "Thank you, Son."

"I'll walk," E.J. bent under the tape and walked through the open gate before the black sports utility sped past him. The gravel road led to a gaggle of fire department trucks. There must have been a truck from every volunteer fire department in the county.

The sheriff's Tahoe stopped before the well location. He probably got flagged down by a firefighter.

E.J. reached the spot asking a firefighter, "Can we go any further?"

"They're finishing right now." The firefighter gestured toward the people walking around the well site, who looked like they were studying cell phones. "Hydrogen Sulfide, Sour gas. They're about to call it clear."

"Sour gas?" E.J. asked.

"Sewer gas, pretender. You ought to know about it; you're so full of it." Sheriff B.B. looked at everyone, presumably proud of his quip.

"A hazard of oil and gas production. My drivers watch videos on how to use meters, but it can't get you in the open," Widow Welchel said.

"Wouldn't risk my life on it, but you're right. There's a little shed where he changed the chart, and it looks like they used it for storage. Bad idea, though they had a meter mounted with the display outside the door like they're required," said the firefighter.

Sheriff B.B. said, "Probably got put on there and then never maintained."

A siren rang out. E.J. couldn't tell the source. However, the message was universal, all clear.

They walked past the pair of large tanks to a little shed where Geoffrey lay. He looked like he might wake at any moment.

E.J. fought the urge to shake the boy's shoulder. Geoffrey never had time to beat the dope. He could never mature now.

Sheriff B.B. called to Son on a hand-held radio. "Deader than a hammer. When the carraway boys get here, tell them to bag him up."

E.J. near jumped toward Sheriff B.B. "You're going to order an autopsy, right?"

"Why? We know what happened. Kid went around with his head up his butt and didn't notice the monitor wasn't working right. Probably high, firefighters told me they saw a meth pipe in his truck."

"Two quirky oilfield accidents in less than a week. While investigating the first one, I develop the kid as an informant, and then he dies in the second. Sound suspicious?" E.J. said.

Sheriff B.B. stepped closer to E.J. "I'm not spending a thousand dollars, so you can pretend you're still a man investigating something."

"I'm not telling you what I'm investigating, but let's add that your deputy and your son is the first one on the scene both times." E.J. didn't back away.

"What you accusing me and my boy of?" Sheriff B.B.'s

chest pushed into E.J.

"Not accusing, only saying it doesn't look good. Spend the money and confirm sewer gas. You don't know if the kid overdosed or a bad batch of meth caught up with him out here." E.J. matched Sheriff B.B.'s tone, certain the two would exchange punches. A fight didn't concern him as much as the fight being captured on a body camera plus a half dozen firefighters, and would Sheriff B.B. get mad enough to draw?

CHAPTER ELEVEN

WIDOW WELCHEL'S VOICE CUT THROUGH THE MASCULINE tension. "Boys, please, if I'd have failed a math test today, I'd swear we were all in high school." Widow Welchel turned to Sheriff B.B. "Each of you gives a little room. E.J.'s not doing any accusing. B.B. A thousand dollars buys peace for this kid's mom and dad. You think they won't remember when they see you driving this seventy-thousand-dollar mon-strosity."

"Get your autopsy, pretender. You can even go. When you get done, you come on over to my office and give me an apology," Sheriff B.B. said.

E.J. took a deep breath. Why argue? He got everything he wanted. E.J. caught a wink from Widow Welchel. This served as additional confirmation. Like he had done for forty years, he told himself, one day B.B., one day.

A quick internet search on his phone revealed nothing E.J. thought dispositive from the scene. Knockout gas appeared as another common name for sour gas because, in large amounts, it caused immediate death. The funeral home bagged and loaded young Geoffrey.

Thoughts rolled through E.J.'s head, looking at the boy. Did turning informant get Geoffrey killed? Well, he really didn't turn informant, did he? This had to be an accident, right?

Looking for a more pleasant thought, E.J. turned to Widow Welchel. Would tonight bring another rendezvous? She had slipped away. He noticed Sheriff B.B. had left as well.

What would Sheriff B.B.'s wife think? Part of E.J. suspected Candy's high school crush on him served as the original impetus for B.B.'s hatred. He'd never known B.B. to step out on Candy, but B.B. sure had looked longingly at Widow Welchel.

By the time E.J. walked back to his truck, he had satisfied himself it was best not to see Widow Welchel. She clouded his mind when clarity was essential. Besides, he needed to call Rebecca.

He cranked the truck. It wasn't like Rebecca not to call him back. "Call Rebecca."

"Anything on Sharla?" A few rings later and the familiar terse tone E.J. had nicknamed Rebecca's prose-cutor voice. They had both been so young. She fought for justice as an assistant district attorney teamed with a crusading detective.

"Not yet, Cooper's working hard," said E.J.

"Is this really E.J. or the black widow girlfriend?" asked Rebecca.

"I don't have a girlfriend, and her nickname is widow, not black widow." E.J.'s mind raced. How did she know about Widow Welchel? Widow Welchel's words rang in his head, "I speak heifer."

"Black widow didn't give you my message, did she?" asked Rebecca

"No. I should have figured you'd have called back."

"Whatever, I really mean whatever, but I'd prefer you not play house while our daughter is missing," said Rebecca.

The blood swelled, pressing on E.J.'s head from the inside. He wanted to yell and curse at Rebecca. She could always push his buttons. Rebecca had been gallivanting with Stuart for who knows how long. E.J. had let his guard down one time after all this time, but he's lambasted for being the immoral one.

He gritted his teeth. Rebecca's tendency to be right, combined or owing to her being smarter than him, had always infuriated him. His nostrils filled with air. She wouldn't set him off this time. "Rebecca, you're right. I'm not making the best decisions right now. All the more reason Cooper investigates."

At first, E.J. enjoyed the long silence. Arguments with Rebecca had crushed him over the years. However, since she blamed him for Konner's death, her voice had become toxic. He wanted to end the call, fearing she would go there again.

"Just don't let her make a fool out of you. Sharla needs you." The softer tone puzzled him. Sincerity from the skilled trial lawyer. What was the world coming to? Maybe she realized twenty years ago he would have come unglued and appreciated the change. No, Sharla had preoccupied her.

"Will you help Rex?" asked E.J.

"You dropped me deep in the grease. Rex had a court-appointed ad litem drawing a nice salary from Rex, of course," said Rebecca.

"Rex thinks the fix is in," said E.J.

"Like maybe the ad litem is the judge's nephew and all the lawyers like him, so he gets a payday to lie down until yours truly drops a skunk in the works. So, I get a bull trial date of Monday and no continuance."

"I never thought they would do you that way. I mean, especially with Sharla. The judge won't give you any time."

"Probably for the best. I can't make a difference looking for Sharla. I always liked Rex."

"No, you didn't."

"No, I didn't." She hesitated. E.J. knew her training demanded she choose her words with precision. "Judge tried to intimidate me in a courtroom full of lawyers."

"No one intimidates you," said E.J.

"No one intimidates me," said Rebecca.

"God help 'em, Beck." E.J. chuckled as he heard her end the call. The anxiety had escaped his body in the closed truck cab, warmed by the noon sun.

In the same instant, his shoulders cringed at the ring of a phone. He touched the steering wheel to no avail; then he realized the burner rang, not his phone. It could only be one person.

"Mr. Blake, is everything all right?"

"All good, brother Jackson. I thought I would extend a little hospitality. We're going to have a little barbeque tonight to honor old Chez."

"Whose putting on the hootenanny?" E.J. asked.

"Oh, our little study group. About seven o'clock. I have a party barn on the lot next to the refinery."

"I will see you then, Mr. Blake."

"Call me Art. See you then."

'See you then.' Was it an invitation to a barbeque or a bullet to the back of the head? There wasn't any way to know. E.J. pulled onto the road, trying to think of a way to discover whether a trap awaited him.

He took Sheriff B.B. up on the autopsy offer. The staff personnel let him sit in Dr. Meecum's office until the doc arrived.

"Remember me, Doc?" E.J. asked.

Dr. Meecum appeared in the doorway wearing a three-piece suit, with blue pinstripes. The baby blue tie with white dots matched the lab coat he lifted from the hook behind his door.

"Walker, Texas Ranger. I haven't had time to work on an autograph. You know they're making a new one," said E.J.

"One show, one ranger, right?" asked Dr. Meecum.

"I think that's *one riot, one ranger*."

Dr. Meecum laughed. E.J. realized the good doctor had made another joke. E.J. figured the dry wit seemed far ahead of him because he kept erroneously assuming the man wasn't as familiar as anyone born and raised in Texas.

The early autopsy work went fast. An external examination revealed nothing to E.J. However, he listened to Doctor Meccum dictate his findings for a digital recording on his laptop.

E.J.'s attention peaked with the terms petechial hemorrhages and foam in the airway. He didn't see any foam, though he recognized the small red splotches in the eyes. E.J. knew Doctor Meecum would look for an enlarged heart and petechiae in the lungs to confirm the findings.

Geoffrey died of asphyxiation. He didn't need to touch Geoffrey to know the cold feel. A different type of strangulation killed the girl hanging from the bridge. How much more pleasant to say. Strangulation killed her.

The image of the girl's neck crashed through his mind. The frantic scratches digging through the light blue epidermis to the leaky droplet of dark scarlet were all he could see. He stared at Geoffrey's neck. Was the pressure of the makeshift noose crushing her windpipe worse than poison, causing drowning in a sea of air? "Was death instant?"

He hadn't intended to speak on the digital recording. Regardless, he wanted the answer. Why didn't it figure into the investigation?

Dr. Meecum pressed a button on the laptop. "Very possibly. Hydrogen Sulfide in large quantities kills immediately. I can't be certain, not yet."

"'Very possibly.' I love the language, doc. How do you know he got exposed to a large amount?" asked E.J.

"An assumption from history. He helps the pumper, and no one has indicated anything more, so I wouldn't expect he stayed long. He checks the well, and the gas overcomes him. If the Hydrogen Sulfide killed him," said Dr. Meecum.

He pressed the button on the laptop. E.J. wanted to ask if there was another possibility like bad drugs, then he caught himself. 'Possible' was a term of art, wasn't it?

Doctor Meecum made the customary Y incision before reaching for the sheers. Despite the odor and the macabre scene from an open chest all the way past Geoffrey's waist, E.J. remained fixated on the neck. In place of Geoffrey, he saw the suicide victim's neck imagining those frantic minutes clawing, then looking up into Sharla's still eyes.

He near back-peddled before catching himself. "Excuse me, doc, it's been a long time. I need some air."

"I'll meet you in my office in about a half hour."

E.J. asked himself, why didn't Cooper call? He answered the question as repeatedly as he asked it. Because she had no leads.

"Can I get you a water or a cup of coffee?" Dr. Meecum asked.

"You have coffee?" E.J. looked at his watch. He had sat there for an hour.

"No, I can make some, though."

"No, no, no trouble. Is it sewer gas?" E.J. asked.

"Can't be certain. Hydrogen Sulfide most likely. I'm still waiting for a full toxicology. However, there wasn't enough urine in his bladder to test," answered Dr. Meecum.

"Toxicology will find it in the blood?" asked E.J.

"No, the reported cases almost never find it in the blood. Hydrogen Sulfide inhibits respiration on a cellular level." The two locked eyes. Dr. Meecum must have expected E.J.'s intended admonishment. "The gas stopped his heart. He died in minutes."

"Could it have been bad meth?" E.J. asked.

"Not likely, but the toxicology can rule it out for certain," said Dr. Meecum.

"While on the subject. Do you have Arnold's toxicology?"

Doctor Meecum opened a different folder and handed him a sheet of paper.

"No street drugs or alcohol." E.J. shrugged.

"Surprised?" Dr. Meecum asked.

"Not anymore. Chez Arnold proved to be an enigma. The proverbial leopard who truly changed his spots, except I think he stole right to the end," said E.J.

Dr. Meecum closed the files. "What really happened?"

"What do you mean? You're the one who tells me what happened."

"No, I opine whether events were possible or probable, remember?" said Dr. Meecum.

"Opine the more probable: An organized ring of criminals steals condensate, what amounts to high-grade oil, by pretending they haul salt water off the wells. Somehow, the ring ties into an Aryan sovereign citizen gang. Arnold appears to have found Jesus, assuming Jesus looks the other way at a little theft. Somehow, he runs afoul of the powers that be and gets himself killed. Later I developed a source where the hot oil is moved. The source, young Geoffrey, likewise gets himself killed. Or hypothesis number two, we have two unrelated oilfield accidents." E.J. had his hands open and extended like he held the two alternatives.

Dr. Meecum leaned back in his chair. "All possible. I can't rule any of it out."

"Doc, did I ever tell you my ex-wife served as an assistant district attorney. How we met."

Dr. Meecum shook his head from side to side.

"I watched her cross-examine this expert witness on a kind of burning bed case, except the shooter had never been abused. Guy still says it's possible she killed the guy out of battered spouse syndrome." E.J. chuckled, recalling the story.

Dr. Meecum leaned forward.

"She tells this guy to look out the window, even opens

it. It's possible little green men are going to land out there and abduct all of us, but it's not reasonable, is it?" E.J. said.

"The why I asked what happened. I checked OSHA records. Two fatalities in the same general area at unrelated sites, rural area, are beyond unusual. It doesn't happen," said Dr. Meecum.

"You're telling me it's not possible?"

"My father taught me an old Ghanaian saying, 'If you're on a road to nowhere, find another road'. Accident is a road to nowhere."

"Doc, you make me believe in the Walker, Texas Ranger school of investigation," said E.J.

"I'm not Walker, more of a Trivette?" Said Dr. Meecum

"Who?" asked E.J.

Dr. Meecum looked puzzled. "Jimmy Trivette, Walker's cool partner."

E.J. debated whether to come clean. Dr. Meecum caught him because he had never seen the show. Perhaps it would prove too jarring to go from hero consultant to zero all in one sitting, at least without actually hearing it out loud.

"Sure, what I can't understand is why you choose the sidekick and not the star?"

"Former Dallas Cowboy and a Texas Ranger. Besides, my father also quoted Micah about walking humbly with the Lord." Dr. Meecum grinned. "Don't you agree?"

"Sheriff Wharton told me to walk humbly less the other fellow doesn't. Then you got to kill 'em," said E.J.

Dr. Meecum's warm smile collapsed. "If you're right about a criminal enterprise, then the people running it killed Geoffrey and Arnold with no provocation. You realize you are next."

"That your way of telling me they're not humble people, doc?"

CHAPTER TWELVE

"CHROME GUN?" A STUPID QUESTION, BUT E.J. DIDN'T want Ed Jackson's new friends to think he possessed any expertise. Nor would he concede he had seen the weapon as Weldon Harris.

Anyway, it was something to say, stupid or not. Silence crushed him in these ruses. Maybe feigning ignorance would explain why he was the only one not wearing a gun.

"Stainless Steel. Didn't Patton say only a pimp in a New Orleans cathouse would have a chrome gun?" The heavy man laughed, then removed an enormous Smith and Wesson six-gun from his holster.

"Pearl grips. Patton carried ivory." Artimus Blake said.

The heavy man broke into a recital of George C. Scott's speech at the start of the movie Patton. He attracted a small group near the picnic table.

More than a dozen men stood around a two-story log cabin. Artimus Blake called it his party barn, while E.J. called it a mansion overlooking a green field and stock pond. People milled around the big sweeping porches.

The men didn't look especially out of place. It could have been a political fundraiser, a charity event, or one of many ranger association supporters' parties, except each individual held an edge. A quality E.J. couldn't stereotype to a certain mode of dress or physical appearance. Artimus Blake looked out-of-place like a supple grass snake in a den of triangular-headed pit vipers.

Everyone openly carried from cowboy rigs to Serpa-style tactical holsters. Leather contrasted with black plastic and nylon, highlighting a virtual gun show filled with high-end pistols and revolvers.

"You're not one of those sweeties who don't like guns?" Further evidence of the beer in the heavy man's koozie wasn't his first tonight.

E.J. considered his response, struggling to contain his hatred over Georgia. He forced himself to overcome the rage swelling within his heart.

Artimus Blake stood. "All right, men, let's have a blessing, and then we'll see if Dwaine's been cooking or drinking."

The men formed near the side of the cabin, facing the pond. They had slid enormous glass doors open, displaying a long-serving style buffet table. The smell of the freshly cooked meat permeated the air.

E.J.'s head followed his nose. Toward the backyard sat two cookers on trailers. A smoke signal rose from opening the second lid. Each trailer spanned about twelve feet, with huge black cylinders connected to rectangular cook boxes and smokers.

What must have been Dwaine and his cook team walked past carrying aluminum pans filled with sausage links, racks of ribs, and briskets? A burnt end laying on top caught E.J.'s salivating attention. The beef and pork aroma combined with the smoky smell finally relieved some of E.J.'s anxiousness. His belly twinged with hunger, making the line in front of him seem longer, then it got longer still.

"Brother Arnold deserves a sendoff. The clouds are parting, and heaven is receiving another giant. A great walking among the mortals." Artimus Blake droned on for some time before blessing the food.

E.J. thought it was a shame they didn't know the man had grown bigger than their collective ignorance. Shame this line's not moving.

The meat satisfied, complimented by a mustard potato salad that wasn't too mushy and spicy pinto beans flavored by the beef. Pecan pie topped with vanilla bean ice cream completed the feast. The crunchy, syrupy concoction topped by a meal made him lose himself for a moment.

He pressed the thoughts of Sharla and necessarily Georgia out as best he could; otherwise, his mind ran wild. Would the Nephilim reveal their secret handshake, study the Bible, commit some crime, or something more nefarious?

In short order, the Bible study theory proved erroneous. E.J. looked up to see Maker's Mark whiskey, decks of playing cards, and poker chips dispensed at each table.

There were six tables, and each had an unwritten hierarchy. A casual observer would have missed the command structure. E.J. spent his life around law enforcement and criminals, both of which maintained rank even when casual.

The heavy man managed E.J.'s table, calling the game, the buy-in, telling stories, and demanding everyone drink on command. "You don't drink, and you don't carry a gun. I'm gonna start calling you sweetie, Sweetie Eddie Jackson. That's your name, isn't it?"

"Where's Artimus Blake?" asked E.J.

"Sweetie Eddie Jackson, got a ring to it? Had a sweetie in my house, called him 'junebug'." Ruckus laughter near shook the table.

E.J. knew a prison reference when he heard it. He wanted to touch his pocket. He didn't because he knew it was the tell they would spot. His heart rate quickened as he looked around the room. How many could he kill if he drew now? Two, three, not likely he could fire the small magazine before the end. Was this the end?

The heavy man continued with his stories, applauded by his friends. Stories and jokes without humor in the punch lines. The content ranged from racist ideology to anti-government rhetoric told in a mixture of prison slang and the language Hall Oglethorpe called 'cracker'.

Nothing E.J. hadn't heard thousands of times going back to the early days of his career driving outlaws to the county lockup. Old school dirtbag ideology mixed with nutty political views, yet this time preached in the wealthy playhouse of the rich by men with money. E.J. couldn't decide whether to act like he couldn't follow the conversation or acknowledge career experience had made him bilingual.

Was this an initiation, a test, or a kill party? Was he the guest of honor? Surely, they wouldn't off him in Artimus Blake's party barn? Where was Artimus Blake? Ask again, ask anything, and it would only confirm they had made him.

'Patience reveals all', as his old Sheriff Wharton used

to tell him. A more useful lesson might have been how not to perspire. They were sweating him both mentally and physically, but to what end?

Did the heavy man read his eyes or his body or his mind? "Blake isn't one of us. Sort of like a ladies' auxiliary." He snickered, which meant the rest of the table snickered.

The heavy man lifted his right hand, displaying the big revolver E.J. had earlier seen up close. The barrel ended in ports designed to diminish recoil. Fine engraving adorned the huge pistol down to the oversized black rubber grip. He viewed the gun from a greater distance, yet he had an opportunity for a calm perusal this time.

E.J. concluded the horse pistol had to be a five hundred magnum or a .460 designed for hunting. Likely, the hand cannon fired a projectile over three times the size of the hollow points in E.J.'s nine-millimeter.

E.J. reached into his pocket as the heavy man lifted the horse pistol. He opened the revolver, dropping the long shells.

The heavy man reloaded one cartridge and spun the cylinder. "We gonna play the feud, boys."

Had the heavy man identified him as Weldon Harris? E.J. studied the crowd, unable to determine if they were the same who watched Georgia's head explode. "What?"

"You know how you join the Kiwanis or the Rotary?" said the heavy man.

E.J. nodded.

"Same kind of thing here. We have to vet you. Know how we do that?"

Laughter surrounded E.J. He shook his head.

The heavy man moved his hand past the gun and

tapped his phone. "It's the twenty-first century, right? Which brings us to the problem?"

"Problem?"

"The only Ed Jackson matching you lives in Center and works in a sawmill. So, Blake wants to know how a sawmill man started driving trucks, especially without a commercial driver's license?"

E.J. leaned back. DPS hadn't updated the old Ed Jackson cover, nor did it really suit this assignment. More contingencies he failed to think through. "I thought Blake was ladies' auxiliary."

The heavy man leaned back as well. For a moment, his upturned brows telegraphed his surprise. "Well, we've more partnered with him than anything else." He cocked the hammer on the massive pistol and swung it toward the open. It exploded, sending the payload through the open carriage doors into the darkness.

The ear-deafening roar near made E.J. wince. He caught himself because he feared giving these fools further satisfaction from his reaction. It would only result in another demonstration by the heavy man. The crowd grew more raucous with the smell of burnt propellant.

The big man lifted another round and dropped it in an empty chamber before spinning it. "I got my own game-show."

E.J. couldn't give away the knowledge learned as Weldon Harris. If the heavy man knew who he was, then there would be no empty chambers. "Russian Roulette?"

"I'm not gonna shoot me." The fat man laughed. "Got a few questions on the application. Wrong answer gets you a spin on the wheel of life here." He pointed the hand cannon and spun it again, cocking the hammer. "Tell us your story."

E.J. summoned his strength, gritting his teeth. He had to pull this off. "I did work in the sawmill. Had a wife and kids the whole nine yards. The wife and I both did a little crank for years. Never a problem, weekend thing. Said it made her stay trim."

A quiet cast over the entire room. E.J. looked around at his audience, moving from eye to eye. "You know how the story goes. It's all bad chasing the first high, chasing the dragon, right?"

E.J. drew a deep breath. "Chez and I met at AA. He prayed with me. I guess you call it sharing his testimony. The real deal, that was Chez. I appreciated his help. I had got myself in pretty deep, owed the wrong people money." He raised his voice yet maintained a shaky quality in the tone. "They were threatening my kids."

"So, he gives you a chance to make some quick cash. What we're supposed to believe?" Said the heavy man. "Well, I don't."

E.J. looked down the barrel, focusing on the hammer dropping in line behind it. Click, this time the room remained silent, beyond still like no one breathed. He asked himself, had he sold it, or was this fool going to drop another round in? How many questions and how many bullets?

The heavy man clapped out of rhythm. Then the entire room made a round of applause. "Till next time?"

"No next time," said E.J.

"Has to be. Game is to the death." The heavy man holstered the enormous weapon.

Almost to a man, he heard comments from around the room. "That was Chez."

"Guy, give you the shirt off his back."

"Sounds just like him."

The tension escaped the room with the same speed with which it had overcome it. E.J. let out a sigh of relief.

The best lies are part truth. Chez had saved him. Only he hadn't done it until now.

Something compelled E.J. to look over his shoulder. The instant he turned his head, his entire body tensed, and he swung his head back. He tried looking around to play it off because the move had been so obvious.

Did he really see Son in the building? He looked again over his shoulder as Son fixed a plate of barbeque, oblivious to what had transpired. The big kid stood in full uniform. E.J. fought the urge to confirm the view.

E.J.'s mind sprung into motion. Why would any deputy be at a sovereign citizens' meeting? If Son made him, the whole line of bull collapses, maybe costing E.J. his life. Did Sheriff B.B. know? Why would law enforcement in full regalia be acceptable in a sovereign citizens' group?

Keeping his back to Son, maybe he could walk out of here, not all that much wiser, yet alive. E.J. glared at the opposite wall sporting Willie Nelson's autographed photos where he had once been a guest.

Such a short time ago, E.J. had consumed a delicious meal like a king, and now he experienced relief at continued breath. Staying even if he didn't ask questions, he feared would look like he was intruding, if not spying.

E.J. rose. Unlike when he arrived, the men at the table extended their hands. The heavy man identified himself as Jonathan Norton before adding, "Call me Norty. No hard feelin's, brother." He cackled. "You gonna be the returning champion next time."

Grateful he had swapped his King Ranch edition at the Marshall yard for an old Devekon work truck, E.J. opened the truck door, nodding to Norty, who stood under an overhead door in an open bay. The drive home gave E.J. far too much time to think.

What had happened? Would Norty have really killed him, or did he somehow palm the bullet? Would he really risk murdering him in front of Son? Son might be crooked, might even be a sovereign citizen nut job, but a murderer?

There were too many incongruent facts to paste into any sort of hypothesis. Nothing made sense about these 'accidents' or the Nephilim or anything else. But the question permeating his being and clouding his reasoning, why didn't Cooper call?

E.J. got the call from Cooper as he pulled into his driveway. She described a new video of Sharla sent to the campus police. E.J. listened to Cooper's description with incredulity. He had to see it.

CHAPTER THIRTEEN

THE VIDEO BUFFERED FOR AN ETERNITY. SHARLA LOOKED much better. However, there were still the telltale signs of an addict. She wore a dark blue blouse with her hair washed and put up in a ponytail.

She identified herself, then made clear she was over the age of eighteen. Sharla made known her intention to withdraw from college. Claiming she suffered years of physical and emotional abuse at the hands of her family, she explained she needed a fresh start. There were no specifics except her parents were powerful people who would not accept her choices or respect her adult status. She hoped the school and campus police treated her with more dignity.

The entire video took only five minutes, yet it presented a game-changer. Cooper didn't argue with E.J.'s protest. She made clear she knew someone had contrived the video to end the search.

Rebecca expressed more outrage. E.J. tried to explain

why the video posed such an impediment, despite its falsity. Of course, she knew the law better than E.J. He elaborated on the policy of both the ranger service and law enforcement.

Cooper would keep working the case because she knew the video was fraudulent. However, without proof, she would be alone. When they needed more help, they could risk entangling fellow officers.

He sat looking across the way at the big vintage Dearborn gas heater, mesmerized by the vent spaces on the grill. From the near darkness of his chair and television tray, he promised Rebecca. "We will find Sharla."

"I've always accused you of being too aggressive. More than teasing you. I know Sharla picked up on it, and I need to say I'm sorry," said Rebecca.

"Sharla called me a jack-booted thug, and your words were, 'I was a walking civil rights lawsuit'," said E.J.

"What I'm telling you is you're good at what you do. She's the only child we have left. Whatever you have to do, to whomever you have to do it, bring our baby home." Rebecca's voice cracked, then steeled, pushing air through her words with great effort.

E.J. exhaled. "If I could, I'd kill 'em all."

"Then kill 'em all," said Rebecca.

She paused, composing herself. "You keep me up to date. If I have to run out of Rex's trial to get there, I will. I can make the drive in two hours."

E.J. thought the flat tone exemplified Rebecca. She wouldn't fall apart because she had this powerful ability to focus herself. He admired the quality, drawing strength from her strength. His jaw tightened. "Jury seated?"

"'Jury seated', already presented openings and called

three witnesses. He gave me ten minutes for voir dire and five for opening. Rex Ashe is being railroaded at super-sonic speed." Sarcasm soaked Rebecca's voice.

"Train's a coming, and you're tied to the tracks?"

Rebecca sighed. "You ought to know. Aren't you hero types supposed to rescue damsels in distress, not help tie them to the tracks?"

"You're a lot of things, Rebecca. Damsel's not one of them."

"I'll need you day after tomorrow, Wednesday after-noon, unless you're following a lead. Then we'll both run out of this thing, and the judge can—"

E.J. cut her off. "I'll be there. Can you get Rex to call me?"

"First break in the morning. I took his phone. I also cleared out the medication these doctors had him on. He stayed so doped up he didn't know his name," said Rebecca.

"Keeping him off the hooch even?" asked E.J.

"I hired a sitter. He knows this is it," Rebecca said.

After eliciting another promise from E.J. to call with any development, no matter how minor, Rebecca ended the call. E.J. pressed the remote, unmuting the old Gun-smoke rerun.

He fell asleep in the chair dreaming he spoke to Sharla. She spooned her cereal, looking out his dining-room window. They spoke to each other, yet E.J. couldn't determine what either said.

Without explanation, they moved to the pond. E.J. watched her cork sinking hard. "Catfish, get it, Sharla."

Sharla lifted the rod and started reeling.

E.J. dropped his pole and ran to her. The taut line

pressed against his hands as he helped lift the fish.

"Is it bigger than Konner's?" asked Sharla.

E.J. wasn't sure what she said. It made little sense. Neither of them mentioned Konner anymore. The pain ran too deep. He shielded his eyes from the sun, turning his hand outward. "What?"

"I have to show Konner. My fish is bigger." Sharla looked so much better than in the videos. Her hair had reverted to its natural color and her sores healed. Death no longer dragged down her hollowed eyes; rather, she brimmed with life and love again.

E.J. lifted the fish, then hugged his daughter. "Honey, there is no Konner. He died overseas in the war on terror."

Sharla looked at him like he had lost his mind. She pointed over her shoulder. "He's putting out hay, Dad, see?"

E.J. turned to witness the tractor drop a bale from the frontend loader. The door opened, and E.J. didn't need to see the face. He felt Konner's presence.

A cavalry bugle blared the charge, sending a troop of men and horses riding hard through the wall. Some black and white movie had replaced Gunsmoke.

He stood groggy, too early to rise and too late to sleep, making coffee a necessity. E.J. brewed a pot, then began his morning routine.

While removing a starched shirt from the hanger, he heard the heavy trucks in his driveway. Throwing the shirt over his shoulders. E.J. grabbed the 1911 pistol from the bed stand.

In the faint dawn, he made out about six people and four large trucks from one-ton pickups to eighteen-wheelers fitted with trailers from flatbeds to cattle haulers. Someone cranked his tractor and began driving toward a trailer.

E.J. stepped on the first of two steps toward the tractor cab, resting the barrel of the forty-five against the thick glass tractor door. The driver depressed the clutch, stopping the tractor, and raised his hands.

E.J. recognized the driver as a local wrecker service owner and pulled the door open. "Alvin, what are you doing stealing my stuff?"

"Man hired me. He's brought papers showing some judge in Houston wants all your stuff taken for Devekon Industries." Alvin pointed toward the working pens. "Little man there."

Before E.J. could reach his cattle chute, he saw him well enough to identify the chief thief. "Mr. Snarky."

Mr. Snarky handed E.J. a folio of court documents, unable to hide a wide grin. "Mr. Kane, I'm directed to remove all Devekon property and make an inventory of anything you may actually own.

E.J. fumed with anger so much he couldn't concentrate on the document. He made a production of calling 911 in front of Mr. Snarky. "E.J. Kane. I've got trespassers trying to steal property I'm responsible for—"

"Pretender, it's all unraveling now. Tell me, who's the big man now?" Dispatch had transferred him to Sheriff B.B.

E.J. pressed the phone, ending the call. In one smooth motion, Mr. Snarky grabbed the phone, causing E.J.'s Colt to jam hard into Mr. Snarky's stomach.

Mr. Snarky's eyes narrowed, and his lips pursed. "Company phone, Mr. Kane."

A newfound respect touched E.J. He had a loaded forty-five caliber semi-automatic pressed into Snarky's gut, safety off, round in the chamber. Who knew Snarky had it in him? Who knew he would have already planned everything with Sheriff B.B.?

E.J. grabbed the phone back. "I'll mail it to you after I get someone to take my contacts and stuff off." Then he lowered the gun while watching a cowboy unload his horse from a cattle trailer. He'd likely be rounding up the longhorns. "Clara Brandis didn't want to be here herself? See the big show?" asked E.J.

"She has to testify today, but she insisted I video the entire event." Mr. Snarky pointed to someone holding an iPad near another moving truck.

E.J. turned, facing the young person. He fumed, feeling like all the blood went to his head. He wanted to curse Clara Brandis. It made no sense to do so.

He breathed deep, looking into the dark sky. Closing his eyes, he turned and walked back into the house to pour himself a cup of coffee. Yak met him at the door, jumping onto him.

"Calm down, boy. It's all gonna be okay." E.J. promised as he playfully rubbed and shook the big dog. Another cup of coffee and E.J. seated himself on the porch, watching the flurry of activity before him.

The sun had risen well into a bluebird sky when Mr. Snarky walked to the porch with the videographer in tow. E.J. took a list from the smaller man; then he stared at the top page of the documents.

"You know, I tried to talk Rex out of buying half this stuff. He had the apartment built in the barn so he could stay between wives and mistresses," said E.J.

"You need to sign at the bottom of page two." Mr.

Snarky pointed to the papers.

"No."

"No?"

"Mr. Snarky, I didn't make Rex sign to leave any of his stuff here. I took care of it because he's my friend and my boss. I promise you, much of the time, I thought about dehorning those cattle."

Mr. Snarky turned to the iPad camera and produced a pen from his tweed sports coat. He extended the pen to E.J.

E.J. ignored the gesture. "Even told Rex Longhorns belong in a zoo, and he went all Gus from Lonesome Dove and threatened to buy buffalo. Buffalo —"

"I'm missing some items, so I'll search your home." Mr. Snarky made the command in a shaky tone.

"No," commanded E.J.

"No?"

"Step foot in my house and you are in the commission of a burglary. Your life becomes forfeit, Mr. Snarky." E.J. looked up, staring into the fear-laden face of the out-of-place urban office worker. It struck E.J. how ridiculous Snarky looked with a rural setting at his back.

"The judge specifically authorized the removal of one Catahoula Leopard dog." Mr. Snarky regained some of his swagger, like he hoped to strike a nerve.

E.J. opened his hand, swinging it over the animal laying on the porch next to his rocker. "Take him—"

Yak rose, looking at Mr. Snarky through what connoisseurs of the breed called glass eyes, what E.J. called a whitish blue. The little man's body tensed, prompting Yak to issue a primordial growl.

Mr. Snarky jumped back, coming off the porch and

tripping over his loafers. As he fell backwards, he pointed to his camera person. She continued documenting his fall.

"Sit." On E.J.'s command, Yak stopped the long low noise and dropped onto his hind legs. E.J. didn't hide his laughter at Mr. Snarky's expense.

Another cup of coffee, and the invasion ended. Mr. Snarky led his motley army of movers from the property loaded with their spoils.

E.J. searched his junk draw for a set of keys. He found them as the phone rang. He accepted the call. "How's the trial, Rex?"

"All bad. Rebecca's a pistol, though. She'll make 'em pay, anyway."

"She did me," E.J. spoke in the same even voice, yet Rex Ashe erupted in laughter.

When the outburst ended, E.J. said, "Glad my matrimonial failure could amuse you."

"Com'on, you got to admit mine has had you laugh and made you good money for a long time. I heard all our stuff got loaded up," said Rex Ashe.

"Your stuff. I only let you keep it here," said E.J. I need to ask something. "Kind of sensitive. Relates to this Arnold case and now a kid named Geoffrey."

"What do you need to know?" Rex Ashe's surprise soaked the question.

"Are there people who can make industrial accidents happen?" asked E.J.

"You mean like arson?"

"I'm asking if you know a guy," said E.J.

"Kyle Limburger, but he won't talk to you. He moved to Tyler, trying to live down a big insurance scam. Heard he got charged in Beaumont. Won't talk to you though, paranoid," said Rex Ashe.

"Got any contact info?" E.J. asked.

"Call old Bill Gleason. He'll find him for you. I got to go," said Rex Ashe.

E.J. walked to the barn. Holes patched with tar dotted the rusty tin. The original structure spawned additions on each side, amounting to storage bays for farm equipment.

He lifted and drew a large dust-coated tarp, revealing an early sixties model Ford pickup. The once mother-of-pearl white had dulled, yet some semblance of the original finish remained. E.J. greeted the antiquated truck. "Are you gonna give me trouble?"

Stale, dusty air assaulted E.J.'s nose after the cab door creaked open. The engine rolled over and then swung the big Y block V eight to life. "Aw, that's a baby."

The road to Kyle Limburger provided more drama than E.J. had expected. Bill Gleason had admonished him. The old man suspected everyone of trying to catch him in his many schemes and frauds from a lifetime of chicanery. E.J. reminded Bill Gleason, he had experienced more than once a gun pointed at him for visiting a residence uninvited. Bill Gleason explained Kyle Limburger posed a risk of booby-traps and exploding ordinance.

Fortunately, Rex Ashe's name went a long way. Like a password, E.J. yelled it across a well-manicured yard next to a golf course. More than a door opened, Kyle Limburger offered him a beverage and a seat on a warm spring afternoon as if he were attending a tea party.

"How is old T-Rex?" asked Kyle Limburger, wearing the distinctive uniform of a golfer retired from his day job.

"Terrible. His family and investors sued him to declare him unfit to take care of himself."

Kyle Limburger shook his head. "You know I heard of you. Lots of stories."

"I hope you'll talk to me, anyway." E.J. grinned, trying to lighten the situation. He looked around at a living space full of the regalia accompanying a golfer's life scattered everywhere. E.J. concluded Kyle Limburger led a bachelor's life.

A smile passed to Kyle Limburger. "You know old T-Rex and I came up together back in the day, back before he got respectable. You know the first hundred million makes anybody respectable."

E.J. feigned relief. "I'm safe."

Both men laughed.

E.J. said, "Rex is like family to me, but nobody ever called him 'respectable'."

"No, they haven't." Both men chuckled again.

"That is kind of what I needed to discuss. I've got a couple of unusual oilfield accidents. Too convenient, and they're mixed up with a scheme to steal condensate." E.J. found the iced tea fresh.

"Tell me what you know." Kyle Limburger's request took a considerable amount of time, despite E.J. supplying the cliff's notes version.

"A smartphone and what's in most people's bathrooms will make you hydrogen sulfide, an easy way to commit suicide. No big deal to get it into a shed waiting on the kid you told me about," said Kyle Limburger.

E.J. nodded.

"The lightning case is more complicated. From what you tell, though, the lightning didn't kill him. Explosion killed him. You can't even be sure lightning hit anything," said Kyle Limburger.

"But you can't make lightning less you capture it like Dr. Frankenstein, right?" E.J. raised his voice in argument.

Kyle Limburger moved an open hand in a pleading motion. "You don't need lightning, but let's say it's the cover story you want to use. It's springtime. Wait till thunderstorm is forecast, then set off your IED."

"Complicated, isn't it?" asked E.J.

"You got a generation of oilfield workers educated by both Uncle Sam and the terrorist of Iraq and Afghanistan in how to rig improvised explosive devices. And what could be a better cover story than a lightning strike? I should have thought of it." Kyle Limburger backtracked. "Of course, not to kill anyone, just maybe a little property damage— You know, for a price."

"Wouldn't an explosive device leave something to give itself away?" asked E.J.

"Who's looking? Some hick sheriff. Even if they call in a ranger or the FBI, likely only one. No offense, y'all are government workers, and it only makes more work when you find something." Kyle Limburger avoided E.J.'s eyes.

E.J. added a touch of sarcasm to the unintended insult. "If we buy the lightning story, then we can get back to our donuts quicker."

After turning down an afternoon on the links, E.J. cranked his vintage pickup with some effort. He would adjust the carburetor when he got home. While driving around the loop, the burner phone went off to an unknown number.

"Jackson, this is Norty. Want to invite you to a little shootin' tonight."

"You gonna shoot in the dark?" Asked E.J.

"Lighted range, come on. Meet some more of the

brothers. Don't let me scare off the returning champion to our little soiree."

E.J. felt a chill up his back. His mind flashed back, and he could see Georgia's fear in the form of perspiration on her brow combined with Norty's foul body odor leading to her death. Was he going to a shooting range to be the target?

CHAPTER FOURTEEN

SURELY NORTY AND THE NEPHILIM WOULDN'T HARM HIM on a public range with a big wig like Artimus Blake. In time, he would surmise there was no public range and no Artimus Blake.

E.J. turned off onto a county road in the middle of nowhere. He drove past an open gas well lease gate, continuing on the gravel road about half a mile.

He parked near several trucks outside a metal shop building on the edge of a pasture. A pavilion stood to the side of the shop, sporting a covered roof and several light poles on each side, illuminating a berm of steel silhouettes. The perfect place to put a cap in the back of someone's head.

Norty and a few other men stood under the metal awning, holding pistols and watching. E.J. elected to maintain the ruse as Jackson. He didn't own firearms, though he couldn't come up with a good plan. Maybe he should pretend he had some familiarity. Muscle memory would cause any use of a pistol to give him away as a former competition shooter, if not law enforcement.

Norty greeted him and introduced him to two other men known as Keyto and Peppy. E.J. used his full Ed Jackson moniker, trying to put an onus on the two men to divulge their actual names. The attempt failed.

Norty dropped semi-wadcutter rounds into his nickel-plated pistol. "It's a 460 xvr from the custom shop. Then I had it engraved and plated."

"Must have cost a fortune," said E.J.

"Used my contractor money from Iraq," said Norty.

"What'd you do over there?" E.J. looked down range at an upper body shaped outline of steel painted white. There were three small rectangular boxes drawn in black sharpie.

"Ordinance disposal. Entire country's an IED. 3-2-1 drill. You know how to shoot it," Norty said.

E.J. looked around. Was he talking to him?

Behind E.J. and from around the front of the building walked Son in full uniform with his gun drawn. E.J. recognized Son's modern polymer pistol in a nine-millimeter probably not loaded with target ball ammunition. More likely, the duty pistol held sixteen or seventeen hollow point rounds. Such projectiles were designed to uncurl like petals on a rose in the human body, ripping a massive wound channel.

The image shocked E.J. He felt his knees weaken, and he pressed his hands on the shelf serving as a firing line barrier. The rough board cooled his hot fingertips.

Son's dark pistol swung forward as he walked past E.J. though the pistol remained pointed downrange. In an instant, he holstered the weapon and raised his hands.

Then a buzzer sounded. The young man's right hand dropped and drew the pistol, presenting it to the target in perfect form. He fired two rounds into the three-inch box drawn on the white target, followed by the two-inch, then the one-inch box. Each round discolored the spray-painted white form, all in the space of a few seconds. Son reloaded and holstered the weapon while staring at E.J.

E.J. knew his charade ended with Son. How long before had they known? Did he blow his cover at the barbeque, or had they known from the start?

Though surely, Norty didn't know he was also the disguised Weldon Harris. If so, wouldn't he already be dead?

"Why don't you take the next target with the Sig you carry in your pocket?" Norty asked.

"Heard you're a legend, pops. I'd like to see it," added Son.

"When did you have me made?" asked E.J.

"Even before the game show. I told the truth about the refinery and Artimus Blake feeling antsy. He called around. There's no Ed Jackson working at any salt water hauler in the area, least not anyway close to matching you," Norty said.

"Why didn't you kill me at the barbeque?" asked E.J.

Norty laughed, swinging his arms open. "Brother, you were never in danger. At first, I thought you had no game; then you took it to a new level. I'm not going to shoot my best contestant."

E.J. lifted the compact pistol from his pocket. "I'm hesitant to fire. I might need some of these rounds later."

"Not tonight, Mr. Kane. I've assured you the Nephilim is the next Rotary club. Tell me, you don't see the destruction of our values. Federal government is openly attacking the livelihood we built Texas upon." Norty shook his head and shrugged his shoulders. "Even if you buy into global warming, why not let innovation solve the problems? We have never treated the economy like a zero-sum game where the builders surrender their hard-earned money to the malingerers and ne'er-do-wells."

"Call it," E.J. said.

"3-1-2," Son said. The timer buzzed.

E.J. raised his pistol, picking up the front tritium sight in the dim light. He fired two rounds in each of the three small rectangular boxes.

Norty laughed, looking at Son, then passed a box of ammunition toward E.J. "Fast. Reload, Mr. Kane. I'm sure Son will test your skill."

"Most guys have gone to a polymer like a P365." Son's facial expression showed he meant the statement to be answered like a question, and E.J. took it though he answered in one word.

"Plastic." E.J. bounced his pistol in his hand, displaying the chunk of steel's heft.

The other shooters became an audience for the impromptu competition. Neither man missed a round, yet the time gap widened in E.J.'s favor. The result shocked Son. E.J. looked into Son's eyes, watching the young man's calm demeanor evaporate. Son kicked the waist-high bench, denoting the firing line. He knocked off the ammunition box.

E.J. turned, ignoring the display. "So, the barbecue, the shooting tonight, all designed to convince me you're just a bunch of misunderstood All-American boys?"

Norty opened his arms, gesturing toward his colleagues

in an expression of childlike innocence. "You can't pretend you don't see the fall of our society."

"How 'bout you tell me what role Widow Welchel and Artimus Blake play in your little civic club?" asked E.J.

"Widow's a wonderful woman. You know she built WelCo from one truck over twenty years ago. She'd pull over on the side of the road to nurse her daughter and then keep rolling day and night. Buying injection wells and trucks," Norty said.

"Can't seem to find anyone not in love with Widow," said E.J.

The happy-go-lucky demeanor drained from Norty's face, raising the nickel-plated monstrosity in the air. "Widow's a fine lady, didn't have everything given to her is all. You better remember it."

"Easy, she's a saint. Mother Teresa sharing God's love with all mankind. Artimus Blake then?" asked E.J.

"Spoiled punk whose Daddy bought him a business to run." Norty laughed.

Son added, "Made a fortune. You know the old joke 'bout making a big fortune into a small one."

E.J. thought Son's mockery of privilege seemed a little rich given his status as a deputy in his father's department. "Y'all aren't going to tell me how the pieces fit together?"

Norty asked, "What pieces?"

"Is Widow Welchel recruiting drivers or supplying targets? Blake the big boss, or only the fence? Nephilim the muscle while Son and his Daddy B.B. provide law enforcement cover?"

Son's fist struck flush on E.J.'s jaw, pinning E.J.'s shoulders to a pole supporting the shooting bench. Then E.J.'s head smacked backward against the post. His teeth clenched hard, cutting down on his tongue. The iron taste of the warm blood coated his mouth. He crouched next to the shooting counter, regaining his balance and trying to defend against the next blow.

E.J.'s head tilted up. He tried to decipher why Son didn't finish him while he had him down, or at least kick him. His mind jumped to notions of striking at the mountain of a man towering over him. No, he had tried to provoke a response with his wild assertions. Son answered the question. His assertiveness proved the veracity of his denial. Were the situation reversed, E.J. knew he would have done likewise.

E.J. reached up to rub his face, now tender to the touch. He had difficulty imagining more extreme offense being taken. Maybe the boy had a little substance to him after all. The thought made E.J. smile even while his cheek swelled and his head ached.

Son extended a hand, and E.J. grabbed it. He stood up, still rubbing his cheek.

Son said, "Whatever's between you and my dad has got nothing to do with me. And I ain't no crook."

"Right now, I won't argue with you, Son. Why are you here? The state tracks this outfit. It's a security threat group." E.J. said.

Norty near leaped forward. "I keep telling you. We're no different from Republicans and Democrats. We're like the Kiwanis, Rotary, Lion club. I'm sure we've got some bad members, but there are crooked police too."

"Sure," E.J. muttered, rubbing his jaw.

"Look, don't you see the working people who built this country are getting the shaft. They sent stimulus checks to child molesters and death row inmates. We're paying for the party. You can't even lock the criminals up without Cadillac health care and sex changes on the taxpayer's dime," said Norty.

E.J. raised a hand. "Spare me." He turned to Son. "He'll keep going until he hooks me. Something libertarian, kind of loosely conservative, but he'll go liberal if he needs to. Then he'll reel me in with some dime store lawyer argument about the 13th and 14th amendments, maybe the tax code from the 1930s."

Son looked puzzled, and Norty chimed in again. "It's not like—"

E.J. stepped toward Norty, startling him into stopping mid-sentence. "My son gave his life in the defense of this nation." E.J.'s harsh tone communicated he held Norty and his purported civic club in low esteem and unworthy of legitimate debate.

E.J. figured he would gain nothing further from Norty or Son. He needed to go home and call Cooper.

The drive home reminded him of what he liked about the fancy company truck, everything. His mind poured over what he had learned. Norty likely duped Son into believing the universe was arrayed against the conservative values he had accepted since birth. Norty and his ilk filled the world with bile, infecting decent people.

Despite his best efforts, E.J. couldn't put the truth together. One guess seemed almost as good as another as to the true nature of the theft ring.

Before he could reach home, Cooper called him. E.J. pulled over, missing the convenience of Bluetooth.

"I've got Taint located," said Cooper

"I'll meet you." E.J. felt his pulse quicken. They finally caught a break.

"No. I'm stuck. Taint's cousin decided he would come to Jesus, but if I leave him, then he'll backslide and tip Taint off. So, we're gonna get a happy meal and coffee together." Cooper sounded irritated.

E.J. put it together. If Taint got word from the cousin, then he was gone, and Cooper couldn't be in two places at one time. She had no one she could count on since the investigation moved off the books. He was her last resort, and he knew her hesitation.

CHAPTER FIFTEEN

"I'LL GO, PUT EYES ON HIM AND WAIT FOR YOU. WHERE'S he at?" asked E.J.

Cooper hesitated. "Taint is wannabe, not banger. I've started calling him a Magnolia Crip."

E.J. chuckled. "There aren't five hundred people in Magnolia. It's like the capitol of redneck-land." His chuckling ended with the realization Magnolia fell in Sheriff B.B.'s jurisdiction.

"Right behind where the old Gulf station used to stand is the Piney Woods version of Compton in Cali. It's Taint's grandmother's house. As soon as I know you are there, I'll start your way," said Cooper.

The old Ford's tires spun gravel before swinging back onto the highway. E.J. wound the Y block as hard as the ancient motor would rev. Despite the massive solid steering wheel, turning the truck required maximum effort.

Magnolia lay on a twisty farm-to-market road off the

highway. More thoughts crowded him on the way. He and Cooper had, without stating it, both assumed Taint sold Sharla into servitude to pay off a drug debt. However, they had been wrong on other cases over the years. If they were wrong, then it could have been Sharla's idea. Both of them could be hiding from their drug dealer.

Perhaps at this very moment, Sharla lay on a couch, either high or crashing. He knew he shouldn't hope. Wasn't this why he shouldn't be working on Sharla's case? His dreams and desires crowded reason from his mind. Was such what Cooper feared. No, Cooper feared more, and E.J. knew for good reason. He contemplated driving onto the porch.

He drove by the structure. It resembled a shed more than a home. Someone had already parked an old truck next to the front steps. No light shone from the one window facing the road.

He turned around in the road, then pulled over and depressed the button on the dash, killing the lights. E.J. called Cooper.

"It'll take me forty minutes," Cooper said.

"Maybe a water haul, anyway. I can't see any lights. There's an old truck in front of the door. Thing probably don't run." E.J. rolled down his window and leaned back in the seat.

After about ten minutes, a car slowed, nearing the house. The older model sedan drove into the driveway. E.J. watched a man open the door and enter the house carrying a bag.

From the expiring beams of the car, E.J. identified Taint and a bag of fast food. E.J. cranked the truck, stabbed the gas, and popped the clutch. A powerful rage coursed through his blood.

Only when he neared the porch did E.J. ask himself what he was thinking? He hoped more than deduced. Taint brought Sharla food. She lived and breathed somewhere between those walls. She needed help. He had to get to her.

The rotten pillar of the porch folded against the thick steel bumper and corner of the hood. E.J. leaped onto the porch. One solid boot crashed into the door, separating it from its hinges.

Taint looked up over a brown bag. He dropped his greasy burrito, trying to scurry backwards in the chair. He landed flat on his back, staring aimlessly at the monster overtaking him. E.J.'s paw grabbed Taint around the collar and threw him into the wall.

"Hey man, stop, stop. Stop," screamed Taint.

"Where's Sharla?" asked E.J.

"I swear, I don't know." Taint saw a massive fist moving toward his eyes, and then there were stars ringing his bell and lifting him from the ground.

"Where?" asked E.J.

Taint spit blood over a swelling lip. "Stop, just stop."

E.J. looked at his hands. The word 'stop' cut through the fog clouding his mind, and slowed the rage within him.

"You wait till CNN gets you. Anderson Cooper is coming back to Magnolia. Solid racism," said Taint.

"Where's my daughter?" E.J. asked.

Taint slid up against the wall, moving toward a small kitchen island in the one large room. "I keep telling you, she left. No calls, no text, she's just gone." Taint used his response as a distraction to slide his hand in a drawer.

He raised a black semi-automatic. Twisting the gun

like a shooter in an action movie, Taint put it near E.J.'s temple. The circular end of the barrel momentarily disoriented E.J.

E.J. swung his right arm into the gun. Taint crunched the trigger. The noise burst through both men's ears. A round ripped through a sheetrock ceiling underlying the tin roof.

The pistol's slide caught on E.J.'s hand, stove piping the spent shell casing. E.J. closed his grip, pulling the pistol into his palm by the barrel. Taint lowered his head as the gun's grip crashed into his skull, rendering him a heap on the floor.

"Get up," E.J. yelled. He shook his head like it would help the ringing in his ears.

Taint didn't move.

E.J. kicked Taint, then kicked him again with greater velocity. He bent down with the barrel still facing him. Recognizing the Glock seventeen, he threw it into the corner of the room.

Taint had a pulse because E.J. confirmed it, although he saw no other sign the man was breathing. E.J. slapped his check, trying to bring him around. The young man reached upward, protecting his head with both hands.

E.J. took a hoodie strewn across the back of a chair and pressed it against Taint's head to stem the blood. He took Taint's cell phone from the table and called 911. The operator told him not to end the call, but he hung up anyway, satisfied they had dispatched an ambulance to the location.

He thought about calling Cooper. What would her old mentor tell her? He had done exactly what she feared. He had lost his cool and pistol-whipped Taint. What about

Cooper's career?

Taint would make a complaint. He accused E.J. of being a racist even before E.J. had laid hands on him. Even if he were willing to lie to protect Cooper, it wouldn't work because she would tell the truth.

The whole thing was wrong. He went after Taint without reflection because his baby girl may have been in trouble. Since birth, he protected Sharla until he failed her. Now she served as a slave to a drug dealer or, worse, worked the streets. He hadn't been there for her when Konner died, combined with the divorce spiraling her drug addiction. His love and good intentions meant nothing now.

He would have gone through Taint regardless of color, but he would never convince Taint of such fact. E.J. stood taking in his surroundings. He had near killed a man yet gained nothing in the quest for Sharla.

The blood slowed to a trickle. E.J. looked at the refrigerator. He found no ice maker. He wrapped a tray of ice in the hoodie and handed it back to Taint. A groggy Taint took it, then pressed the hoodie to the top of his head.

"Where's my gun?" Taint asked.

"Where's my daughter? You should know I don't need a weapon to kill you," said E.J.

"Man, I keep telling you. I don't know. I want her too," said Taint.

"Who did you sell her to?" E.J.'s hand slapped Taint's throbbing head.

"All right, all right. His name is Sug. Look, she would work for a guy named Geirmo one time. Sug tricked us. He took her." Tears streamed down Taint's cheeks. Taint yelled over and over. "He took her. He took her."

E.J. bent back down and grabbed Taint by the collar. "Where do I find, Sug?"

"We met him at a motel in Lufkin. I waited in the car. I went back to the room, and they were gone, out the back window, I guess." Taint gasped for air.

"He's your drug dealer. You don't have any way to contact him. Bull," Taint's warm sticky blood covered E.J.'s hands. The house smelled of blood, greasy fast food, and the sweet-sour odor of mildew and decomposing garbage.

"I got a number, but it just keeps ringing. We always made the drop at the hotel." Taint rocked back and forth on the floor.

"You're an idiot. A mark playing wannabe gang banger, the Magnolia Crip," said E.J.

"I know, I know. I should die." Taint hit the floor with his first.

"Then why didn't you tell the truth instead of giving me the activist routine?" asked E.J.

"Kill me. I don't deserve to live," said Taint.

E.J. shrieked in unexpected agony. He instantly recognized the technique and the weapon, an Asp baton. The force drove him to his knees. Even before he heard the voice, E.J. knew the source. The next strike didn't resemble a precise tactic; rather, this blow evidenced rage. His ribs ached, and his gasping breath shortened.

"I feared you'd beat the kid. Not his fault your daughter wanted darkie love and crystal meth." Sheriff B.B. yelled at the top of his lungs. He swung the heel of his work boot onto E.J.'s head, jabbing it to the stained, nasty floor with such force E.J.'s skull bounced, throwing dirt and trash from the carpet upward.

CHAPTER SIXTEEN

E.J. COULDN'T CLEAR HIS HEAD ENOUGH TO PLAN A DE-
fense. He had prided himself on keeping his wits when
others panicked. The steel toe of the boot kicked through
him as E.J. rolled his body into a ball. Consciousness fast
escaped him.

Son's voice cut through the haze, swelling E.J.'s brain.
"Stop—" In E.J.'s mind, the world spun forward, then spun
backwards prior to turning dark.

A wet coldness woke E.J. He rolled over a small drain
in the floor. The icy cement felt good against his swelling
face. Pain throbbed through him. He figured he was laying
in the drunk tank of Sheriff B.B.'s jail. Sheriff B.B. stood
over him, holding an empty five-gallon bucket.

E.J. spit blood toward the drain. "You have to take me
to the ER. It's a civil rights violation."

Sheriff B.B. mocked E.J.'s voice, trying to repeat the
demand. He laughed even louder. "Oh, that's rich from
you, pretender. You're off the books. I know you know

what it means."

E.J.'s mind tried to reconstruct the night's events. He didn't recall being booked into jail. Surely B.B. wouldn't kill him. At one time, they had been friends. Then he caught himself in his own lie. No, not friends, though they had known each other all their lives. So long that E.J. couldn't recall what B.B. held against him.

"You know what off the books means. No records you're here. You know I don't wear a body cam and don't have one in my personal truck." Sheriff B.B. threw the bucket across the small room. "No security camera caught you being brought in."

E.J. tried unsuccessfully to rise. The floor had the additional advantage of keeping the room from spinning. He fought back nausea in his throat. "What is it, B.B.? Did I beat you racing on the schoolyard? Steal the gal you had a crush on?"

The Asp snapped from palm length to near two feet. "You really don't know, do you?"

E.J. continued spitting blood into the drain. "Curiosity is flat killing me."

"Always sarcastic, mister pretender. I caught you trying to kill somebody, a black somebody, and you got the gall to tell me I'm violating your rights," said Sheriff B.B.

E.J.'s arm straightened, making progress toward rising at least to his knees.

Sheriff B.B. stepped on E.J.'s shoulder. "I can charge you with aggravated assault with a deadly weapon. Maybe I can get your buddy Hall to hook you up with some federal charges for trying to lynch that boy. Maybe one of those federolly hate crimes."

E.J. rolled to reach the wall hoping to rise. After many

failed attempts, he stood. Sheriff B.B. had left the room.

In his place stood Son. "You gonna make it?"

"Least if you book me in, I can see a jail nurse," E.J. said.

"Nobody is booking you. You're not being charged, pops," Son said.

E.J.'s knees wobbled, yet he caught himself. "Your dad made a list. He makes me sound like some kind of grand dragon serial killer public enemy all rolled into one."

Son took E.J.'s arm, near lifting him. They walked through the steel door. "Nathaniel Raney, a.k.a. Taint won't press charges."

"You're kidding." E.J. laughed until pain constricted his lungs.

Son shook his head. "Got right in my father's face. Dad threatened to charge him, so Taint tells Dad he's calling the NAACP for harassment on Dad."

E.J. thought back to a broken young man in tears, begging to die. Maybe it wasn't an act or a con. Maybe Mr. Nathaniel Raney regretted whatever part he had played. Taint's words rang through his ears, "I should die."

But it always takes two. Rebecca was right. Rebecca is always right. She held a high opinion of the kid. Could be Sharla pulled him down. What a terrible thought. More than a thought, it made sense.

Walking out of the jail, the early morning sun hit E.J. across the swollen eyes. "What about Cooper? Did she look for me?"

"Yeah, Dad told her we weren't holding you and to kiss off. You know how he can be," said Son.

"Didn't she find my truck at Taint's little hideout?" asked E.J.

"We impounded your truck. It's in our forfeiture yard. Had to use a wrecker. I couldn't get it started. Like does a crank flip down from somewhere in the front?" asked Son.

E.J. said, "Sometimes the starter hangs. Got a broomstick in the bed to beat on it."

Son handed him his wallet, his keys, and the pistol. "Almost kept your little Sig."

Their gaze locked. E.J. asked, "What're you doing?"

"Don't worry, I wasn't going to steal your World War One tech," said Son.

E.J. thought about thanking the young man for saving his life. "No, I mean you're not what I thought you were."

Son looked down and started walking toward the forfeiture lot. "Can you drive home, or do I need to take you?"

"Going to Houston today." E.J. got behind the wheel. He knew he needed to call Cooper. He would do it after he got cleaned up and spent a few minutes on ice, preferably all of him on it. Then travel to downtown Houston driving a pickup that came off the assembly line when Houston had six million fewer people.

"Whew, Rebecca hunting you," Rex Ashe flipped a cigarette butt into the shrubbery.

"Mad?" asked E.J.

"Enough to give you another beating. Who'd you cross?" Rex Ashe said.

"Next break. I better find Rebecca."

Rex Ashe pointed toward a busy Franklin Street. "What about your truck?"

"Figure towin' is cheaper than parking down here." E.J. swung his hand up at the downtown skyline. "God didn't intend for people to be stacked up like sardines."

Rex Ashe yelled as E.J. entered the building. "Closing in on you, huh?"

E.J. had navigated several large court buildings over the years. This one proved equally challenging.

"Any lead on Sharla?" Rebecca met him in the hall, then she turned, walking back the way she came.

E.J. matched her pace. "Nothing to speak of. I'll update you later."

Rebecca started in a whisper, then increased her volume. "Where have you been? Why did I give you a time? You look like a black widow mated with you!"

E.J. spoke, however, Rebecca proved louder and quicker. "They're railroading your best friend into the nut-hut, and you can't be bothered to show up. And when you finally show up, you look like somebody locked you in a closet with a rabid bobcat."

E.J. laughed until the pain crunched through his jaw. "I'm, I'm sorry, Rebecca."

"You got lucky. Judge tells pointless stories takes forever in between berating me with the jury in a box. But there's no time to prep you, so sit on the bench. You're under the rule." Rebecca pointed at a marble bench along the wall of the crowded hallway before she exited to a perpendicular hallway next to a sign designating the county court at law by number and judge.

E.J. didn't need the rule explained to him. Being prohibited from discussing the case or listening to other witnesses wasn't much inconvenience. Unlike Rebecca, E.J. didn't favor courtrooms.

Trials weren't about truth. Like any trial lawyer, Rebecca held to the battles of competing stories idea. E.J. accepted the concept with a caveat. Story trumped truth.

The cold seat matched the overly air-conditioned space. The hallway stretched for a football field dotted by several ten-foot open spaces between the long slab pews. Dizziness prohibited him from looking at his phone. He watched people in the hallway to pass the time.

E.J. spied Widow Welchel. He rolled forward, trying to force his aching back to rise when Clara Brandis caught the corner of his eye. The two women embraced. Did he see Widow Welchel and Clara Brandis embrace like family?

A long distance down the hall, the two women spoke and then separated. Clara Brandis took a seat on the rock bench. Widow Welchel stepped into her distinctive walk toward the courtroom. E.J. lifted a discarded newspaper over his face until she passed.

A bailiff stepped into the hall and called, "E.J. Kane."

E.J.'s shoulders made a little involuntary shudder after entry. The packed dark courtroom hid the tremendous wealth at stake in the trial. Tables strewn with papers and other materials were stacked end to end with attorneys and clients before a small gallery packed with people.

He took the oath before continuing to the witness stand. Sensing the stare of everyone in the room, E.J. became self-conscious over his raccoon eyes and battered face. He wore a dress shirt with heavily starched blue jeans.

Whatever his role, the jury wasn't expecting it. They looked like they were awaiting a dental appointment.

Rebecca began her examination with the usual name, education, experience, and occupation. E.J. answered the questions on autopilot. Then something caught his attention in the crowded gallery.

Widow Welchel was sitting close to a woman, closer than seemed normal. Finally, his mind clicked on the woman, and the entire picture came through his thoughts, Clara Brandis' family photo.

The powder blue eyes showed strong like her mother's. Widow Welchel had to be the woman's mother, which made Widow Welchel Clara Brandis' mother-in-law. What in the world did the connection mean?

Widow Welchel's words came back to him, 'She rebelled and I'm still coming to terms with it'. Of course, Widow Welchel would have seen it as rebellion. A woman who reveled in her sex appeal and enjoyed all things men had raised a gay daughter.

Rebecca walked him through his long association with Rex Ashe. Ashe's own son-in-law had targeted the wealthy oilman for a ransom plot. The ne'er-do-well kidnapped Rex Ashe's granddaughter. E.J. caught the case as the ranger assigned to the county where the son-in-law abducted her.

E.J. fired his forty-five seventy through a hunting cabin wall, then stormed the structure. His bravery earned a commendation, though the story didn't end entirely happily. The events achieved a powerful bond between Rex Ashe and E.J.

When E.J.'s career ended in disgrace, Rex Ashe provided a soft landing. E.J. proved valuable to his wealthy benefactor. Rebecca skillfully soft-pedaled Rex Ashe's juvenile hijinks.

Rather than a womanizer, he followed his heart into sometimes ill-considered decisions. Later, Rex Ashe paid enormous sums only to discover the objects of his affection didn't want him. Rather than alcoholism, he built an early distillery, jump starting vodka and later whiskey production in the Lone Star State.

E.J. glanced into the gallery occasionally. He needed no further proof Widow Welchel favored Clara Brandis over Rex Ashe, yet she provided more. After staring daggers at E.J., those distinctive eyes rolled back under long lashes toward the frosted and perfectly quaffed blond hair.

The only woman he had slept with since his marriage ended, and she amounted to the enemy. He had to ask himself, how does one achieve such a level of stupidity? Then he gazed again toward those brilliant orbs, still magnificent, despite the disdain they displayed for him.

The exciting pout of ruby lips pursed to kiss or laugh at him told him what he knew. Men were stupid or predictable, depending on one's viewpoint. Even now, when he knew she stood arrayed against him, he allowed her to pull his attention from the only woman he had ever loved. E.J. renewed his effort to ignore Widow Welchel and her brood.

Rex Ashe's business ventures failed spectacularly occasionally, yet Rebecca painted him with the romantic brush of an early wildcatter bringing prosperity and wealth to hard rock scrabble farmers. Rex Ashe didn't fail at fatherhood; rather he raised feckless brats who turned on him for money. We could say the same of investors whom he made wealthy. They applauded him as an eccentric genius. Then the first real rough patch, and they all wanted off the Rex Ashe merry-go-round.

Despite frequent, sustained hearsay objections and instructions to disregard when E.J. strayed too far into what he had heard others say, Rebecca presented a powerful portrait of a loveable rogue and brilliant entrepreneur. E.J. played his part. Both communicated their sincere view of Rex Ashe in their mind's eye, and the jury paid more attention. A woman on the far end nodded to E.J. when he tried to explain why he valued his friendship with Rex Ashe.

E.J. watched Rebecca catching glimpses of the clock located over the jury box. He knew she looked to stretch his testimony to after five. Lawyers liked to end the day or even take breaks at high points.

However, the judge wouldn't contribute to the plan. He refused to recess. "Your witness, Mr. Baker."

A petite, bald man tapped the microphone. "Mr. Kane, my name is Richard Baker. Given your attorney, I mean Mr. Ashe's attorney's late entrance in the case, we agreed to you being called without advance disclosure on a witness list or being given the opportunity for deposition."

E.J. thought it was a little thick. Maybe the man wanted a medal for letting Rex Ashe have his day in court. He knew the attorney intended to show the jury he was magnanimous, allowing a paltry argument for the other side so long as he could strike it down.

E.J. looked at Rex Ashe. He suspected Rex knew he wanted to apologize for not helping more, and they both knew neither man could escape their past. E.J.'s credibility faced nuclear attack over his forced retirement.

CHAPTER SEVENTEEN

RICHARD BAKER MADE SURE HE HAD EVERY JUROR'S eyes on him. "This is my first opportunity to meet you. Puts me at a certain disadvantage, so you forgive me if my questions aren't clear, and I'll restate them. I'll endeavor to show the jury facts without so much opinion."

Rebecca leaned forward, yet didn't object to what amounted to the lawyer testifying.

E.J. suspected she knew the judge wasn't having any of her objections. "Yes, sir."

"May I approach the witness, Your Honor?"

The judge made a grand motion. E.J. saw Richard Baker had some paper in his hand.

He extended the paper to E.J. "Can you identify Petitioner's twenty-five?"

"It's an inventory," E.J. answered.

"But you recognize the items on this inventory, right?" asked Richard Baker.

E.J. started to answer, then Richard Baker stepped to

the document camera and blew up the list, beating him to the punch. "Fifteen registered longhorn cattle, a one hundred horsepower John Deere tractor, a bass boat, and this goes on for a couple of pages?"

"Yes."

"Yes, is all? All you have to say?" Richard Baker gestured an open arm to the jurors. "Every one of these items is Devekon property, correct?"

"Devekon or Rex Ashe one. Didn't know there was a difference," said E.J.

Richard Baker pointed back at the list, enlarged on monitors between each juror and a screen for E.J. and a big screen past the jury box. "There is another page very similar to this one, correct?"

"Yes."

"I mean, Rex Ashe had given you something like a million dollars in personal property, right?" asked Richard Baker.

"No," said E.J.

"What do you mean, no?" Said Rex Ashe.

"Rex kept his stuff there, and the values on this list are wr—"

Richard Baker interrupted. "Devekon employees recovered all these items at your home, right?"

"I tried to explain—"

The judge cut him off this time. "Yes or No, Mr. Kane."

"They recovered them," E.J. said.

"In addition to your one million in personal-use property. You got a nice salary, correct?" asked Richard Baker.

"Yes."

"You make well above six figures a year, plus retirement, insurance, and fringe benefits, right?" Another point to which Richard Baker saw fit to draw each juror's attention as he asked the question.

"Yes," said E.J.

"May I approach again, Your Honor?" The judge nodded, and Richard Baker stepped to the witness stand. "You recognize the truck in this photo?"

"Yes."

"You know this truck alone lists for over a hundred thousand dollars. One of your fringe benefits, correct?"

E.J. answered, "I don't know what it cost."

"But it's your benefit, like Magnum P.I. gets the use of the Ferrari from Robin Masters. Good work if you can get it, right?" asked Richard Baker.

"So, huge salary, Ferrari to ride around the island, sorry, loaded pickup and about a million dollars in other toys. What you're worth, right?" Richard Baker made a puzzled look to the jury.

"What?" asked E.J.

"I mean, it's the value of your services, right?"

"I don't know, said E.J."

"You don't know what others would pay you?" asked Richard Baker

E.J. knew Richard Baker had played him well. The lawyer had reduced him with mockery so much he could finish with his professional disgrace.

E.J. and Rebecca had discussed whether to even call him or whether to address the issues indirectly. In the end, Rebecca decided there was no stealing Richard Baker's thunder. He had an ace, and it couldn't be made a duce, no matter the sleight of hand.

E.J. gazed at Rebecca. She no longer held any measure

of control. Rex Ashe owned all this stuff, yet the company accountants valued it. The wealthy valued their items in rich people's fashion. Sure, at a fancy registered sale amongst millionaires, a five-hundred-dollar longhorn cow might bring ten thousand.

Rex Ashe mingled at such events because someone there had a lease or a work-over rig or a frac outfit he needed. The same with the bass boat. Rex Ashe needed to take out-of-state investors to Lake Fork and Toledo Bend. They whopped water for those big Texas bass while Rex Ashe talked them up, raising funds for the next big play. E.J. had never used the boat.

Rex Ashe couldn't store all his junk in downtown Houston. E.J. realized Richard Baker already knew such, yet he had taken the jurors too deep into envy to listen to rational explanation. Trying to explain how the wealthy achieved more wealth and how exclusive and ridiculous their soirees seemed to the rest of us wouldn't endear E.J. to the jury.

Rex had even insisted on the truck because E.J. represented Devekon. Nobody will lease their land or invest with an energy company where the head of security beat his starter with a broom handle. In Rex Ashe's words, "To sell the dream you have to live the dream."

Richard Baker's voice boomed through the ire fogging E.J.'s brain. "Mr. Kane, do I need to repeat the question?"

"Yes."

"You make a huge salary, significant fringe benefits, and the use of about a million dollars in personal property. I asked if other companies would pay the same because it's what you are worth?" Richard Baker smiled.

E.J. knew the lawyer smiled because he had used the opportunity to make a mini jury argument. "I don't know what folks would pay me."

"Well, let's take the Texas Department of Public Safety, for example. What would they pay you?"

"Nothing."

"What?"

"I'm not eligible for re-hire with the department." E.J. struggled with the words. He tried to stifle the anguish. The bitterness had subsided, yet the heartsickness had never left him.

"You resigned during an internal investigation?" asked Richard Baker.

"Yes." E.J. gritted his teeth.

"An internal investigation into your conduct arising from an incident where two fellow officers lost their lives, correct?" Richard Baker no longer smiled, yet E.J. knew the attorney relished the kill.

"Correct." E.J. glimpsed Widow Welchel, moving onto the edge of her seat. Her cold glee made him sicker.

"In fact, I understand there were law enforcement assets at your disposal which you chose not to deploy?" Richard Baker said.

E.J. glared at Richard Baker.

Rebecca stood to object, yet before she could speak, the judge raised a hand. "Overruled."

E.J. hadn't looked to her because the objection only highlighted the damage Richard Baker inflicted on him. E.J. knew Rebecca understood the fact; however, she couldn't stand to see him suffer, even knowing the judge intended to shut her down. She also knew E.J. hadn't included Sheriff B.B. in the operation because Sheriff B.B.

took money from the target.

Richard Baker looked from the jury to E.J. "Let me ask something simpler. What happened to your face?"

E.J. glared at Widow Welchel. It made sense now. She had moved to the edge of her seat because Sheriff B.B. had told her, hadn't he? "I got hit."

"You got hit. A law enforcement officer had to pull you off a young black man whom you near beat to death last night. Isn't that how you got the bruises." Richard Baker's voice reached a crescendo as he played his Perry Mason moment for all it was worth.

E.J. did his best not to look at Widow Welchel. He didn't want to give her the satisfaction. He breathed in deep. "No one made a complaint, and I wasn't arrested."

"But you're not denying you were hit by a law enforcement officer?" asked Richard Baker.

"No," said E.J.

Richard Baker said, "Let's get back to Rex Ashe, shall we."

"Please." E.J. did not intend the comment as sarcasm; however, he noticed several jurors fought back smiles. He took it as further evidence Richard Baker had thoroughly skewered him.

"May I approach, Your Honor?" Richard Baker retrieved an exhibit from the table by the court reporter. "Allow me to show you what the court has admitted into evidence as Petitioner's exhibit number one."

E.J. took the document and struggled to make it out without his reading glasses.

"Forgive me. I should have put it on the projector." Richard Baker walked to the document camera.

E.J. deciphered the paper, recognizing some sort of

medical record for Rex Ashe. His heart sank, and his mouth gasped at the word jumping off the page, Alzheimer's.

CHAPTER EIGHTEEN

RICHARD BAKER ASKED FOR A RECESS, AND THE JUDGE gave him the end of the day on a high point. E.J. had known he should hide his surprise, however, knowing the action necessary and achieving it were two different things. Why had Rebecca let him walk into Alzheimer's? How could Rex Ashe ever win?

The shock passed, and E.J. fumed as he stepped down from the witness stand. He stepped directly to Rebecca and Rex Ashe.

"Not here," said Rebecca.

"Where?" E.J. growled in a low voice.

"A colleague loaned me his office, a short walk away. You'll update me on Sharla on the way," said Rebecca.

Along the way, E.J. downplayed the whole Taint story, though he shared the gist of what happened. A 'short walk' E.J. decided denoted a Houston distance because it wasn't a short walk, and it did nothing to calm him down.

They rode an elevator to the fourth floor of a bank

building and embarked into an empty reception area. Then Rebecca took him into a conference room with old-style leather-bound books along the walls.

The long day spent trying to recover from Sheriff B.B.'s beating him increased E.J.'s ire at being hung out to dry. "Alzheimer's is a little fact y'all could have shared."

Rex Ashe shook his head from side to side. "I'm sorry. I didn't tell anybody. Doctor lied to me."

"I made a strategic decision. To win," said Rebecca.

From the bewildered look on Rex Ashe's face, E.J. could tell she didn't include Rex Ashe in her plan. "How appears to be a mystery, Rebecca. Your strategy is so super top-secret neither your star witness nor your client knows what it is."

"You're Rex's best friend. You know everything about him," Rebecca said.

"I really don't," said E.J.

Rex Ashe added, "I'm no charity case. Besides, we don't take long walks on the beach together, Becca."

Rebecca didn't hide her irritation. "My point is E.J. knows you better than anyone, and the shock showing on his face to the jury told them he didn't think there was any way on earth your mental faculties were compromised."

Both men looked at each other. E.J. knew Rex Ashe well enough to know he thought Rebecca's reasoning sound. E.J. conceded the same to himself, though telling Rebecca she was right was unnecessary. Rebecca knew she was right, and he suspected she knew he knew.

His speculation proved correct. Rebecca's face relaxed, and E.J. decided she had forgiven him for not appreciating her genius. He had to ask himself whether Rebecca's theatrics would be enough. The trial didn't appear to be going well by any measure.

"I'm taking Rex Ashe to the assisted living center—"

Rex Ashe interrupted, "More Prison, it's like a giant field of rotting melons."

"You know I'm following the court directives. Sorry." Rebecca turned to E.J. "I was asking if you have a place to stay. I'll drop you after Rex. He told me you got your truck towed."

E.J. exhaled. "Been a bad day."

"You don't have anywhere, do you?" asked Rebecca.

"I'll be all right," said E.J.

"He's got nowhere, Becca. Probably figure he'll sleep in his truck when he finds it," said Rex Ashe.

E.J. gave the old man a stern look. "Why didn't you tell me?"

Rex Ashe looked at his Italian shoes.

Rebecca intervened on his behalf. "You know Rex. He won't cry to anybody. I couldn't get him to show emotion even when he testified. He is in the early stages. With a little help and planning, he should have a long time before he can't—" She paused, unable to find the words.

"Before I play with doll babies and start slobbering all over myself," said Rex Ashe.

Rebecca snapped at him. "No one said that."

E.J. thought no one had to say it. Fear must have crushed his old friend. Rebecca was right. There were people capable of planning for a debilitating illness and discussing treatment options rationally. Then there were stubborn, overly proud men; men like Rex Ashe, who would rather curse the darkness consuming him than ask for a match.

The diagnosis only increased E.J.'s support for Rex's

position. No one should tell anyone how to spend their last days, at least not until they pose a real danger to themselves or others. In time, maybe Rex would summon the additional courage necessary to face the monster consuming him.

"You'll stay with me. I need to print a few pages, and then we'll take Rex back." Rebecca insisted, as denoted by her sharp tone. "Besides, I intend to grill you about last night's events. Your account seems a little sketchy to me."

"All right, I owe you the truth," said E.J.

They argued on the way back to the hotel. She had insisted the room was a suite with plenty of space. He had to admit it sounded better than sleeping in the truck at an impound yard.

The suite stretched across most of a floor. E.J. observed an impressive view of the city. "Stuart is going to be okay with all this? I don't want him to think his girlfriend's husband is trying to steal her back. I don't want to hurt his feelings."

Her look gave E.J. the response he knew well. It asked whether he really wanted to fight more tonight? His headache remained unalleviated despite a near overdose of aspirin.

E.J. asked, "You want to make the point I can help take care of Rex tomorrow?"

Rebecca opened a diet soft drink. "We've done what we needed to do with you."

"Then I can go home and try to help Cooper?"

Rebecca pursed her lips and shook her head. "Maybe in the afternoon, unless Cooper gets a lead and needs you."

"What's the hold up?" asked E.J.

"I got a surprise for your black widow girlfriend."

Rebecca laughed.

E.J. winced. "I'm going home in the morning."

"No, I'm serious," said Rebecca

"You need to hear me say I messed up," E.J. said.

"You have no idea." Rebecca started laughing again; then she trailed off toward the bedroom.

E.J. lay on a couch thinking about Sharla and whether anything Taint said could lead to her. He had talked to Cooper on the way to Houston. She would interview the hotel manager and workers, but neither thought it likely a no-tell motel would produce much in the way of identification.

He couldn't sleep, so he called Cooper. Much like he thought, the hotel resulted in a dead-end even after Cooper recruited the local Sheriff to interview the owner and staff. They went over everything again, and neither investigator could decipher a lead.

E.J. had thought to pack a bag. It did him no good in the truck. In the morning, he found his truck in a tow yard. He tried explaining how he managed security for Devekon, and he had been late for court. The implausibility of a large energy company executive driving an old truck brought giggles.

E.J. cleaned up in the courthouse bathroom, managing a clean shirt and khakis. He arrived a little late, which drew a dirty look from Rebecca and a smile from Rex Ashe.

The court excused E.J. Whatever Rebecca had in mind; he wouldn't be testifying. E.J. felt relieved taking a seat in the courtroom behind Rex Ashe on the opposite side of Widow Welchel. She high-headed E.J. walking in as if she didn't see him.

Rebecca called one of Rex Ashe's accountants. The

bookkeeper presented charts and records. The presentation pointed out Rex Ashe's philanthropy. He still paid employees whose injuries prohibited them from working. Rex Ashe provided a hand up to his employee's children in the form of scholarships. There were gifts to support parks, hospitals, and the arts.

Richard Baker didn't address the charitable contributions. Instead, he concentrated on Rex Ashe's waste of vast sums on questionable relationships, parties, and gambling excursions.

Richard Baker pointed to E.J. using the records to address the many purported heirs and would-be children of Rex Ashe. E.J. had investigated these false paternity suits, common law marriage claims, and harassment allegations.

E.J. thought maybe at least the jury would know he had earned his big salary over the years. What a stupid thing to take pride in.

Rebecca stood and said, "Call Jonley Ruth Cannatella." No one moved as the bailiff called the name in the hall. Rebecca looked right at Widow Welchel, and to E.J.'s surprise, she rose.

Widow Welchel came forward and was sworn. Richard Baker approached the bench without asking this time. The other lawyers huddled, making a rugby scrum in front of the bench.

They looked over their shoulder as they spoke, as if they could see whether the gallery and jurors heard their words. When they whispered, they couldn't hear each other, so they spoke up and repeated themselves until everyone in the room heard.

The judge had not placed Widow Welchel under the

rule. In fact, she had sat in the courtroom the entire trial. Richard Baker and the judge seemed quite perturbed.

Racheal said, "Your Honor, I am calling her in rebuttal to the Petitioner's case. I couldn't foresee all the potential witnesses the petitioner would make necessary."

Richard Baker asked, "What is she rebutting?"

The judge laughed along with the other lawyers.

"Your entire case amounts to fraud, and this witness will prove it. Without her, I shall have to make a bill of exceptions to seek a mandamus ordering her to be heard," Rebecca said.

The judge stopped laughing.

"Your Honor, I see no reason to delay or even address such a frivolous issue when I trust the jury to see through Counsel's farce." Richard Baker made the statement louder and with a flourish, obviously for the jury. He stepped back, and all the lawyers followed suit.

"Please state your name for the jury?"

"Ruth Welchel, but everyone calls me Widow Welchel."

"I will call you whatever you prefer. However, your name is Jonley Ruth Cannatella, correct?"

"Correct, but I prefer Welchel, my late husband's name."

"You weren't ceremonially married. You proved up a common law marriage in probate after his death, correct?" Rebecca said.

"Objection, Your Honor. Isn't there a point?" Richard Baker stood, opening his arms to the jury.

"Your Honor, she buried five husbands, took everything each one had, stepping up in class every time. We think the pattern will be important," said Rebecca.

"Move along." The judge said.

"Tell the jury, what do you do for a living, Mrs. Welchel?" asked Rebecca.

"I run a salt water injection company. Salt water is a byproduct of hydrocarbon production. I transport and dispose of it by injecting it into old, non-producing wells. It's an environmentally and naturally safe way to dispose of the salt water, and, over time, it increases the pressure in the formation, sometimes resulting in improved production of surrounding wells." Widow Welchel spoke to the jury like they were prospective investors.

Rebecca said, "Congratulations, you have made money and done the world a service, haven't you?"

"I like to think so," said Widow Welchel.

"You're going public with your company, WelCo has gone from nothing to an expected thirty million and yet still small compared to Devekon, right?"

Widow Welchel answered the question in a deadpan tone. "Everything is small compared to Devekon."

"Who runs Devekon?" asked Rebecca.

"Rex Ashe."

"No, I mean currently. Who?" Rebecca asked again.

Widow Welchel looked at the jurors and then E.J. "Mrs. Kane, you'll have to tell me." She wanted to make sure the jury knew Rebecca either had been or was married to the witness from yesterday, E.J. Kane, tarring Rebecca with the broad brush used to paint E.J. as a greedy leach.

"Clara Brandis serves as chief financial officer, and currently, she is in charge of day-to-day affairs, correct?" Said Rebecca.

"If you say so," said Widow Welchel.

Rebecca asked, "Tell the jury how you know Clara Brandis?"

Widow Welchel looked straight ahead, no longer making eye contact with the jurors. "She is my daughter-in-law."

"Daughter-in-law and parent to your grandchild, correct?" Said Rebecca.

"Correct," said Widow Welchel.

"She also serves as manager of a limited liability partnership named Couriville Holding Company, correct?"

Widow Welchel paused before answering. "If you say so."

Rebecca leaned her head where Widow Welchel had to look at her, then made a circular motion with her hand. "But you would know because Couriville Holding Company is owned by another company whose sole owner is Jonley Ruth Cannatella, correct?"

CHAPTER NINETEEN

E.J. SAW RICHARD BAKER TURN AND MOUTH SOMETHING to one of the other attorneys, probably the name Jonley Ruth Cannatella. E.J. had been shocked, yet he took comfort from seeing genuine surprise on Richard Baker's face.

Rebecca had let her question linger in the ether long after Widow Welchel's acknowledgment. Rebecca built a sense of suspense, inviting speculation. Why would Widow Welchel put Clara Brandis in charge of some shell company and use a different, although her legal name? Has she done something she didn't want people to know?

"Devekon is publicly traded, correct?" asked Rebecca.

Widow Welchel answered in a monotone. "Yes."

"You used Clara Brandis and Couriville Holding Company to buy a large number of Devekon shares, didn't you?" Rebecca asked.

"Free country and an excellent investment." Widow Welchel looked up, avoiding Rebecca's eyes.

Rebecca looked down and up, then to the jurors. "Free country, but Devekon shares are pricy even in a downturn, right?"

Widow Welchel nodded.

"In fact, you've done everything you can to raise cash and dumped a vast amount into Devekon shares. It's why WelCo is going public, right?"

"Which question should I answer, Mrs. Kane?" asked Widow Welchel.

"You are also either receiving Devekon shares from other purchasers, or you are using other shell companies to purchase the shares because they are all ending up in Couriville Holding Company. So, tell the jury, which is it?" asked Rebecca.

E.J. could sense Richard Baker's nerves fraying. Richard Baker leaped to his feet. "Your Honor, I have to object because we have strayed far from the issue."

"Sustained," bellowed the judge.

"Your Honor, may I respond?" Said Rebecca.

The judge nodded, and Rebecca turned to the jury. "Your Honor, the fact that Mrs. Welchel spent her life leveraging her late husbands for their wealth and has recruited her daughter-in-law to control a multi-national corporation by institutionalizing my client is exactly why we are here."

Richard Baker screamed, "Mistrial," as Rebecca tried to talk over him.

The lawyers mobbed the judge's bench, and then he sent the jury to the jury room. Soon, the legal arguments degenerated to assertions of personal honor and ethics.

E.J. didn't follow the argument. He lost himself in the speculation Rebecca's investigation raised. Had Artimus

Blake or others like the members of the Nephilim paid Widow Welchel her cut in Devekon stock? It appeared too bold to believe, using Devekon's own condensate to pay for Devekon's stock.

Was Widow Welchel the mastermind of the entire crime ring? Were Artimus Blake and the Nephilim her yutzes, or were they willing co-conspirators all the way to the plunder of Devekon.

Time he concentrated on what he knew rather than speculation. Clara Brandis participated to the full extent of the takeover of Devekon. Little else appeared certain.

Assuming Widow Welchel murdered Arnold, why? What about Geoffrey? The motive for Geoffrey appeared obvious. Geoffrey provided little information, but in time he either could have done so, or the killer believed he knew more. Who knew about Geoffrey? Who had he told? What had he done?

E.J. tasted bile in the back of his throat. He put his hand over his mouth for fear he might vomit.

The judge banged the gavel, scattering the gaggle of lawyers before him. "We will recess for the day. Briefs submitted by eight a.m. on whether an instruction is sufficient."

The tone reverberated through the courtroom. Rex Ashe relished in the judge's ire. E.J. witnessed the smile so long gone from Rex Ashe's face. He hadn't realized it was missing.

Rex Ashe pulled at E.J.'s elbow. "Rebecca needs to talk to us. We whopped 'em all today." He guided E.J. to a conference room down the hall outside the courtroom.

Rex Ashe tried to strike up a conversation about a deer hunting property he had once owned in South Texas. They had shared some good times on the ranch, yet E.J. continued to mull over the revelations about Widow Welchel. How did he let Widow Welchel play him for such a fool?

Rebecca swung open the door. "Not as I had hoped. Nonetheless, we won the day."

"Did you need me to see for myself how big an idiot I am?" E.J. asked.

"Added benefit. I needed you here because I think she is stealing from Devekon, and I can't figure out how," said Rebecca.

"E.J. will." Rex Ashe placed his hand on E.J.'s back.

E.J. nodded. He still suffered from a kind of shell shock over the revelations. Added to such, Rex Ashe had never been a touchy-feely person. Perhaps the stress had worn the once-powerful captain of industry, or could it have something to do with the Alzheimer's?

Rebecca placed a hand on her hip, showing E.J. that she had expected more of a response from him. "Well?"

"I don't know."

"Then I'll let you go help Cooper, and you can keep thinking on how Widow Welchel's getting the money for all the Devekon stock in between leads because I know you know something. I see it in your eyes, Elliott."

E.J. turned and left the lawyer and client. He needed answers. Calling Cooper brought no new leads, he decided he needn't rush home.

A red corvette stood out in any small town in East Texas. However, there was a plethora in downtown Houston parking garages. He found a quiet corner, and the stakeout ended about thirty minutes after it started.

"You played me for a fool while Rebecca saw right

through you. Men really are stupid, aren't we?" E.J. yelled across the parking garage.

"I told you, predictable, not stupid. Certainly, I'll admit your ex-wife revealed my designs early. Still, whether I keep Rex Ashe locked in a nursing home or the doddering fool gets released makes no difference. I have the company." They had closed the distance. Still, Widow Welchel stepped closer to E.J.

"Worth the blood of innocents? Geoffrey was just a kid." Said E.J.

She rolled her eyes. Telegraphing her opinion, the remark posed a juvenile question. "Such a series of unfortunate oilfield accidents."

He needed to step back to preserve his space like the action would end the violation. The first woman he had slept with since Rebecca. "I'll prove it. I'll see you rot in a cell."

Widow Welchel invaded his space further, pulling the phone out of his pocket. She checked it. "No passcode, no facial recognition, so twentieth century? Anyone else would record me."

E.J. lowered his gaze. Then he swung his head up to glare into her ice-blue eyes.

"You killed Geoffrey. So proud to tell little ole me you had an informant in the bad man's refinery, and the boy would tell you who killed my beloved employee. I had to kill him. Somehow the kid knew." She inhaled as she spoke, pouring the thick Louisiana accent like sorghum molasses oozing down a stack of buttered pancakes.

"He knew nothing. The kid went to his grave thinking Artimus Blake killed Arnold," said E.J.

"Artimus Blake. Predictable and useful," said Widow

Welchel.

"Sheriff B.B., Artimus Blake, me. You slept with all of us?"

"Not me, baby." Widow Welchel batted her lashes, relishing the masquerade. Like turning a light switch, her tone and cadence became seductive perfection. "Arnold got greedy, pieced too much together, like your Rebecca. Your innocent Chez the troll blackmailed me."

E.J. snatched his phone back from her hand. He swiped his index finger over the icon for the app Rebecca had installed.

Widow Welchel looked puzzled until two more touches of the screen resulted in her voice broadcast from the device. Terror replaced the puzzlement, and as quickly as it appeared, she washed the emotion off her face.

He took no satisfaction in this moment. His mind chided him for stupidity. She would face justice for her crimes, but the price had been far too steep. Widow Welchel stood on the precipice of her promised land, yet he alone blocked her path. Her face cringed as the recording of their recent conversation played on E.J.'s phone.

The light blue eyes stared up at him again. "You ever want to see your daughter again?"

"What? What?" E.J. grabbed her by the shoulders, restraining himself from shaking her.

"It's not enough to navigate the sex trafficking sites. You have to know the players and which key opens which door," said Widow Welchel.

E.J. lifted the phone to her line of sight. "Anything to save Sharla."

"Predictable." Widow Welchel beckoned E.J. with

haunting eyes. However, this time E.J. saw through the overt seduction. The guilt and shame of succumbing to her charms turned his stomach, loading sour-tasting bile in the back of his mouth.

"Where is she?" He demanded at the top of his lungs. "Where is she?"

CHAPTER TWENTY

E.J. YELLED, "TELL ME, DO YOU HAVE HER?"

Widow Welchel rolled her eyes. "Of course not."

"But you know where she is?" asked E.J.

"Curiosity as much as anything. Took me about three hours on the dark web—"

E.J. cut her off, screaming. "Where?"

Widow Welchel stepped back while staring at E.J. She raised her arms.

E.J. spread his hands to make them less menacing. He had never had such an overwhelming desire to kill a person. It burned through him like a flare, illuminating the darkness. He knew his entire body shook, yet he couldn't succumb to rage. "Where?"

"I almost told you. I really wanted to tell you. Then I thought, what else would he have to do except investigate and defend his friend? Plus, I suspected the day might come when we needed to reach an understanding," said Widow Welchel.

Still no answer, yet he had to stay calm. He leaned his head back. A short time before, the woman had captivated him. Now her heavy perfume, combined with a day spent sweating on the witness stand, repelled him, turning putrid in his nose. He couldn't step back further. He had to do whatever to find out what she really knew.

"Tell me where she is?" E.J. made his best attempt to maintain an even tone.

"Give me your phone," said Widow Welchel.

E.J. complied.

"The heifer showed you how to use a recording app. I didn't see that one coming." Widow Welchel shook her head.

"What do you want?" asked. E.J.

"I need to know the recording didn't upload to a cloud or get transmitted to another phone." After making several selections on the phone, she looked around the parking garage before grinning. "Concrete and steel. Gotta love it," said Widow Welchel.

"You can erase it. Gone forever the way I understand phones," said E.J.

She pressed the phone. "Gone forever."

E.J. echoed her. "Gone forever."

"Can't erase you," Widow Welchel said.

E.J. responded quickly. "I'm disgraced. You saw the testimony yesterday, plus I obviously have a bias to lie on you. No one would ever believe me." Would it be enough? She had killed Geoffrey because she thought maybe he had something on her. In time she would kill him too, but give him long enough to get to Sharla, and it wouldn't matter.

"I'm going to need your gun too," said Widow Welchel.

"No."

"Not even to save your daughter?" Widow Welchel asked.

"No. Because if you kill me, then she dies too. I'm your pigeon so long as I can save her." E.J. saw lakes of ice replacing the inviting pools of blue light, which had so fascinated him.

"Aren't you John Wayne types supposed to keep your word forever?" She rolled her eyes.

"You have my word. We're at a standoff. All I can do is all I can do," said E.J.

Widow Welchel pursed her lips and her eyebrows arched. "Oh, I believe you."

E.J. hoped it was enough. He made the promise sincerely, though he knew she would play for the opportunity to kill him at a time and terms of her choosing. Her coldness chilled him. Com'on, tell me where.

Widow Welchel's thumb and finger moved across her phone and E.J.'s phone with impressive speed. "I've transmitted it to your phone. What I have is the site she was advertised on. It's not her, but that doesn't matter. Her pimp uses the number. Hopefully, she is still with him because she has been sold a couple of times already."

E.J. extended both hands for his phone.

Widow Welchel showed him a screenshot of what purported to be a dating site with the explicit sexual depiction of a young woman. "We got lucky she's still using the name Sharla, so call and ask for Sharla to arrange a hookup. I'm pretty sure she works out of a motel in Shreveport, but I didn't get that far."

E.J.'s head bobbed up. "You spoke to her?"

"Yes," said Widow Welchel.

"But you're—"

Widow Welchel looked at him like he should know better.

"Right." He nodded. "You really spoke to her."

"E.J., she's not your little girl anymore. Probably hasn't been in a long time." Widow Welchel extended her hand. "We have a deal."

He looked at it for a long moment.

Widow Welchel asked, "Would you rather seal our little deal like we did the other night."

He turned his gaze.

She flipped a hand through her bright beach blond hair, passing E.J. a disdainful look. "You're kind of whole-grain toast in a wonder bread world."

E.J. stepped around her.

"You're not going to get my door? Not very nice, John Wayne," said Widow Welchel.

E.J. kept walking until he reached the elevator. He parked on the top of the parking garage. A habit formed when he drove a much bigger truck. The uncrowded roof proved amenable to parking a big vehicle.

He stood in front of his old truck, looking at his phone. E.J. had been told deleted data on a computer could be reconstructed while deleted cell phone data could never be recovered. Should he call Hall and ask what the FBI could do? No, nothing mattered except Sharla. It sure looked like Widow Wechel knew what she talked about. She probably knew ways to harm Sharla too.

He touched the phone to his ear. "Rex."

"E.J."

"Rex, do you have your gun collection, the old Thompson."

Rex Ashe laughed, "Rule number one: when they

decide you're senile, take all the machine guns."

"What about your target pistols and ARs, your silencers?" asked E.J.

"They only got what I had at the house. I still got a few guns in my office at Devekon. Silencers on a pair of them. But you know I can't get in there. Think that's why they left 'em there," Rex Ashe said.

"Your big office?" asked E.J.

"Yep. What do you need my guns for?" Rex Ashe asked.

"Best you don't know," E.J. said.

"Tell me. I'll claim I forgot if they ask me, same as you never told me." Rex Ashe chuckled.

"Rex, why didn't you tell me?"

"It's not all the time. I have good days and bad days. Today's a good day. I wasn't about to waste good days talking about bad days." Rex Ashe's voice cracked across the phone transmission. "Besides, Rebecca saw one of my episodes...."

Rex Ashe trailed off, fighting back enough emotion to speak. "She looks at me with pity, and I can't take it."

"You take care, Rex." E.J. ended the call.

E.J. suspected his identification card and codes remained active. The security cameras at the bank building would catch him, but the security staff likely had no reason to stop him. To the unsuspecting, it would look like he ran to the office after closing time to get something for Rex. Even walking out with several obvious gun cases shouldn't raise suspicion.

This all-assumed Clara Brandis hadn't sent a memo and revoked his codes and credentials. E.J. bet she didn't want the additional attention formally firing him would raise with the security team he had hand-selected and hired. After all, he figured she stood neck deep in a theft ring and possibly more.

About an hour later, he loaded three thick, solid polymer gun cases in his truck. His luck had held. One of the security officers had even offered to help him carry the weapons to his truck.

E.J. passed Minute Maid Stadium, the large air-conditioned home of the Houston Astros. E.J. and Rebecca had taken the kids almost every year. Rebecca hated baseball. Still, she endured it largely without complaint because Konner and Sharla loved going to the games.

He thought he smelled the odors of 'distinctive ballpark cuisine' as he drove on the freeway. Sharla had insisted on using the ridiculously commercial term for junk food. E.J. had spent far too much money on concessions for the kids.

E.J. exited the interstate and pulled over to the side of the service road. He needed to call Rebecca. Could he call her and not reveal his source? What would he say? Widow Welchel would figure it out if he divulged anything, and then Rebecca's life would be in danger if it wasn't already. Sharla had to have one parent survive all of this.

"Come up with any ideas yet?" asked Rebecca.

"I got a lead on Sharla," said E.J.

"What?"

"All I can tell you, Rebecca—"

"What is going on?" asked Rebecca.

"All I can tell you is I got a lead," said E.J.

"I'm her mother and you won't tell me?" asked Rebecca.

"I can't."

"Whatever you are protecting me from. Stop. Losing

my law license, making me a party to something illegal, I don't care." Rebecca's voice cracked.

E.J. decided she must be crying. He could never stand up to a woman crying. Silence overcame both of them because he couldn't muster the courage to hang up on her.

Rebecca could interpret everything Widow Welchel sent him better than he could. Rebecca's duty required using the information to help Rex Ashe. E.J. had given his word, plus more the information would make Rebecca a target for Widow Welchel.

A couple more bodies would not stop the takeover of a global energy corporation. The super-rich had a phrase for what taking Devekon amounted to, generational wealth. Against his better judgment, he had to say something. "Rebecca, I'll bring our baby girl home."

"Next week would have made thirty years," Rebecca's tone softened.

E.J. thought about it. It was their wedding anniversary. Thirty years evaporated, and he stood at the altar. He could see the joy in her eyes, right down to the smell of the flowers enveloping him for a split second before the blare of the freeway noise snapped him back.

Rebecca had said something during his reminiscing E.J. didn't hear. Emotion welled in his chest and rose through his throat despite his best efforts to stop it. "I'll bring our baby girl home."

"I know. Thirty years and you never broke a promise," said Rebecca.

"There's a lot I'd like to say. I'm not going to, though," E.J. said.

Rebecca released some tension with a half chuckle.

"You know, I didn't mean all that stuff about Stuart.

He's a pretty good little fellow." E.J. didn't want to end the call. He felt like he would lose the connection forever.

Rebecca's laughter turned to tears. "It was a cheap shot about your career. I'm sorry. I know you'll bring her home. It's what you do."

CHAPTER TWENTY-ONE

SON CAME TO THE DOOR. HIS MUSCULAR PHYSIQUE poured into small shorts and a tee-shirt proclaiming across his chest, "Life is too short to drink cheap beer." The puzzlement expressed on his face told E.J. this had to be one of the last events Son had expected.

"Need a favor," said E.J.

Son's brows furrowed more. "You sure you came to the right place, pops. Favors down the street to the right."

E.J. looked down. "No way around the ask. I need help."

Son opened a screen door, inviting E.J. into the small home. It looked like a rent house for a bachelor. Mismatched furniture, a weightlifting bench, and guns in every corner adorned the room.

Son offered E.J. the recliner in front of the television. Son took an armchair and lifted a beer from a coffee table. "Beer?"

"I'll pass, thank you." Beer and dirty clothes didn't

make an enticing aroma to E.J. He had thought his days of bachelor life had long passed.

"You got me curious, old-timer," said Son.

"You never met my daughter, Sharla, did you?" E.J. asked.

Son shook his head, showing no.

"She won't know you," said E.J.

"What does it matter?" Son asked.

E.J. took out his phone. "My daughter took a bad path. She's turned to drugs. I don't have to spell out for you how the life goes bad for a young woman."

Son looked at E.J., then he looked away and raised the Michelob to his lips. "I'm sorry, but what do you want me to do about it."

The older man swiped the phone and began showing screenshots. His hands trembled so much; Son pulled the phone from him.

"It's not her pictures. I've been told if you call the number and ask for Sharla...." E.J.'s voice cracked and trailed off.

Son shook his head. "There's nobody else who can call? You got no ranger friends or FBI friends?"

"It's all off the books. I shouldn't have the information. I can't reveal how I got it. You know what I'm saying." E.J. said.

"Yeah, I know. Why you bringing me in?" Son asked.

"They'll all lose their jobs or worse, but not you. I can't see B.B. firing you because of some questionable infor-mation. And I think I sold you short as a lawman. I think maybe, just maybe, you know where the deer are, as the old-timers used to say." E.J. said.

Son raised his massive arms. "My dad might fire me

for helping you, period. He's not as crooked as you think, only sort of bent."

"I'm sorry. He's your dad, and he is what he is." E.J. looked into Son's eyes as if he were looking into his own for a split second. He saw the inverse. How they could say the same of Sharla. The truth neither man spoke, yet by their gaze acknowledged Sharla is what she is or what she has become.

Son broke the painful silence. "We find her, and she won't go with you, or she'll run away, right back to the pimp. We've both seen it."

"Then you'll help me?" E.J. asked.

"Go home, try to rest. I get to talk to her. I'll call you." Son transmitted the screenshots to his phone.

"Try to arrange a meet," E.J. said.

"I'll come get you if I find her," said Son.

"No. You won't be in this any further. Set the meet, then I'll go, not you," said E.J.

Son nodded. E.J. stepped through the screen door into the darkness.

The soft bite in the air had given way to a warm breeze from the south. No moonlight shone, and there were few stars. E.J. peered into a pasture formerly alive with the reds and greens of Arrow leaf clover. A dark void looked back at him.

E.J. glimpsed movement, a paleness in the field. He had pastured the horse here to graze the clover, though he still couldn't make the animal's form out.

The white patches made a surreal movie running toward him. Sunshine stopped at the fence, and he felt the horse's nostrils exhaling air on his hands. "She'll come home, Sunshine. I promise."

His forehead fell forward, touching the horse's head. The weight of all the lost opportunities with Sharla had played through his mind for days. Banks no longer held back the river of misery. E.J. thought how odd the animal consoled him when he could never cry in front of Rebecca. Sharla needed him to share their grief. At least, that was what the counselor theorized before they stopped going to the sessions.

"She's coming home, Sunshine. I can't lose another." E.J. straightened and put one foot in front of the other, moving toward the house.

Three watertight crush-proof cases were laid out on E.J.'s floor. The cases alone must have cost Rex Ashe a considerable amount. E.J. had a mental checklist of ammo, clips, functioning and familiarity with each gun.

Twin ARs chambered in three hundred blackout with a huge number of magazines connected by couplers. Rex Ashe's favorite pistols lay side by side; Staccato 2011s fitted with silencers.

The textured feel of the grips connected to his hand like the final Lego brick to an elaborate model combined with the feel of the cool steel frame, slide, and barrel. Stepping out of his door, E.J. spotted a five-gallon feed bucket under the security light of his barn.

Fire erupted into the pitch-black like it extended from his fingertips, propelling thirty-four nine-millimeter projectiles into the white shape bouncing until there remained nothing except the horse feed supplement in a pile. The odor of burnt gunpowder hung in the air. Then he lifted each weapon, working the slides to chamber rounds, dropping magazines, and repeating the processes.

A truck engine woke him. E.J. looked at the TV tray for

his phone. No one had called or texted. He walked out his door to headlights moving down the long driveway.

An eighties model GMC Jimmy jacked up and sporting deep dish chrome wheels approached. The two-tone blue and white sports utility vehicle predated the term. It stopped in the yard and Son stepped out. He wore all black, and he had traded his customary leather rig for a tactical configuration in black nylon and polymer.

"What do you think you're doing?" E.J. stepped off his porch.

"Your model T won't get you to Shreveport."

"No model T," E.J. asked himself why Son said it. The kid must have meant it in sarcasm. "It's an American classic."

"No, this is a restored classic. Look, pops, I'm not putting you down. I'm just saying, without a broom handle or going downhill; you can't start that thing." Son chuckled at his little joke.

"You're not going," said E.J.

"They're expecting me. If I don't show up, they'll know somethin's up." Son displayed a Glock pistol in his waistband, complimenting the one in his tactical holster.

"You had to show your face?" E.J. asked.

"More than that, pops," Son said.

E.J. nodded. "Sorry. I didn't think it through. Not a technology guy. Never done an internet hook up."

"I bet you were a player back in the day with some smoke signals, pops," said Son.

E.J. stepped back. "You're quicker witted than I thought."

"I'm a lot more than you thought. You need me. Take my help," said Son.

"Why do you want to risk your neck for me?" E.J. asked.

"Pops, you're kinda famous. In your day, if you could have ridden with Wyatt Earp, you'd have done it."

"I'm not stopping to hunt Miranda cards. I'm shooting center mass until I find Sharla. At best, I'll be the lead on CNN, and at worst, I'm not coming back." E.J. made the speech without emotion.

"You owe it to your daughter. Pops, I'm watchin' grass grow in twelve-hour shifts. Roustin' drunks and chasin' cows back in the fence. That's why I hung out with the Nephilim. I need the action, and you need me."

E.J. recalled Konner volunteering for combat. He recalled the burning thirst for excitement, what Rebecca described as reckless machismo. She could never understand why Konner had to seek hazardous duty.

Was he seeing too much in Son, too much of himself, too much of Konner? Maybe it wasn't there. E.J.'s mind swung back to the task at hand. "Where are we going?"

CHAPTER TWENTY-TWO

"SHREVEPORT. LET'S GO." SON SAID.

E.J. loaded his gear into Son's truck. They flew down Interstate Twenty while E.J. debated whether to involve Son further. Much as he disliked B.B., he wouldn't wish the death of a child on anyone. No, he would turn Son around before the shooting started.

Once in Shreveport, they exited off twenty onto Allendale. The phone announced they had arrived at their destination, a rundown, multi-story building.

"Let's park a couple of blocks away. Can you find somewhere where your ride won't get stripped when we get out of it?" E.J. said.

"Maybe a pretty good drive," Son said.

E.J. and Son wore their shirttails out, dark baseball caps, and loose jogging pants over their dark blue jeans. They kept a fast pace, moving down the street past several adult-oriented businesses.

They opened a door to a foyer covered in dilapidated

peeling wallpaper. The smell of urine near punched them backwards. Son pushed the button for the third floor, then stopped the elevator.

E.J. watched the numbers change on the center sign above the elevator. He had devised a simple plan. Son enters room 309 and confirms it's Sharla while E.J. waits outside. If it's her, Son opens the door and nods, pretending he heard a noise. E.J.'s position would also have a strategic advantage.

He knew pimps positioned themselves close to their workers. If one came running to the room, then he would have to go through E.J.

The elevator doors opened, surprising them.

"Hey, hey, hey man, got to take care of the room, man. My hotel." The stranger's eyes blazed an intense red, with his pupils dilated. He more slobbered the words than spoke them. He wore a filthy pair of coveralls.

E.J. pulled him out of the elevator and activated the third-floor button. Son followed the numbers on the doors to 309 down the hall to the right. He knocked and then entered before there was a response.

E.J. slid down the wall onto the nasty floor, grateful for the sweat pants over his jeans. Sliding his hands in his pants, he touched the pistols and leaned against the side of the wall. He wanted to look like a passed-out bum, though he hadn't counted on a rancid meat odor assaulting his nostrils.

E.J.'s gaze alternated between the elevator and the door, each about twenty feet away. Out of the corner of his eye, he saw movement past the elevator. A work boot came bounding from a door into the hall. This had to be the pimp looking to roll Son for an easy score.

E.J. came up with a pistol in each hand. The man wearing the work boots recoiled, losing his balance trying to get back inside the doorway from where he had appeared. E.J. figured he'd come back out armed and likely with help.

Son made no signal, and E.J. decided the plan went off the rails. He leaped into the door of 309, swinging the door open as he fell through. A startled gunman had the drop on Son and Sharla. E.J. fired two rounds through the man's forehead.

"Let's go," screamed E.J.

Sharla shrieked. Son pulled her down behind the couch. Then E.J. saw the wall leading to the next room had been partially removed. A hoodlum wielding an AK-47 rifle raised up. The rifle flashed, roaring through the room.

E.J.'s pistols exploded, continuing until the hoodlum dropped to his knees. E.J. motioned through the haze with the gun to Son. Son dragged Sharla by the arm into the hallway.

Before they reached the elevator, work boots cut loose with an automatic weapon from the corner of the doorway where he had entered earlier. The wall erupted in splinters. The whiz of bullets moved air and pressure toward the elevator. E.J. fired his Staccatos, emptying the rest of the magazines into the doorway as the elevator doors closed.

He jammed new clips into the mag wells as the elevator descended. E.J. saw Son had his gun drawn. "You concentrate on Sharla. I got this," said E.J.

Sharla continued screaming. She looked gaunt, covered in sores, and haggard. E.J. fought the urge to embrace her, to hold her near him. He had remembered on the drive to Shreveport walking into Sharla's room when she was a baby. He would stand at her crib listening to her breathing, shocked at how small she compared to his hands.

Now guns extended from his fingers like additional appendages. He threw himself out of the doors and onto the floor. Firing in each direction, he lay down a blanket of bullets.

Son lifted Sharla like a sack of feed over his shoulder and scurried through the door. None of the ne'er-do-wells tried to run the gauntlet of lead E.J. laid down. He compressed his knees and placed a hand on the floor, lifting himself. Hitting both releases, he dropped the clips into the lobby.

E.J. reloaded on the run. A thousand needles stabbed his knee joint, trying to crush him into submission. Yet E.J. couldn't surrender to pain and exhaustion. He couldn't slow. One boot landed after another until he was within a block of Son's vehicle.

He hadn't been able to see Son, yet he took comfort in such. The muscular young man likely ran fast, even with a woman slung over his shoulder.

E.J.'s eyes feasted on the white and then royal blue of the Jimmy. It drove toward him and barely missed connecting. The metal of the passenger door handle felt cool against E.J.'s hand. He flung himself inside, and the force of acceleration threw him into the seat.

Sharla continued screaming. The shrill noise pained E.J. setting fire to his ears and head. Sharla moved away from him. Thankfully, she couldn't get out because there was no rear passenger door, unlike modern trucks and SUVs.

E.J. wrestled with a dry throat, trying to find his voice. They were going too fast. "Slow down."

"Let me get on the interstate," Son yelled.

E.J. reached for Sharla, trying to comfort her. His efforts failed. Sharla continued to thrash around in the back bench seat, screaming incoherent shrieks. How could he help her? How could he calm her?

E.J. laid his seat back to block her, then he climbed over the console, getting his boot stuck before finally falling into the back seat. She clawed at him. He felt a searing sensation and reached up, touching warm blood.

Despite her emaciated state, E.J. spent all his diminishing strength to hold her. He fought to gain a tight grip. They had reached the interstate. Son cruised a smooth eighty, not fast enough to draw attention on the interstate.

E.J. saw the rest area. They were crossing into Texas. Sharla's imitation of a banshee subsided. Still, E.J. dared not let her go. He maintained control over her arms for fear she would strike him, maybe hit Son and then cause him to wreck. Facing the front, Sharla could not bite him despite efforts to turn her head and chomp at him.

A million thoughts raced through E.J.'s mind. Were there enough security cameras along his path to connect them to the GMC Jimmy? Could any video have caught their faces enough to identify them? Would the police put enough effort into the investigation to do so? Would there be an outcry in the community, or would a couple of dead thugs be a typical night in the rough part of town?

What about Sharla? Should he get her to a hospital now? If he didn't, then could he find a rehab tomorrow? Could she die of withdrawals? Would she report him for killing her captors? Were they really her captors? Was his baby girl still somewhere trapped inside a hardcore addict and prostitute? Would she ever be all right? There were no answers to the endless questions.

CHAPTER TWENTY-THREE

SHARLA CALMED, AND E.J. STROKED HER HAIR. HIS HAND slid along a ratty tangled mess until he held some strands in his hand, having fallen from her head. Her strawberry-blond hair had been replaced by a foul-smelling platinum yellow.

One thought overcame him, Rebecca. Rebecca would know what to do. Both his kids had always run to Rebecca with their boo-boos, and later they took most of their problems to Rebecca. E.J. had wanted to be more approachable to his kids. He could shoot, fight, and build. Still, it was always Rebecca who could lift their spirits.

As a Dad, he had never had a relationship where they shared the heartbreak of being jilted or any of the awkwardness and angst of adolescence. E.J. had told himself they just preferred talking to their mother, but now he asked himself whether he had really been there for his kids. The answer tore his heart open all the more. A void expanded into the pit of his stomach until he thought it couldn't get any vaster. Such a chasm separated him from humanity, from what he had always believed was his ideal family.

He pulled his phone while he held Sharla. Her attacks had devolved to squirming in his arms before reaching an uneasy acquiescence.

"Rebecca, I got her."

Silence poured over the phone. "Rebecca? Rebecca?"

Through sobs, Rebecca answered, "Yes, yes, yes. Is she okay?"

"I don't know? I think so. She's in rough shape," E.J. said.

"Is she hurt? Can I talk to her?" asked Rebecca.

"Probably not. She's calming. Withdrawing from drugs. Meth, coke, heroin, maybe all of it. I don't know. Not sure what to look for," said E.J.

Rebecca whispered into the phone, "Does she need to go to the hospital?"

"If she goes to the hospital, then she could eventually check herself out, and we will never find her the next time. I don't know what to do." E.J. drew a deep breath before exhaling over the beginning of tears watering the corners of his eyes.

"Then no. Take her to the house, and I'll meet you there." Rebecca's voice strengthened.

Another pause overcame both of them, then Rebecca made a faint snicker.

"Somethin' funny?" asked E.J.

"First time you've ever admitted you don't know what to do?" Rebecca said.

"Another first, I never tried to take care of our kids without you either."

"You'll never have to. Keep her safe till I get there," Rebecca ended the call.

E.J. knew 'the house' could only mean their house together now, his home.

Son exited the interstate and turned onto the highway. "She must be better."

E.J. kept rocking Sharla back and forth, trying to keep her calm. "Some." He thought about asking Son to slow some. They were nearing home and unlikely to be stopped for speeding and even less of a risk of being connected to the Shreveport shooting. So there seemed little need for Son's aggressive driving.

When the GMC pulled into his driveway, E.J. felt a sense of euphoria. The enjoyment lasted no time. Sharla wailed again. She struck at E.J. while he pulled her out of the back seat.

Ill-prepared for the blow, E.J. stumbled backwards. Sharla broke free, hopping through the red dirt gravel of the driveway in bare feet. She reached the grass and took off. Still, her emaciated form proved no match for Son's speed.

He placed an enormous hand on her flimsy pink camisole, pulling her backwards long enough to reach around her with his other arm. She kicked and fought, to no avail. He could manage her with one hand and use the other to keep her snapping jaws out of range.

Son lifted her, dragging Sharla toward the house. "Want me to zip tie her?"

"No, let's get her to her room." E.J. helped him manage Sharla until she went limp in futility.

Her room looked exactly like she had left it before college. E.J. got the young woman to the bed. The white bedspread contrasted against her filthy wisp of a gown. Above her head, a poster of Taylor Swift hung. The icon appeared in black and white except for vibrant red lips.

E.J. held Sharla on the bed, marveling at the room's décor. It befit the honor student and teenager from a few short years ago. How did we get here?

"I'm gonna go," Son said.

E.J. couldn't rise without releasing Sharla. He looked up at Son, fully appreciating how wrong he had been about this big man. Son stood larger than his father in character and honor. "I don't know how to say thank you."

Son shook his head from side to side, flashing a huge, tooth-filled grin. "Rode with the legend. Thanks enough."

"Leave the door open. Yak will come up soon, and Rebecca won't be long," E.J. said.

"Need to get rid of those pistols. Want me to do it?" Son asked.

"You're in too deep already. Go."

E.J. leaned back against the headboard, waiting on Rebecca. He realized, 'How did we get here?' didn't matter. How do we get back? That was all that mattered.

He heard Yak before he saw him. The dog laid down at the foot of the bed. Yak never failed to surprise. E.J. had long been convinced the same high-strung animal which had to bark down every creature on the property from two-thousand-pound bulls to armadillos picked up on the moment and behaved in accord.

E.J. hummed a low shushing sound to calm his daughter and lost track of time.

Rebecca startled Yak long before she entered the room.

E.J. saw her and slid his compact Sig Sauer into his pocket. "Hold, Yak. Hold. Sit."

What's more, she had brought someone. A medium build woman with high cheekbones who peered at him from the doorway, holding something he couldn't see from his angle.

"This is Vanessa. Vanessa, this is E.J.," said Rebecca.

E.J. acknowledged the meeting with a nod, yet didn't risk getting up for fear Sharla would see an opportunity to bolt. Vanessa nodded in return.

"Vanessa freelances for me as a nurse breaking down medical records. We made a deal. I've hired her to take care of Sharla, but when she thinks we have to, we get her to a hospital. No arguments. No questions," said Rebecca.

E.J. looked back at Vanessa. "Fair enough. Proud you're here, ma'am."

"Leave her to us. I'll let you know if we have to take her," Rebecca said.

E.J. stepped into the hall, followed by Yak. His back ached. He had exhausted himself, yet he knew he couldn't sleep. He didn't really know if Sharla knew who he was. She never acknowledged him. How can she not recognize her own father?

Standing on his porch, the dawn washed over him and Yak. The pallet of colors pouring out on the green hills and pine trees gave him pause. Anything so grand couldn't have been an accident. But if there was a God, then why? Why so much suffering and torment?

The doubt brought forth what old-timers would have called his raising. An immediate admonishment as stern as any he would have faced in his youth from his parents, his grandparents, from his Sunday school teachers chiding him. They would demand he give thanks for recovering Sharla and set aside his mortal attempts to order a universe broken by man's rebellion from God.

E.J. saw a black bundle on a lawn chair. Likely, Son had wrapped the Staccato pistols in the black shirt and oversized jogging pants that Son had worn the prior night. E.J. picked up the bundle and carried it to the barn.

Sunshine stood over two hundred yards away from where E.J.'s property fell into a creek bottom. The horse heard him, and a lifetime of running to the barn for feeding time moved his head and heels into the air. Before long, the trot had turned into a gallop. Sunshine gobbled up the pasture between them.

Yak barked while E.J. fed the horse one small scoop of feed and closed the surrounding stall. He stood there, loathe to bother an animal while it ate.

"You didn't believe me, did you, Sunshine? I told you I'd bring her home." E.J. stepped across to his tack room, absorbing the sweet smell of leather conditioner. He touched the leather saddle seat, his favorite a Billy Cook because the saddle fit Sunshine so well.

Then he grabbed the blanket and bridle. In a moment, he had the horse saddled and stepped into the stirrup, finding his seat.

He forded the creek and rode into an overgrown system of sloughs which his family had owned for over a hundred years. Reeds, thistles, interspersed by occasional willow, bois d'arc, and massive water oaks checkering across the swampy ground had assured this ground never saw a plow.

He rode deep into this wilderness, coming to a massive slough. It was too wide and deep to be seined for catching crawfish or mudcats. He removed his shirt and jogging pants, leaving himself clothed in an undershirt and blue jeans. The weapons tied to the clothing would sink into the mire forever.

Near ten thousand dollars worth of guns sucked forever into a bottomless swamp, produced a curious amusement making him grin. A moment of levity soon ended when he thought about how long it would take to replace what he had taken from Rex Ashe.

He took a different path back over higher ground in an easy lope, then unsaddled Sunshine. His wife's familiar roadster and a suburban he assumed driven by the nurse remained in his yard. It was a good sign they hadn't deemed it necessary to take Sharla to the hospital.

E.J. walked across the yard from the barn until he froze, recognizing a scraping shrill indomitable voice. He heard Rebecca yelling, thankfully not at him.

She held the cell phone, walking onto the porch. "No, you listen to me. You turn down a twenty-year lawyer for a continuance when her child has a life-threatening illness, and there will be attention. The kind of attention an uncle padding his nephew's fees doesn't want."

E.J. assumed she talked to the judge about delaying the trial. Despite supporting Rebecca and Rex Ashe's position, he couldn't help but feel sorry for the judge. Once Rebecca determined to make a scrap of it, she sliced a man like a Ginsu knife on an infomercial.

"Send your bailiff. I'll get a selfie of him cuffing me at my daughter's sickbed. I need the photo for your next election. I know, how 'bout, I blow it up poster-sized when we go in front of the ethics commission." Rebecca paced across the porch.

Law enforcement is the application of government legitimacy to keep the peace. The endeavor was necessarily political. Such demanded pragmatic forgiveness by E.J. to remain standing despite absorbing the opponent's best blows and returning as good as he got. Surviving amounted to victory enough. However, for Rebecca, once crossed, she crushed the transgressor under the heel of her expensive shoes.

Rebecca walked off the porch, then past him. She continued her rant, no doubt getting the better of the judge.

E.J. stepped into his living room. He smelled bacon frying in a pan. Maybe Sharla wanted some breakfast, and the nurse was cooking it? That would be too good to be true.

E.J. walked into his living room and turned on his television. One of the Shreveport stations included a twenty-four-hour news channel.

In short order, E.J. learned his delusive hopes the killings wouldn't be reported were dashed. He heard the standard call from authorities for persons with information to come forward. They would not release the names of the deceased at this time.

In his mind, he knew he acted in self-defense and regretted nothing. The men stood between him and the safety of his daughter. As if he had neared her crib to hear her breathing while these men tried to end her life. He neither pitied nor hated them; therefore, how could one experience remorse?

No one would believe he acted in self-defense. People acting in self-defense didn't leave the scene. They didn't take the fight to the enemy, nor did they destroy evidence like the weapons used. These were all circumstances consistent with murder.

Walking onto the porch, dark thoughts consumed E.J. A lifetime of work as a lawman could end in disgrace. Convicted police faced constant terror and suffering in prison at the hands of criminals. He had no confidence in his ability to handle what was likely an eventuality. Could he face the disgrace? Could he handle the torture or choose to die on his own terms?

CHAPTER TWENTY-FOUR

"WE FOUND A FACILITY IN SAN ANTONIO," SAID REBECCA.

"San Antonio?" E.J. asked.

"Five months," said Rebecca.

"She still hasn't spoken to me, and I got to send her to San Antonio for five months," said E.J.

E.J. turned his back to her, looking over his porch to the place where he should have had his garden. He failed to plant this year for the first time. "She still won't see me?"

"She doesn't say it, but I think she's mortified over what she's done. Drugs, prostitution. Could you face your lawman father?" Rebecca stepped around him where he had to look at her. "The same Daddy who doted and spoiled her."

E.J. raised his voice. "This is my fault?"

"I didn't say that," said Rebecca.

"You blame me for Konner and now Sharla. Maybe you should have got your head out of trying to make Konner's death a grand conspiracy and seen the signs of drug addiction." E.J. became cognizant he might be overheard and reduced his volume.

Rebecca looked back at the house. "You're right. I indulged her. We both did, Elliott."

E.J. looked down. "When are you leaving?"

"Tomorrow morning," said Rebecca.

"So Soon?"

"We were lucky to get her in. Really lucky." Rebecca's voice softened, and she placed her hand on E.J.'s shoulder. "Venessa says she needs medication, medication she can't proscribe to combat the withdraws, a treatment plan. It's going to be bad."

"You blame me for Konner because you think I pushed him into needing to prove himself. There's more truth to it than I want to admit, than I can admit. I won't lose my daughter the same way. I can't." E.J. turned to face Rebecca.

"What do you want to do?" Rebecca asked.

"I'll park the truck in the pasture. She'll think I went to town. I'll walk to the barn. You get her out there. Tell her to see her horse." E.J.'s eyes pleaded.

"It won't go well," said Rebecca.

E.J. begged her. "Give me the chance. Give Sharla the chance."

Rebecca nodded, and E.J. prepared for the ruse. When he got back to the barn, he fed the big gelding and shut the gate in his stall. He stepped into the original barn, now little more than a tin shed, looking more like a mismatched addition.

A heavy wooden stool stood behind a miniature table under an ancient pair of cabinets. The peeling paint and half-hanging cabinet door revealed the cans of nails his grandfather straightened when rain prevented more fruitful work.

The wait seemed interminable. His mind played through scenarios, what he should say, then, how she would respond, followed by so many contingency plans.

E.J. stared at the old piecemeal tin wall. He told himself nothing was gained from writhing in misery, yet he couldn't tear himself away from feeling sorry for himself.

He should be grateful Sharla lived, grateful Rebecca and Vanessa would soon escort her to a rehabilitation program in San Antonio, and grateful someday there would be an opportunity to make amends to Sharla for all the mistakes running through his memories.

His mind stepped back to his previous tomboy daughter fishing in their stock pond. E.J. retied hooks, cast rods, and undid bird's nests of line in the reels as quick as possible, all to keep his angel fishing.

The little strawberry blond miniature of Rebecca looked up at him, holding the rod dangling a perch which looked barely hooked. "Daddy, why doesn't Konner go fishing with us anymore?"

She drew the line at touching the cool, slick fish no matter how much E.J. encouraged her. "I don't know. Suppose he's getting to the age where he thinks his girlfriend is better company than his dad and kid sister."

"I'm not a kid."

"No, you're growing up too. Pretty soon, I'll be fishing all alone." He recalled sarcasm jumping to his mind. He could get his hook in the water. Then his mind took him to the hospital, where a proud Rebecca placed Sharla in his arms at her bedside.

The fish jumped off his thumb, flopping back into the pond. "Daddy, I'll never leave you. Who would take my fish off?" Said Sharla.

What a great day it had been. E.J. shuffled forward on the stool. He heard the footfalls and voice of Rebecca nearing the barn.

E.J. could hear Rebecca coaxing Sharla. For the first time, Rebecca spoke to Sunshine like a pet. She addressed Sharla in a similar tone. As if it would be the greatest event of her life if either complied with a request.

E.J. turned around the corner. He chose the approach because he stood between Sharla and the house. She could run, yet it would be more difficult.

E.J. pleaded even before she could see him. "Please, Sharla, let me talk to you."

Sharla screamed.

Rebecca reached for Sharla. Sharla's confusion about where to run was all the hesitation Rebecca needed. She wrapped around the girl.

E.J. stepped toward them, and Sharla's shrieking reached a glass-shattering volume. "Sharla, I just want you to know I love you. I love you." He turned and walked back the way he had entered the barn.

The yelling subsided about the time he reached the back of the structure again. His plan failed. Perhaps it had been more a hope than a plan.

Would Sharla ever be Sharla again? Was she mad at him? Was she ashamed or some combination he couldn't understand?

CHAPTER TWENTY-FIVE

REBECCA HAD SPARED HIM THE, "I TOLD YOU SO." E.J. took the gesture as a statement on his current pitiful nature. Stuart had joined them, taking his Land Rover because the vehicle accommodated five.

E.J. sat on the porch, staring down his driveway. His phone rang. "Hello."

"Listen carefully." Hall Oglethorpe spoke in a slow, deliberate cadence.

"Cooper is on her way. She intends to ask you something about Arnold, but it's a tactic. Her real goal is to feel you out about how you got Sharla back and the killings in Shreveport last night."

"How does she know?" E.J. asked. "Rebecca, call and tell her?"

"God Bless America. Doesn't matter. Listen to me."

"Why would she ask me about Shreveport?" Said E.J.

"Drop it. No time!" Hall took a deep breath and continued.

"You will tell her you joined Amy and me for dinner. We ate roast, mashed potatoes, purple hulls, and hot water bread. Then we watched The Man Who Shot Liberty Valence. She'll buy it. We both quote John Wayne all the time. You got here at six and left about eleven."

"What do I tell her about how I got Sharla?" asked E.J.

"I can't come up with all of it," said Hall.

"What's she got connecting me to Shreveport?" asked E.J.

"She used some FBI cyber unit. I suggested smoking out Sharla. They had it narrowed down to an outfit in Shreveport and one in Houston. Looks like it was Shreveport," said Hall.

"I can't lie to Cooper," said E.J.

"You're protecting Cooper and keeping your word to whatever informant you must have used," Hall said.

"I can't let you risk your career," said E.J.

"Amy and I agree. It could have been Shasta." The call ended.

The phrase 'keeping your word' hung in the dark spring air. Why couldn't he break his word to the lying, thieving murderer who played him for a fool? More than a fool, a man succumbing to his lust. She deserved worse, and he had never lied to Cooper.

And yet he knew he would lie to Cooper, because it wasn't about Widow Welchel. He engaged in deception, even lying when unavoidable. Shreveport wasn't the first time he had taken a life when necessary. Still, he had never broken his word once extended. Since Konner's death, there had remained little sacred in his life, and yet this precept of manhood remained inviolate for him as it did for his father and grandfather.

He wouldn't get Cooper killed. Since he hypothesized Widow Welchel's guilt in the courtroom and foolishly played the hunch to her face, his life had been worthless. She would have to come for him when the right accident opportunity afforded itself. Why take Cooper to her death, too?

He thought of Cooper's family. Her children without a mother. Tell her children, her husband, the parents what? What would she have died for? No, even if he would break his word, he wouldn't pull others into his mire. Cooper was innocent. She might have even found Sharla with more time. There was no telling what other leads she was working on and risking her career to do it.

Despite staring at the road, he didn't see Cooper's headlights until she stopped. The beams woke him from his introspective misery.

"Why haven't you called me?" asked Cooper.

"Rebecca called you," E.J. said.

"She didn't know how you got her back or where you were last night." Cooper stared into E.J.'s eyes.

The lights from Cooper's Explorer timed off. E.J. drew comfort from the darkness. It released the pressure from Cooper.

"Not much to tell. I took Hall and Amy up on a dinner invitation."

"What did y'all have?"

"Purple hulls, hot water bread, roast and potatoes." E.J. had deliberately changed the order. His experience with contrived alibis from suspects proved a perfect recitation right down to the order conveyed suspicion.

"Sweet potatoes?" Hall knew she was coming because she had interviewed him. She had set a trap for him. Roast most often was served with halved potatoes, but it could have been baked potatoes or another variation like sweet, baked potatoes, or even fried.

"Mashed." Friendly curiosity doesn't extend to how to prepare potatoes for dinner. No, he couldn't sell it if he didn't call her on the question. "You takin potato recipes?"

She ignored his question exactly the way E.J. expected. "What did you do after dinner?"

"What do you think? Get Hall and me together. We watched the Duke save a pilgrim." He didn't add the plot revolved around John Wayne protecting Rance Stoddard and his dream of civilization from Stoddard's own commitment to honesty. The parallel to Cooper wasn't lost on E.J. the movie must have leaped out to Hall.

"So, how did you get Sharla home?" asked Cooper.

E.J.'s mind had calculated his response from the time Hall called. Weak liars needed some element of truth to wrap around. He settled on a kernel of truth. "One of my informants came through. Dealer at a crack house in Marshall. All I had was an address. Sure enough, I found her, ran a john off, and insisted the trafficker let her go. I persuaded him."

"Who's the informant?" asked Cooper.

"Promised not to give 'em up. Gave my word," said E.J.

"Drug dealer?" asked Cooper

"Got nothing but a street name," said E.J.

"Address?" said Cooper.

"No, you could work backwards, and it would reveal my informant," said E.J.

"Did 'persuasion' involve a gun?" Cooper spoke in a tone near mimicking E.J. A skill she had mastered to tease him in more light-hearted times.

"I didn't kill anybody in Marshall." E.J. fought the urge to look away from her. Even in the poor lighting, the movement would be noticeable.

"In Marshall, huh?" Cooper moved her hands.

Experience told E.J. she likely placed her hands on her hips. Part tell and part feigned doubt to test the story. "Why aren't you tickled to death? We got lucky. You and I both know luck has a big play in the good outcomes."

"I guess I just need to talk to Sharla. Can I see her?" asked Cooper.

"Rebecca took her to rehab, some private facility in San Antonio. You know you still haven't asked how she is?" E.J. had learned from Rebecca, access to Sharla at first would near take a court order for anyone except immediate family on her visitor list. Ultimately, Sharla might unravel the whole ball of lies. If she did, then so be it.

"Rebecca told me she was pretty shook up. Why didn't you call me?" Cooper sounded genuinely perplexed.

Even in the dark, he could sense Cooper's movement. She stepped toward him in a challenge. "A Texas Ranger kicking in the door on a tip from a criminal. You know how it is on the news. It's always grandma's house, and she didn't know her baby ran drugs and girls from her house. Ranger going rogue. It'd be worse than when the Department ran me off."

"What about after?" Cooper's tone became more accusatory.

"Still would have insisted on my informant, and I gave my word. We both worked too hard to get you that peso." E.J. pointed toward the badge, glinting despite the darkness.

"Don't expect you'd let me look at your phone?" asked Cooper.

"Don't expect," said E.J.

Cooper stepped back. "You know the technology's come a long way. I can geofix your phone."

E.J. struggled to keep the anxiety from his voice. He hadn't thought that through. How could he be so careless? "You need a district judge warrant, requested by the elected DA. Wouldn't you think I'm smart enough to turn it off or leave it?"

Cooper paused, and E.J. suspected his bluff proved successful. He had taken her off her prepared script, off her game. All talented investigators had been stuck many times in the no-man's-land of knowing something and nothing solid to support the elaborate construct of inferences necessary to prove it.

Cooper was good. Early, E.J. had witnessed the powerful intellect, dogged determination, and her rigorous right and wrong view of the world. His only knock on an otherwise brilliant detective. One had to appreciate gray, if for no other reason than because the people you were chasing saw so much of it.

"Let me get you a glass of tea," said E.J.

"No. I can't stay. Got sidetracked. I really came by to give you some of Arnold's property to return to his widow," said Cooper.

"What?" No one ever returns evidence in a murder investigation, and why use a private security contractor to do it? It made no sense.

"She insisted. Hounded the DA until he got a district judge's order. Sentimental value stuff, an AA coin and his Bible."

"Okay, but why me?"

"You will not believe this, but Sheriff B.B. came across a little arrogant, and she won't speak to him or anyone in his department." Cooper made the comment, tongue firmly in cheek.

The mere mention of B.B.'s name caused E.J. to remember the force of the sheriff's steel toe boot to his head and stomach. A moment so vivid he could taste the iron flavor of blood in his mouth again.

He didn't realize a reference to the man would cause such an emotional reaction within him. Fighting the urge to ball himself into a smaller target, E.J. asked, "Why didn't she want you?"

"Asked for you and I didn't figure it was a big deal. Probably really was an accident, anyway. So, what does it matter if his kids get his Bible instead of locked in an evidence box forever?" asked Cooper.

"Rex Ashe insisted I convey his sympathies. I kind of made an impression at the funeral home," said E.J.

Cooper walked back to her explorer. When she returned, E.J. had the door open. They stepped to his dining table.

Cooper displayed a document signed by the truck driver's widow giving E.J. the right to take possession of the items, a district court order to release evidence, and one large brown paper evidence bag covered in initialed red tape.

E.J. drew his pocketknife from his jean pocket. The yellow handled Case sliced through the red tape, revealing a cardboard box and a much smaller paper bag.

Upon looking at the contents, E.J. signed Cooper's receipt, releasing one AA chip and one bookmarked Holy

Bible in gold lettering encased in a leather-bound cover closed by a small gold clasp.

Out of habit, he closed both the bag and box, looking to Cooper for evidence tape to seal and initial them.

"No need to reseal them," Cooper said.

"Right. I'll run them to her tomorrow."

Cooper nodded. "I figured you would want to do it, so I asked if she was home tomorrow. She's taken some time off from work."

"Hard time?" asked E.J.

Cooper nodded. "You were right about Arnold being the real deal. A genuinely reformed outlaw trying to get out."

"Sort of restores a little faith in humanity," said E.J.

Cooper looked down. Perhaps E.J.'s comment resonated. "E.J., I'm sorry if I gave you a hard time."

"You did, and apology accepted. He patted Cooper's shoulder. Both knew it served as his equivalent for a hug from more expressive people.

It wasn't any awkwardness or concern owing to their respective genders. Displays of affection weren't natural to E.J., so he avoided them. He regretted not being more affectionate to Konner and Sharla. Now, he would hug Sharla every time he saw her if she would let him.

All the way to the Arnold residence near Nacogdoches, he thought about lying to Cooper. She didn't believe him, however, she could point to nothing strong enough to poke a hole in his story. Given such circumstances, what would she do?

If she thought there was even a small amount of evidence incriminating him, then she would list him in a contact log, noting she had inquired about the Shreveport killings. Once the investigation slowed, the officers from the Louisiana Bureau of Investigations would go through all these referrals and eventually interview him.

On the other hand, she might believe it didn't rise to the level to place any suspicion on her old training officer and choose not to embarrass her mentor and herself, as well as the ranger service.

He would have chosen the latter. In fact, it never would have reached such a point because he, like Hall, would have let the gray inherent to a broken world color their vision.

Cooper wouldn't do so. She marked a great leap forward in law enforcement. E.J. had to be cognizant of the prejudices of his era while they only existed for Cooper when painted upon her canvas by others. Her inflexibility in the law kept her on the straight and narrow, well ordered. The world wasn't well ordered, and her inability to apply such truth caused her to suffer a shortfall of humanity for all its foibles and grandeur.

Between Nacogdoches and Garrison, the forest grew dense. Enormous oaks punctuated thick stands of pine and sweetgum, closing all around. The Arnold home made a better impression than others on the county road. Brick covered the house, and perhaps the structure encompassed three times the size of the lesser white frame homes and trailer houses.

E.J. speculated most of the houses were kin to Arnold and his wife. Like his own family prior to the era of internet love, attraction was limited in distance. In his youth, he had mocked it as inbred. However, now he held an appreciation for their shared heritage. White, African American, and Hispanic didn't separate them as much as the pine curtain they lived behind.

Chez Arnold had proven E.J.'s theory by overcoming prejudice. E.J. had intended to follow up with the man's wife. However, developments moved him in other directions.

He knocked on the door. The woman pictured at the funeral home, Arnold's widow, answered the door.

"Come in." She motioned to a seat on the couch near what must have been her chair based on the cup of hot coffee sitting near it on a small table.

"Mrs. Arnold, is this a good time to visit?" The aroma of her coffee drowned out the unmistakable smell of diaper cream.

"Now I'm April. Chez's momma was Mrs. Arnold. She liked to point out I was an in-law."

E.J. didn't intend to stir up anything. He suspected the normal tension with a mother-in-law might be aggravated considerably by overcoming race even in the modern times. Besides, wouldn't the mother-in-law have been an in-law under that reasoning? "Yes, ma'am"

A shriek broadcast from behind the house through a screen door, and E.J. shuddered, moving his hand toward his pocket.

April Arnold yelled in an instant, "Bisbee, stop aggravating your sister. I'm talking to the sheriff." In a softer voice, she turned back to her guest. "I was a little older than Chez. Way too old to start over, but my grandkids. What can you do? Their momma chose drugs. Hate drugs."

"Yes, ma'am, drugs are a devil all to themselves," said E.J.

"Chez loved all the babies. There were no 'steps', to his

children, his grandchildren."

"I've discovered he was an exceptional man." E.J. admired Chez's family picture from the funeral tribute. The affectionate looks cast by all of them were indeed enviable. "You know I'm not a sheriff? More like security for Devekon Corporation or was, but that's a long story."

"I know, but I like you better than the sheriff. He's a jerk. What kind of grown man calls himself B.B.?" asked April Arnold.

E.J. chuckled before he could cut it off. His laughter struck him as unprofessional, yet she had pegged B.B. "I wanted to ask you a question at the funeral home, but it seemed like the wrong time. Do you know the where-abouts of your husband's cell phone?"

She giggled, then exploded into a gregarious, full laugh. "Chez wouldn't carry his cell phone for nothing. He had an old flip phone, and rarely did he take it anywhere. I used to yell at him about me and the kids being in a ditch, and no one could get him. In one ear, out the other."

"So, he didn't carry it on his routes?" asked E.J.

Her face made a scowl. "It's back there in his nightstand where he kept it. I saw it yesterday. Why?"

"The modern thing is to track people with their phones. Sometimes we only get the general cell towers they pinged off, and sometimes we get exact GPS." E.J. looked downcast.

"Why you want to know where Chez was?" asked April Arnold.

"Just trying to be thorough. Forget it." E.J. said.

"Do you know the sheriff here, Li'l Jim Duckett? Such a good man. I sat with his momma for years. He called B.B. to get Chez's coin, and B.B. acted smart with him."

"Yes, ma'am, I know him well enough to know not to be smart with him," said E.J.

She laughed. "Where are my manners? Would you take some coffee?"

"Very kind; I'll take you up on it."

April Arnold moved to the next room and returned with a dark mug accented by a lighter handle and top, a style E.J. remembered because his parents had a set.

"Ranger Cooper and the DA got a court order, and I'm here to return the items you requested from the WelCo truck." E.J. lifted the small bag and the box. He removed the coin and handed it to April Arnold.

She near leaped toward it. She grabbed the chip and held it up to the lamplight. "He showed it to all the children and the grandchildren. So proud. He had several of them." She held it high. "His favorite."

E.J. opened the box and removed the Bible.

April Arnold gasped. "Oh, his Bible." She clutched the clasped volume to her chest. Tears formed in the corner of her eyes.

E.J. leaned back on the couch. He wanted to give her a moment, except there was no way to do so.

After a long pause, she looked up at him through tears. "He studied it all the time. Full of notes. He wrote everything in here."

"Yes, ma'am." E.J. didn't know what else to say.

April Arnold began shaking her head. "I can't; I can't have it here."

He looked at her, unsure of what to think. The Bible meant everything to her. So why wouldn't she 'have it here'? It made no sense. "Your husband kept it close in the truck's console." Experience taught him loss and emotion made little sense.

"He always kept it close. He used to tell me if anything ever happened to him, this book would take care of the children and me. Everything I ever needed was in here. I just smiled and went on because I knew I would die first." The last statement brought a grin through the tears. "I'm really a good bit older."

E.J. wouldn't take the leather-encased book, despite her efforts. "Give it to your children or save it for the grandchildren."

"No, it makes it too real. I know I'll cry every time I see it. I don't know why they sent it. I only asked for the coin," said April Arnold.

E.J. expected someone; maybe the DA figured because it was a Bible, perhaps it would be a family heirloom. They would want to hand it down through the family. Or maybe they deduced there was no evidentiary value to it, so why not return it? Especially if the woman had been insistent about the coin. No one wanted this bothersome woman coming back in two years raising a fit again. He took the black and gold Bible back from her.

She exhaled, taking comfort in the fact E.J. had relented.

"He said this would take care of you and the children." E.J. held up the leather-bound volume with the little gold clasp and triangular fold-over cover.

"Oh, he went on and on about it. Never kept it far from him," said April Arnold.

"I've heard of people hiding their wills, stock certificates, treasury bonds. Anything like that in here."

April Arnold laughed. "He made a lot of money, but he couldn't keep it. He bought everything for everybody and gave to every hard case who put their hand out on both sides of our family."

E.J. pressed a button on the clasp and lifted the cover. He carefully angled it to one side and thumbed through it, hoping to find some document of value. Then he turned the Bible in the opposite direction, likewise carefully angling where the contents would divulge themselves or fall out.

"Told you," April Arnold said.

E.J. noticed all the handwritten notes scribbled between verses. It wasn't tradition in his family to take notes in a Bible. He had near fell over when he first saw Rebecca do it. They'd taken a study about experiencing God's love before the kids were born.

"You take it. Cooper told me about your daughter. I didn't know how to bring it up, but I've been praying for her ever since I heard." April Arnold took a deep breath.

E.J. thought Cooper had no business telling his misery. However, the woman seemed so genuine in her consolation, he changed his mind. "Thank you. It must have helped. She came home yesterday."

"Is she okay?" asked April Arnold.

"Drugs are the devil," E.J. made the comment while his eyes focused on a note between two verses in Romans. He held up his hand to stop April Arnold from speaking, and he turned the page, then the next page, and thereafter.

"What?" April Arnold asked.

"Shhhh—"

"What is it?" For the first time since he had known her, April Arnold's tone approached insistency.

"It's a ledger. Dates, drivers, wells, volumes, delivery locations, amounts." E.J. thought Widow Welchel killed

Arnold for this ledger. How she did it wasn't entirely clear, yet the motive was now certain.

More than blackmail, he had recorded her operation in great detail. From here, they could trace the money back to Widow Welchel.

CHAPTER TWENTY-SIX

E.J. SWORE APRIL ARNOLD TO SECRECY BEFORE LEAVING with the Bible. Despite not bringing her wealth, the Bible's pages held a treasure. A way to stop a killer. And a way to do it without breaking his word.

It couldn't stand on its own. He needed to pass it along after he had established in the mind of Cooper and Hall that Widow Welchel masterminded the ring. She arranged accidents to murder whistleblowers. The notes never specifically mentioned Widow Welchel, yet her drivers and trucks comprised the volume of the operation.

They had to see her for what she was. Neither would have the opportunity he stumbled across. As ill-prepared as he had been for Rebecca's courtroom theatrics, Widow Welchel had been less prepared. Rebecca had jousted Widow Welchel off balance. Then E.J. pressed her with the perfect combination of punches.

In hindsight, the ambush he laid in the parking lot seemed haphazard, as if he inadvertently stumbled into the truth and, once stuck, couldn't extricate himself. E.J. seized upon the fact only Widow Welchel knew the identity of his informant before capitalizing on the only potential solution, albeit impossible to his lust-struck mind.

Did he really capitalize? What good was a confession he couldn't use? What if he could turn the tables? Was there a way to catch her without breaking his word, preferably before she found the appropriate 'accident' for him?

On the drive home, E.J. called Rebecca. She brought him up to date on Sharla. Rebecca and her colleagues highly recommended the people in San Antonio. The primary doctor there was a Mark Grayson.

Dr. Grayson advised Sharla had a good chance at a strong recovery; however, setbacks were common, so common most measured success in how short and intermittent she suffered a relapse. Recovery posed a lifelong challenge.

The news didn't surprise E.J., though he heard the despair seeping into Rebecca's voice. She suffered the slow realization her daughter would suffer consequences forever. This time E.J. tried to lift Rebecca's spirits. "She will be alive, safe, and loved."

Rebecca had to return to Houston for the trial. Dr. Grayson assured her she could do nothing for Sharla until family counseling began at the start of week two. She also extracted a promise of constant updates from the recovery caseworker. The treatment center assigned a social worker to Sharla.

Rebecca joked the other lawyers' gravy trains were ending. She took credit for stopping Rex Ashe from being assessed the tab for all the padded legal bills. Oddly enough, all the parties reached the point they thought the evidence should be closed and the case submitted to the jury. Tomorrow would be the last witnesses and the fight over the charge or instructions to the jury.

"We close day after tomorrow, and E.J. rent a car, don't risk your rolling wreck," Rebecca said.

"You didn't used to say that about my make-out wagon." He could imagine Rebecca rolling her eyes at his lack of couth and maturity.

Her failure to take the bait proved she wanted E.J. there, despite her unwillingness to say so. Rex Ashe also wanted him there.

"I caught a break on the truck driver's death I've been working on. It's kind of a delicate state. If I can be there, I will." E.J. promised once more to do everything he could to get to Houston for Rex.

He called Kyle Limburger. Kyle didn't answer, and his voice mailbox was full. People facing felony indictments weren't always reliable. E.J. decided he had no choice. He tore out for Tyler. Likely he'd find Kyle Limburger on the links.

Arriving in early afternoon, E.J. confirmed his conjecture: Kyle Limburger stood on the eleventh hole, yet already playing the nineteenth. The sharp odor of meta-bolized alcohol emanating from Kyle Limburger made E.J. step back.

He willed himself forward. Blue jeans, boots, and a pearl snap shirt weren't golfing attire on a spring day, and E.J. didn't want to draw attention. It didn't seem possible, much less likely any word could get back to Widow Welchel or any of her conspirators, but why take unneces-sary risk when he preferred a low profile.

"How's my boy, Rex?" Kyle Limburger said in a slurred stammer.

"We'll know tomorrow. He's waiting on the jury to tell him if he's stuck in a nursing home or cranks out a few more years on the merry-go-round," said E.J.

"You're not dressed for golf. I got clothes and clubs, join me." Kyle Limburger leaned toward E.J. spouting fire breath. "Might have a little totty too." Then he repeated the phrase, amusing himself, "totty too."

"Please, Rex and I need your help. Concentrate, remember, I asked you about a supposed accident involving lightning. You mentioned the tanks might be blown apart with an IED, especially if no one was looking."

"I remember." Kyle Limburger took a seat on his cart.

"How could somebody fool the pathologist into thinking the person got electrocuted?" E.J. asked.

"You misunderstood me." Kyle Limburger paused.

E.J. asked again, "Can an autopsy tell the difference between electrocution and lightning?"

Kyle Limburger shook his head like he needed to clear it. "How many lightning deaths has your pathologist worked? How many has your crime scene team worked? Is it a direct strike, contacting some object while the object's struck, flash discharge where it hits something nearby?"

"I don't know," said E.J.

"Didn't you fire the early non-lethal weapons with wires and electrodes where you could keep zapping five-second bursts until the battery wore out? Long after the poor soul became a crispy critter."

"I never thought you could keep zapping them," said E.J.

"Come on, you're making this too complicated. The biggest thing about homicidal accidents is being willing. You guys want to close them, the family wants to close them out. Only the murderer profits from murder." Kyle Limburger stomped his cart and was off.

E.J. yelled, "Thanks."

Dr. Meecum seemed vastly better than any pathologist E.J. had ever encountered. Still, everything Kyle Limburger said made sense. What better way to murder someone than an accident, more than an accident, an event universally accepted as an act of God, right?

E.J. didn't relish driving back to Nacogdoches, so he called Dr. Meecum, despite never expecting to get a doctor on the phone without an appointment.

"Doc, I can't believe I got you."

"How can I turn down the man who knows Walker?" asked Dr. Meecum.

"I really wish we were in person, because I got to own up to something, Doc."

"What?" asked Dr. Meecum.

"Walker is kind of an inside joke between Cooper and me. The way CSI is so far from your profession. You know how it all comes so easily, and we can't compare to this image in the minds of people. So, I think Cooper didn't think there was any harm in zinging me with a little joke. I'm sorry it was at your expense," said E.J.

"Oh." Dr. Meecum said.

"I feel bad about it because instead of being honest, I went along. I suspect Cooper and I both thought it odd that such a bright guy bought into our little show," said E.J.

"You never did security or stunts for Chuck Norris?" The disappointment in Dr. Meecum's voice ground into

E.J.'s conscience.

"No, I met him one time at a banquet, heck of a nice guy," said E.J.

"So it is still a little true?" Dr. Meecum asked.

What did it matter? He had come clean. What did it hurt to find a little common ground? "I suppose so. I promise I'm going to give it another chance, put it in the rotation with Gunsmoke. Doc, how many autopsies have you done or observed on electrocutions?"

"One."

"Chester Arnold?" asked E.J.

"Yes."

"Doc, when I took a course one time on non-lethal electric weapons, mostly about how to keep them from being lethal. They had a video where this two-thousand-pound bull dropped to its knees from a taser-type device. Anyway, it's amazing it doesn't kill folks. Something about the voltage and the amps being the right combination," E.J. said.

"Makes sense," said Dr. Meecum.

"A good connection and proper spacing between the electrodes becomes important. I got the idea, one in the top part of the torso and one below the waist on the other side," said E.J.

"So, the current passes through the heart?" Dr. Meecum asked.

"Right, so you see if someone continued pressing the trigger, sending a continuous jolt or altered the device—"

"Non-lethal to lethal." Dr. Meecum surmised.

"Exactly, so did you note any tearing in his clothes or any punctures, even small ones on his upper or lower body, probably on his back, posterior side?" E.J. asked.

"Let me get my notes."

The Doc didn't rule the idea out of hand. Trying to drive a pre-power steering vehicle while concentrating on a phone call, even with a speakerphone, proved too challenging for E.J.

"Are you still there?" Dr. Meecum asked.

"Go ahead, Doc, and spare me the jargon. I used up about all I know trying to ask an intelligent question."

"I noted a small puncture mark on his upper left torso, however, I don't see that I noted another." Dr. Meecum's normally steady voice had slowed communicating doubt.

"Doesn't mean there wasn't one there. I mean, they are made by small hooks, not much bigger than a good-sized needle," E.J. said.

"I could have missed it." Dr. Meecum sounded contrite. "I hope I haven't failed justice."

E.J. envisioned an image of the downcast doctor. 'Failed justice', watching old school hero programs, judging by his office pictures, a good family man, and a Christian worldview all wrapped in a doctor's package. The guy was like a kid or something. "No, Doc. You've done the Lord's work trying to piece together Chez Arnold's story."

A fear of failing justice reminded E.J. how many times during his career he agonized with the weighty duties before him. A time when the awesome dignity and majesty of serving as a guardian of everything his neighbor held dear inspired and renewed him. What he liked about the doc was how much he reminded him of himself before Konner's death, the scandal, the divorce all flattened the faith, love, and inspiration in his soul like a ball of flour under a rolling pin.

"Ranger?" Said Dr. Meecum.

"Call me E.J. I'm still here. I need to ask you something else."

"What is it?"

"Pray for my daughter. She's in rehab in San Antonio." E.J. thought it odd to ask for prayer, yet he was desperate, and he couldn't do it for himself.

"What is her name?"

"Sharla," said E.J.

"Then I will pray for Sharla and you."

"Thanks, Doc."

E.J. debated whether he should put Hall and Cooper together, given Cooper's suspicions. It didn't matter if she wanted to dig into his story, then she would dig. It was probably better to face her together. Separating witnesses proved a valuable technique for reaching truth, and E.J. preferred Cooper not to reach all the truth.

However, he desperately needed her and Hall to reach a level of truth. E.J. arranged the meeting at Cooper's office.

Despite only having to negotiate the old truck across town, Cooper and Hall arrived before E.J. at the DPS headquarters. He tried to dispense with pleasantries, though Cooper's offer of coffee proved irresistible. The aroma struck him as more vibrant, despite probably having stewed in the pot most of the day.

"I knew you knew more than you were telling me yesterday," Cooper said.

Hall's surprised gaze turned to E.J.

E.J. thought, come on, Hall, don't make such an amateur tell. E.J. spoke quicker. "There are things I can't tell you, and I can't talk about. The way it is."

Cooper smiled. "'Way it is'."

"Cooper got me thinking about this geo-tracking idea," said E.J.

"Before long, they won't need us. Whole planet tracked and videoed," said Hall.

E.J. had the same thought initially, but not now. "They may need us even more." He took the Bible out of a cardboard box and put it on Cooper's desk. Then E.J. opened the clasp and laid the leather flap back.

"I got saved, but that doesn't mean we have to open the meeting with a Bible reading," Hall made a lone chuckle at his joke.

"Open it to any page you want," said E.J.

Cooper turned the leather cover, stopping to read the notes. She looked at E.J. "This was in Arnold's truck."

Hall raised from the chair, turning to ease the difficulty in reading the document.

Cooper pointed Hall to one entry. "We knew they were running hot oil, condensate in salt water trucks. There's no actual record, no way to prove who took what, when, until now. Trace the sales to checks, and you'll find who profited."

Hall appeared to pick up fast. "So did Arnold mastermind the operation? I mean, you got wells getting hit in four states."

"No. I can't tell you why Arnold recorded all these. Was he trying to get out? Disgruntled with the big boss? Or wanted blackmail ammunition? I expect we'll never know." E.J. said.

"So, everything my informant told me was true?" Cooper asked.

E.J. nodded.

Hall said, "Gives us who ran the whole thing and had a reason to kill Arnold."

"He's in a WelCo truck. These are all WelCo drivers. Can't be a coincidence. This outfit is run out of WelCo," E.J. said.

They both nodded in agreement. Now E.J. needed to take them as far as he could.

"This book is the motive to kill Arnold. The only plausible person is the mysterious big boss, and such a person had to be connected with WelCo. Arnold owned a flip phone, which he never carried. It was a recurring source of irritation to his wife," E.J. said.

"Right, a man who makes a written record in a Bible won't use an excel spreadsheet on a tablet or phone, will he?" Hall said.

E.J. looked at Cooper. "I bet you already got a list of WelCo phone numbers to compare to Arnold's phone before we knew he didn't really have a phone."

"I'm sure we have a list in the business records we subpoenaed," Cooper said.

Hall jumped ahead of him. "You want us to run those numbers and see if any WelCo employees pinged off towers near the Martin number three prior to the 911 call."

"I figure the big boss won't leave this task to underlings, too dangerous. The kind of killer who mimics accidents, avoids attention and takes few into their confidence. Likely a small built person because they even the odds with electricity and gas. I found everything I needed on the internet, including a recipe to make and store hydrogen sulfide," E.J. said.

Cooper quipped, "Can't make lightning."

"No, but you and I have learned what it means to 'ride

the lightning'. Come on, it's the same thing. After Arnold got juiced, then all somebody had to do was keep popping him or alter the device. Improvised explosive devices are even easier to find in how-to manuals than swamp gas," said E.J.

"And none of us were really looking hard for any of it. We wanted to see natural causes between our bias and B.B.'s bumbling. We'll never know what was out there." said Hall.

"We had tunnel vision. Nobody makes lightning," said E.J.

"All right, we find a target. Still kind of thin, isn't it?" Cooper asked.

"Whoever it is will sing because you're already humming the tune. You copy a few pages from this Bible. Person might even recognize Chester Arnold's handwriting. You'll be holding three aces for hole cards." E.J. made sure he had their undivided attention.

Hall said, "Okay, I'll bite. What are we holding?"

"What gets all criminals, arrogance. The target doesn't think they can get caught, so they'll assume you have an informant. Which means they will assume you know more than you do, right? Second, the copied pages reveal a good number of drivers who can all be turned. A fact obvious to the ringleader. You're being courteous by going to the source before working backwards from the little fish. Third, the target won't know Arnold didn't name them because you'll only give them a sample of his Bible. They'll assume Arnold spelled it out because they feared blackmail. You'll have a confession and a deal."

"You're not leading the interrogation? Odd, you live for this stuff." Cooper said.

"I'm more useful on the outside," E.J. said.

"Why?" Hall asked.

"I've told you all you need to know. I will not tell you all I know." E.J. stood to take his leave.

"Well, hallelujah to you too, patriot." Hall likewise stood.

E.J. said, "I'm no expert, but I kind of believe if this 'saved' business was really takin', then you wouldn't still want to cuss."

Hall descended into a series of curses without the moderation of excessive patriotism.

"Glad you cussed me. I don't feel so bad about taking your car to Houston tomorrow." E.J. extended his hand to receive the keys. "Cooper will take you home, and you can check out a ride from your favorite Uncle, Sam."

Cooper asked, "Why are you so sure your plan will work?"

"I have full confidence in both of you," E.J. said.

"Not likely, more likely you know who the target is. Still no assurance, especially not getting a confession on a capital murder," said Cooper.

"Make sure you have the DA ready to deal. This isn't some junkie trying to score enough for an eight ball. It's a big-time scam stealing royalties from the little guy, the royalty owners." E.J. turned and left them.

CHAPTER TWENTY-SEVEN

HALL'S LEXUS ATE UP THE OLD EAST TEXAS FREEWAY like a kid chewing a chocolate bunny's ear on Easter morning. E.J. would arrive during the lunch break, when Rebecca expected to start her closing. He really didn't care about hearing from the other side.

The judge and the lawyers stacked the deck against Rex Ashe, and for E.J., their bull amounted to bragging about swindling his friend. At least Rex had a chance. Rebecca would give as good as she got and likely a lot better.

E.J. parked in the garage. Despite the maneuverability of the Lexus, he parked on the roof, more accustomed to accommodating his three-quarter-ton truck. He walked to the elevator, where he got a shock.

"Figured you'd park up here." Widow Welchel appeared without warning.

"You peg a man pretty good, don't you?" asked E.J.

"Predictable." Widow Welchel answered. "You don't

return my calls. I like to keep my men close."

"Think I can undo your spell with distance." The elevator doors opened.

"First time for everything." Widow Welchel blocked E.J.'s path. "I need to know we still have a deal, no matter the verdict."

"Look, I got my daughter back, and I'm grateful. I haven't gone back on my word and don't intend to." E.J. tried to step around her, but the doors closed.

The sun beat down on the concrete roof to the parking garage. Houston deteriorated into an inescapable sauna around the start of summer. E.J. surmised Widow Welchel had been waiting for some time by the way her makeup had run, despite the best work she could pull off with the equipment in her purse.

She gritted her teeth, staring him down. "We're not done here."

E.J. marveled at how the incredible blue eyes no longer held any mystery for him. An odd thought went through his mind. Maybe Chester Arnold had once succumbed to her charms like he had. Maybe he should have looked at passages about monsters and witches in his Bible. He hadn't read all the notes or even skimmed them.

She picked the wells, and he assigned the drivers. Otherwise, how would Arnold know all he had recorded? She wouldn't have trusted him with so much information if she didn't have him under her spell, keeping her men close.

Just when he had decided Arnold was a good guy, he had proven predictable, too. Well, E.J. really couldn't throw stones at Arnold or any of the woman's paramours.

"Don't you look at me with your self-righteous contempt. You, you, you gunned down two men and would have killed twenty to save your daughter from her own rotten choices."

E.J. stared into pools of blue ice.

"You think I'm recording you the way you recorded me." Widow Welchel turned her scowl into amusement. "No, you're too smart to fall for your own trick. Besides, I don't need you to admit to anything. I know what you did." She made a gun motion with her thumb and index finger, then blew the top of the pretend smoke off the mock barrel.

"What now?" E.J. asked.

"You admit you're no better than me. The men you killed only gave your daughter the chance to earn what she wanted. Be modern and call it sex trafficking if it makes you feel good, but it's just pimps and prostitutes. Way it's always been, they need each other—"

"Shut up." E.J.'s arm erupted forward before he quickly stopped it. Rage poured through him, and he shuddered.

"Hit me. You think men haven't knocked me down all my life. Why can't I provide for my daughter, my granddaughter, so they will never have to know the abuse I did? They'll never be at the mercy of anyone, never be beaten, raped, humiliated." Widow Welchel stood looking up at his face, near spitting the words at him.

"You only had to kill what? Two maybe three people for enough wealth to last generations, right?" asked E.J.

Widow Welchel stepped back. "I'm sorry about the kid. I really didn't know what he knew. As for the troll Arnold, you're a fool if you believe he found Jesus. He blackmailed me."

"I kept my word. Still, I figure it's only a matter of time before I have an accident." E.J. stepped back, hoping to release some of his own rage and tension.

"Don't need it. I have insurance. No one will believe you killed those men in self-defense. You murdered them for embarrassing your little girl, really embarrassing you. Not about her virtue; it's about who you are. Rogue lawman, former ranger, ought to make some headlines. Enough to follow your baby girl forever. And you know what they'll do to a pig in the pen."

E.J. tried to set the heel of his foot in hopes he could stop his body from shuddering. He couldn't hit her, couldn't strike out at her, and yet she appeared to him as an evil apparition threatening everything he loved. Frustration confounded him.

"Now we have an understanding, don't we." Widow Welchel stepped aside.

E.J. took a step forward, and she moved again to block him.

She said, "Say it. I need to know you know."

"I understand you."

She moved again, and he entered the elevator. He exited the parking garage and walked across the street to the courthouse. Somewhere, the hatred consuming him subsided.

Was he that much different? Or was she the rarest of all victims? The weak, the powerless prey who somehow scratched and clawed her way into changing her stars? Or was she as evil as he had believed? Weren't both of them trying to navigate a world vastly different from the traditions and values instilled in their youth?

Like a gator surviving the strikes and onslaughts of her

own kind to one day rule the swamp. Little wonder such a creature couldn't fathom empathy for any but her own.

Rex Ashe stood crestfallen in the hallway. E.J. saw no point in asking him how the earlier argument had fared. He could tell by the long face. All seemed lost.

Rebecca did not look nearly so downtrodden. E.J. had seen the look on her face many times. She looked like a bomb ready to ignite. How many times had he witnessed her prepared for battle?

He once compared her to a triple crown-winning thoroughbred outclassing her competition. Rebecca didn't care for being compared to a horse. The more E.J. had tried to explain, the worse he had made the situation. Hence today, he said to her, "You look ready."

Rebecca laughed, "They're at the gate."

"And they're off," E.J. said. Out of his peripheral vision, he saw Widow Welchel escorting her daughter and Clara Brandis into the courtroom. E.J. leaned toward Rebecca and spoke in a soft tone. "Looks like the other side rang Rex's bell pretty good."

Rebecca answered in a whisper as she walked. "You know the whole great wealth, great responsibility deal. The idea he can't be trusted with great power, too irresponsible. Gave him the 'me too', climate change, corrupt politics, blame. Pretty sure Rex invented cancer."

For so long, Rebecca spoke to him in anger that E.J. had forgotten her quick wit and sarcasm. When an outlaw had escaped justice on his watch, her razor wit and gallows humor ironically comforted him.

In his mind, their mix of the traditional and non-traditional made their relationship exciting. A warm glow enveloped him, thinking about how he had missed their interchanges.

A quick look back at Rex Ashe's face shattered the fuzzy moment. Rex feared nothing, and yet here he stood on trial.

E.J. took a seat in a pew behind Rex Ashe. The judge did not appear pleased as he took the bench. The lawyers approached, and this time managed a quiet bench conference. Thereafter, Rebecca stood and began the pleasantries to start her argument.

She stood behind Rex Ashe. For a moment, she paused, then put her hand on his shoulder. "Today is the day I've longed for. She lifted her arms up with open hands. You see, for a person who built a life on his terms. An amazing life. He took the zero-sum game and the cards we all get dealt, then Rex created more cards. Wealth to power a corporation, to contribute to his state, his nation, universities, untold charities, and philanthropic activity. He did it in a brutal business, and he never forgets the lessons he learned.

"Lessons about people, values that tell us who we are. When an employee gets hurt, you take care of them and their family for however long it takes. And he made mistakes, admitted mistakes, lapses in judgment made worse by alcohol and chasing all the wrong members of the opposite sex. True, all true. The downside to life on his own terms.

"Yet it's the only life he has ever known. This is the trial for his life. What someone like him is facing is nothing less than a death sentence. I'll sit down in a minute, no longer standing between my friend and the end of everything he is. I no longer have any way to defend him. You are charged with determining whether to take away his right to life, liberty, and the pursuit of happiness, those bedrock inalienable rights which led our ancestors to forge government to protect them from their neighbors, from government itself.

"Do his sins merit such an awesome punishment, and even if so, are you the ones to mete it out?"

She paused and paced back behind Rex Ashe, placing her hand on his shoulder again. "I don't presume to tell you there'll ever be a happy ending. Either way, Rex knows he's in for a fight. A battle with a disease which will eventually take all he has. A disease his pride wouldn't let him admit to his friends and family, probably not truly to himself. She turned and extended her hand to E.J.

"There are many who love Rex and will move heaven and earth to protect him. To create the safety net, he needs. I know I will—"

"Objection, Your Honor." The youngest opposing lawyer stood.

"Sustained," said the judge.

"Move to strike."

"Granted."

Rebecca stood with her mouth open. E.J. knew she never intended to respond. From what he had seen, it would have done no good. She wanted the jury to know the process wasn't fair.

E.J. silently applauded her advocacy. The jury knew she and E.J. would take care of Rex to his last breath, if not their own. Who couldn't trust that? E.J. saw she deliberately drew the objection because it made her point. The perfect time to tilt to the offensive.

Rebecca took a deep breath. "So, why are we here?"

Then Rebecca turned, looking at the pew occupied by

Clara Brandis, Widow Welchel, and her daughter, drawing the jury's attention to them. "Couriville Holding Company owned by another company owned by Jonley Ruth Cannatella. Why? Why use holding companies and limited partnerships under different names? Why?"

Rebecca stared at the three for a long time before the judge started to speak, and she started her argument again to get ahead of him. "To buy publicly traded stock anyone of us could buy over the counter? Why hide their identity? Odd, because the company needed capital. The banks holding the notes knew it."

She stepped back into the well of the courtroom. "Is that why the banks forced Clara Brandis on Rex Ashe as the new Chief Financial Officer of Devekon? Odd, once in the position, Clara Brandis becomes the whistleblower? What's more, she separates Rex Ashe's friends from Devekon."

Rebecca paused, drawing the juror's attention to E.J. "The bankers make money because of this infusion of capital into a company in trouble. Where does the money come from? Odd, again, we go back to mysterious companies and partnerships ultimately traced to Jonley Ruth Cannatella, better known as Widow Welchel. Where does she get the money? We ask, but the bankers don't ask, do they?"

Rebecca leans against the jury rail. "We don't have to be Shakespeare to know, 'Something is rotten in the state of Denmark'. I don't carry the burden of proof. It's not my obligation to tell you why you're really here. Why this court, this process is being used, weaponized to steal vast energy holdings."

She looked around the courtroom. "Everybody gets

something, from the lawyers to the bankers, to everyone else except you. You, like all the trappings of this court, get used to make the theft legal. Make these lawyers stand up and answer. We know they won't tell you why Clara Brandis and Couriville Holding Company leads to Jonley Ruth Cannatella and Widow Welchel, and she leads back to Clara Brandis."

Rebecca turned and pointed to Widow Welchel in the gallery, "Make them all come clean."

CHAPTER TWENTY-EIGHT

AS PREDICTED, THE FINAL SUMMATION DIDN'T ADDRESS Clara Brandis, nor Widow Welchel, nor WelCo, nor stock purchases, nor the source of the money, nor the purpose for masking of identities. Rather, the lawyers hammered on their strength, the diagnosis of Alzheimer's, and the ultimately poor prognosis therefrom combined with a company run to the precipice of destruction by mismanagement.

Rebecca's compelling argument buoyed Rex Ashe's spirits. So much so that Rebecca had to press her nails into his hand to keep him from rising out of his seat in indignation at the insults of the following lawyers. The jury deliberated for about two hours before asking to go home to return the next day.

Still, Rex Ashe gained some of his old swagger. The three old friends enjoyed a quiet meal in Rex's favorite restaurant. Rex ate like he wasn't under the care of a cardiologist, a garden salad in a vinaigrette, warm buttered rolls, steak covered in blue cheese, and more butter on a baked sweet potato.

Rebecca alluded to the unhealthy nature of the fine meal, prompting E.J. to whisper, "We get to be near eighty, then we can talk."

The next morning, the bankers nodded to Rex Ashe again, and the lawyers acknowledged him. E.J. saw the relief on his old friend's face. Whatever the verdict, it couldn't be more devastating than the one delivered by the doctors, and what's more, Rex no longer had to face it alone.

About one-thirty, the jury sent out a note. The judge read the note and his response from the bench to the jury. E.J. had often seen correspondence from the court sent back via the bailiff, however, Rex Ashe distrusted the entire process, and Rebecca's dander was up.

"How much stock did Welchel and Brandis buy? Did they control the company? Where did Welchel and Brandis raise the money to buy the stock?" The judge read the questions in a flat tone, looking at each word.

E.J. fought back a chuckle until the last question caused him to release it.

"Why won't you let Rex Ashe's lawyer answer objections? To which the court replies: You are to be bound by the instructions the court has heretofore given you and continue your deliberations." The judge asserted a stern countenance, turning to the jury after reading the last sentence.

Rex Ashe whispered to E.J., "Man, don't look happy. Good sign."

E.J. decided it was all a good sign. He wasn't the only one sharing this opinion. As far as the bankers and institutional shareholders were concerned, the trial ended there.

E.J. and Rex Ashe passed their time in the courtroom recalling goose shoots, elk hunts, and Rex's grandchildren. He expressed his intent to make amends with his children, which led to E.J. sharing the truth of Sharla's drug addiction.

The seriousness of the subject caused a pause in the conversation. E.J. looked up to see Hall and Cooper walk into the courtroom. They spoke to the bailiff in hushed tones. Thereafter, the bailiff called out the name, "Ruth Welchel."

Widow Welchel rose and walked forward, trying to make eye contact with E.J. He declined the invitation, watching her from his peripheral vision. She walked in slow motion, well aware they would take her into custody, yet they didn't cuff her. Rather, they escorted her out the door.

A part of E.J. wanted to take over the interrogation. It occurred to him there might not be any questioning. She might demand her lawyer. No, Widow Welchel thought far too much of herself, and she would be curious about what they had on her.

She would talk at least to the point of trying to figure out whether he broke his word. What if she assumed he had told the authorities she killed Arnold and Geoffrey?

Would she reciprocate naming him as the killer of the sex traffickers in Shreveport? Would Cooper believe her? How would she do it without admitting her involvement, and how much involvement did she have? Did she really only research Sharla's location, or was she orchestrating the captivity? Widow Welchel said herself Sharla had been sold a couple of times. Did she buy her to gain leverage over E.J.?

E.J. assumed by having the bailiff call her name, they were arresting her and offering a custodial interview as opposed to a non-custodial. She would talk either way, yet she was far too smart to admit much. Hall had proven his skills in interrogation. Hall had the additional advantage of being counted upon to reduce any value Widow Welchel might seek from her knowledge of the Shreveport killings.

"That's your FBI buddy and Cooper. Wonder what they got her on? Whatever it is, I expect she's good for it." Rex Ashe spoke in a soft tone because the courtroom had turned silent, despite a small crowd.

"How well did you know her?" E.J. asked.

"I didn't, not much anyway. Why?"

"I'm asking if you were an easy mark and how she knew it or if she targeted you because of something personal?" E.J. could see in Rex Ashe's eyes the man knew what he really wanted to know. Was she a spurned lover? Given what he knew about Widow Welchel, wouldn't she have used her wiles on Rex Ashe? Wouldn't it be like shooting fish in a barrel?

Rex Ashe eased back a short distance and laughed. "I figure I'm the only fellow who hadn't been sparking the woman."

"You enjoying being holier than thou?" E.J. asked.

"After all the lectures from you? It's like catching your Sunday school teacher in a liquor store," said Rex Ashe.

"Laugh it up, so long as you're enjoying my misery," said E.J.

Rex Ashe nodded toward Widow Welchel's alluring form before stepping through the door. "Bet it wasn't all that miserable."

E.J. fought back the urge to cuss him. He had earned the rebuke even if he hadn't lectured Rex Ashe every time E.J. had rescued him from some pretty face bent on stealing Rex's money, and there had been a lot of them.

Rebecca stepped back into the courtroom and walked toward E.J. and Rex Ashe.

E.J. asked, "How's Sharla?"

"Caseworker says she's making progress." Rebecca shrugged.

The response seemed so brief to E.J., so shallow. He wanted more, some understanding of how she progressed. When could they see her? What was she like? Asking more would only torture Rebecca. She had to be suffering from the same need to know more.

"Learn anything from the lawyers?" Rex Ashe asked.

"It's over as far as the lawyers are concerned. Even if they deliberate much longer, the lawyers are ready to non-suit. The banks decided Clara Brandis is gone," Rebecca said.

E.J. asked, "Gone, just like that."

The bailiff shut the door with a thud, and within seconds, the judge sat on the bench. "Bring the jury in."

E.J. preferred the simplicity of guilty and not guilty. He didn't care for special issues. The series of questions answered by the jury seemed unnecessarily complicated. As best he could tell, Rex Ashe won every issue, though he waited for Rebecca to nod to him.

Rex Ashe hugged Rebecca in triumph. Rex Ashe stood, then turned to embrace E.J. Each attorney congratulated Rex before many of the jurors congratulated him.

After all the well-wishing, Rebecca motioned to E.J.

and pulled Rex Ashe into the jury room. She asked him to have a seat. "You're the conquering hero today, but we have to talk about where you go from here."

Rex Ashe said nothing. He looked at E.J.

E.J. said, "He knows."

"E.J. and I are going to San Antonio tonight." She smiled. "We're going to get to see Sharla tomorrow. What are you going to do?"

"I thought I'd have another steak, maybe a totty to go with it," said Rex Ashe.

"Why I hired you a nurse. He will make sure you get home and be there if tomorrow is not as good a day as today."

The comment cast a shadow on Rex Ashe's elation. "'He', you got me a male nurse. I could probably do a female nurse, but not a male."

"Think she's ahead of you there, Rex," said E.J.

Rebecca turned to E.J. "We have an appointment in family counseling at two o'clock tomorrow."

Devekon returned E.J.'s company truck, which meant he no longer needed to borrow Hall's Lexus. Discussion about returning the vehicle offered an opportunity to get an update on Widow Welchel's interrogation.

E.J. let several hours pass, trying to make sure he couldn't interrupt anything before calling. "Hall, I need to return a fine automobile."

Hall laughed. "Really? Why you called?"

"Might be a little curious."

"Well, I don't have to tell you, you were right about a cell phone owned by WelCo being at the Martin number three for about forty-five minutes before the well fire gets reported," Hall said.

"Forty-five minutes, long time," said E.J.

Hall paused before adding. "Long enough to bring down the lightning."

"What I figured."

"You also figured the number traced back to the primary phone for Ruth Welchel. Also, put her at the well site prior to Geoffrey's death. Too much to be a coincidence."

E.J. asked, "Did she talk?"

"Oh, she talked. Tried desperately to figure out what we had on her. Didn't want to give us anything," said Hall.

"Did she float an explanation for the phone location?" E.J. asked.

"Cooper and I decided we didn't want to divulge our cards without being certain of getting something back," Hall said.

"So, you didn't arrest her?" E.J. couldn't check the incredulity in his voice. This was unthinkable. How could they mess up a case he handed to them with a bow on it?

Hall's tone grew more solemn. "We talked to the DA. The phone puts her at both crime scenes, if they're crime scenes. The Bible's notes are circumstantial evidence she must have run the theft ring—"

"She's the only one who could," E.J. interrupted.

"Right, but all circumstantial," Hall said.

E.J. felt the pressure erupt from the pit of his stomach through the trunk of his body and out of his head and hands. "You let her go. You just let her go because she didn't confess. What's wrong with you people—"

"Easy, easy. You think Cooper and I would quit. You know better. Cooper's way smarter than you are, anyway."

Hall's attempt at trying to assure E.J. served only to

further enrage him. E.J. yelled into his cell phone. "Geoffrey's life wasn't worth your time. Is that what I tell the kid's parents? Never got a chance to beat the dope." The parallels between Geoffrey and Sharla had consumed him of late.

Before Sharla's battle with addiction, drug abuse happened to other people, the weak people. Understanding the complicated struggles of Geoffrey and Arnold in the context of Sharla had proven unsettling.

Hall fired back. "Cooper worked the drivers listed in the Bible. She recognized one of them on parole."

E.J. asked, "She turned one?"

"More than turned one. Got him to call Widow Welchel," Hall said.

"One party consent call?" E.J. asked.

"You bet your Sweet Uncle Sam."

E.J. didn't foresee this strategy. Cooper showed her genius. But would Widow Welchel fall for it? Especially after he had already sprung a similar trap on her earlier. "She admit anything?"

"Not entirely, no, not on the murders anyway, but she denied little. Cooper drew up a little script where this guy claimed we were trying to turn him. Welchel figured out it was a line, but not before she admitted she ran the theft ring."

E.J. said, "Pretty good."

"My U.S. Attorney really liked the part where she offered to give the driver's family money if he did time for it. Even if we never make the murders stick, this is a big-time criminal enterprise over four states," Hall said.

"Will we get some federal truth in sentencing?" asked E.J.

Hall paused before answering. "There's a fly in the ointment."

"Huh?"

"She's got something she wants to trade. All she'll tell us is it's a dirty cop murdering some gang bangers," said Hall.

"What's your boss say is the price of poker?" E.J. asked.

"You of all people know the politics. Stealing, drugging, even murdering is all on the back burner to get a shot at a rogue cop. Been like that for years. I can't promise the deal won't get made."

"How much time before the other shoe falls?" E.J. asked.

"Her lawyers want to meet directly with the United States Attorney tomorrow. You know I'm telling my boss it's bull."

"But it's not your call," said E.J.

"No, it's not my call," said Hall.

"I better let you go," said E.J.

"One more thing. There's another phone there at the same time as the WelCo number," said Hall.

"Who?"

"Not WelCo. Don't know, it's a burner. Warrant didn't give us enough window to see before or after," Hall said.

"So, she had an accomplice?" asked E.J.

"Can't say for sure. Call logs aren't showing calls between these phones, so could be she kept a burner. There are some calls from WelCo's landline to the burner. Who knows?" asked Hall.

E.J. exhaled. "Welchel, and she's not telling, right?"

CHAPTER TWENTY-NINE

"AND HOW DOES THAT MAKE YOU FEEL?" THE COMMENT passed in a monotone, with no emphasis on the therapist's expressionless face.

How did she think he felt? His daughter told him he had been a controlling jerk her whole life. She might as well have blamed him for pushing her into addiction.

"Dad doesn't have feelings or moods or anything normal," said Sharla.

Did Sharla really think so, or was she still playing him trying to get back to the drugs? Maybe she could guilt him into taking her out of here? Who knew? He couldn't tell, and this supposed therapist couldn't find his backside with a GPS.

The therapist raised a hand to end further discussion. "What is more important than what your father thinks is you, Sharla. You have to want sobriety for you."

For her, what about her mother, her late hero brother, everyone who loved her? Seemed like this was all about her choices, which had gotten them all into this mess. E.J. wanted to leave. He had been glad to see Sharla, though this entire process proved unproductive.

E.J. looked at his watch. A pained, cold chasm opened through his insides. All the way to San Antonio, he couldn't stop himself from daydreaming. Despite Rebecca's warnings, he clung to the idea Sharla would embrace him.

The fantasy began dissolving at his first impression of the rehabilitation campus. The place looked too white, too sterile, too somber. A whole hallway decorated with those ridiculous landscape pictures reciting a word, like determination or courage. If they had landscapes, then how about some oil paintings or photographs of sites from Texas like the Trinity River or the Guadalupe Mountains?

Even this 'family conference room' appeared barren. The therapist started with a poor impression by calling E.J. down for trying to hug Sharla. Sharla had no intention of letting him hug her anyway.

His watch read two-thirty. A kind of mercy ended the long-awaited visit. Things would be better now. Rebecca would join him and the therapist while Sharla walked back to her room.

Rebecca wore a downcast countenance. Perhaps despite her warnings to E.J., she too had raised her hopes only to see them dashed by reality. It was supposed to be a long, hard road, but not this hard.

Rebecca asked, "She's medicated, isn't she?"

"We have a psychiatrist assigned to review all medications. We're still trying to stabilize her right now," said the therapist.

E.J. asked, "Dr. Grayson, right?"

"Correct."

"So, is it temporary, or will she be on medication from now on?" asked E.J.

"There's no way to know until we have more time. Some people become addicted because they already had mental health issues; they self-medicated." Dr. Grayson opened a file. "We have to identify her triggers to change the behaviors."

"Can you give us a better idea how long she will be here?" Rebecca asked.

"You have to look at this from Sharla's point of view. She didn't see it as being held against her will. Kind of Stockholm syndrome thing. She identifies with her captors. She feels sorry for them, and as horrible as it sounds, she wants the life because she gets to chase the high she experienced." Dr. Grayson looked at E.J. "Can you tell me about how you found her? All I have is second-hand."

"Nope."

Dr. Grayson scowled. "Just called you from Marshall, and you go get her—"

Rebecca interrupted. "That's right."

E.J. thought she answered a little quickly. Of course, he never expected Rebecca to believe the story. Whatever their many differences, he knew Rebecca would be fiercely grateful and protective of both Sharla and him.

He couldn't get any lower. It sounded like Sharla wanted to return to a life of addiction. She might even mourn for the men he killed.

The drive home should have taken six hours. Rebecca begged him to stay in San Antonio. E.J. didn't want to spend another minute there. Seeing Sharla hadn't been the tonic he had hoped.

In his mind, scenes of home played. The hardwood bottoms, pine forest, and the pastures of his farm passed before him. Even his overgrown and unworked garden called to him. He thought about how he needed to get his peas in the ground. He would spend tomorrow tending to his plants.

The drive took longer because E.J. drove through the hill country, leaving San Antonio. He stopped at the Medina River. The river reminded him of a family trip with Konner and Sharla.

He remembered teasing Sharla like Rebecca's ongoing joke about whether Sharla was Mommy or Daddy's, girl. Sharla had insisted she would always be his girl.

Sharla urged Sunshine into the river, despite the horse's reluctance. A beautiful fall day surrounded by the reds and golds of the river valley foliage. He recalled the crispness of the fall air saturated with the smell of rain.

Fearing she might be too inexperienced to handle the horse on unfamiliar ground, he stuck close while Rebecca and Konner rode ahead. He had always watched out for her. How did they get to a sterile hospital room where no affection passed between them?

E.J. arrived well after dark. He went out to the barn and fed Sunshine. As had become his custom, he had a long heartfelt discussion with the skewbald paint.

It occurred to E.J. Yak hadn't jumped on him. Despite Sunshine's objections, Yak drank from Sunshine's water trough. A float kicked the water on and off.

He looked at Yak's bowl. The animal still had some feed in the bowl. The big dog took care of himself mostly. E.J. thought of Yak as more of a guest than himself as Yak's owner. Maybe he'd taken off in the woods chasing hogs.

"Yak, Yak." A few more attempts gained him nothing.

E.J. stepped onto his porch, exhausted. Driving wore E.J. out. Despite a career on the road, he'd never cared for it. He looked around his shoulder at the farm in the darkness, asking himself why did he stay here?

Like old man Copeland with the meth addict sons, he had a sacred obligation to pass his heritage to his children. Konner suffered death at the hand of terrorist thousands of miles from home and what would become of Sharla?

There were so many memories of Rebecca and the children. So many better times, combined with the pain of how it had all ended. For the first time, the place felt foreign now, somehow menacing. Nothing remained here of the life he had built, still he knew he could never leave.

He chuckled to himself, remembering how he chided Copeland for holding such a reverence for dirt. He took a deep breath, then looked down. Like Copeland and so many others, some strand deeply intertwined in his DNA connected E.J. to the land.

Inside the doorway, he flipped on the light, and it flashed over the nickel-plated hand cannon aimed at him. E.J.'s eyes focused on a dark hole the size of a quarter before it expanded several times larger.

"Hope you don't mind me takin' your chair. I reckoned I might have to wait awhile. Got to finish our game." Norty cackled, amusing himself with his wit.

A mournful whine drew E.J.'s attention. Yak lay in a pool of blood in the corner. Ire near raised E.J. into the air. What kind of low trash can't even kill a dog, right?

He should have seen Norty coming. Another phone at the crime scene and Norty had the explosive ordinance skills necessary. Plus, Norty defended Widow Welchel even though Welchel didn't make apologies for who and what she was.

E.J. closed his fist, trying to gain composure. Soon he would die, and the knowledge gave him a strange peace, so long as he killed this cackling pig, all would be good. Could he close the distance to the big gun and cram it down Norty's throat?

E.J. continued to concentrate on the weapon aimed at him. He saw no opportunity to draw his pocket pistol.

The enormous round barrel swung, motioning for him to sit. E.J. slumped into a soft cowhide chair. His mind raced with thoughts about somehow distracting Norty for a moment. A moment would be long enough.

"You're wishin' you hadn't shown me the Sig you carry in your pocket. Can't reach it, can you, Mr. big man?" Norty yelled, "Draw."

E.J. didn't move. Norty began laughing again. "You should see your face, Mr. shootist. Mr. big time killer. When you smoked those guys in Shreveport, did you give 'em a fair shake?"

"Figured you loved Welchel, but I didn't see all this coming." E.J. looked to his TV tray, where Norty had several heavy zip ties.

Norty took his left hand and threw them at E.J. "Tie your wrist to the chair arms. Rules of game."

E.J. feared this was his last chance, yet there wasn't a chance or a choice. No time to reach for the semi-automatic in his pocket. He left the plastic ties loose.

Norty rose and took several steps toward him. He took his left hand and jerked the end of the plastic cuff until it bit into E.J.'s wrist and pressed his flesh hard against the cool ebony-stained wood of the chair.

"Are you just love-struck muscle, or does she let you and your neanderthals taste the profits?" asked E.J.

"Nephilim." Norty snarled. "You never understood." He stepped back across the room and twisted the knob open on the big vintage gas heater.

E.J. thought, who would believe such an accident. "Y'all getting lazy."

"Oh, it's all very intentional. Sad story, so sad, man had it all." Norty turned to face E.J. "Respected career, high and mighty ranger. Beautiful wife. Two kids. Man had it all."

"Nobody will believe it," said E.J.

"Hero son dies in the war, right? One of the dumb ones. Then Mr. big ranger flubs up, gets folks killed, and has to resign." Norty waved a hand across his nose, acknowledging the powerful odor from the gas filling the house.

Then Norty bounced in delight. "New game show. I call it; this was your life."

"You can spare me the rest," E.J. said.

Norty continued hooraying at his joke. "We haven't got to the good part. Mr. big's wife leaves him for another man and his daughter? She starts a new career on her back to support her habit."

E.J. pulled against the straps and swung his legs up. His legs could move, yet his arms were immobile.

"So, baby girl, streetwalker gets an employment opportunity in Shreveport. Till Daddy comes over and kills everybody. Hard on a working girl, Daddy killing all her customers and bosses." Norty shook his head in a mocking gesture.

"Nobody will believe it," said E.J.

"Sweetie, they'll believe it. Because this puts Mr. big

man over the edge. There was a meeting today with the U.S. attorney where Widow Welchel told it all, and then Mr. big man found out from one of his buddies. Lawman, turned outlaw, facing pen time for murder. I can't figure out why you didn't blow your head off years ago." Norty's cackling morphed into howling, then sneered. "Sweetie."

The disparaging way he spit the word 'sweetie' and the look in Norty's eyes told E.J. somehow the gang leader had put together that E.J. was Weldon Harris.

Norty ended all possibility of further doubt. "Never could hit nothing with those little guns, much less a fella's kneecap at thirty feet. Decided way too much coincidence. Man same build, same skill with pocket guns, and enough brass to come into my house—"

Norty stopped mid-sentence then waved the enormous pistol jabbing it in the air at E.J. "Why are you smirking?"

"Ponderin' on how I'll feel when I kill you."

"What?" asked Norty.

"I don't drink cause the first time I killed a man, I got to liking liquor, and it scared me," said E.J.

"You think you can appeal to my conscience. If I kill you, I'll fall apart like you did." Norty threw his head back with raucous laughter. "Tell me, maybe we got enough time. I mean, I got time, anyway."

"Good shoot. Guy's momma didn't see it. She painted her son's name in blood-red paint on the door of my old white truck. Took years fore I took it off," said E.J.

Norty made a motion in front of his eye with his free hand like wiping great tears. Then he cackled again. "Mark of Kane."

"Figure I'll have a drink when I kill you."

Norty stopped laughing.

"Make me a toast to Widow Welchel's sweetie. I should have known. Women like Widow Welchel don't want their virtue defended, but you did anyway. You're like one of those French fellows who like their gals running with other fellows," E.J. said.

"You're not gonna get a rise out of me." Norty pointed the gun at E.J.'s head.

"Cuckold, that's the word they call y'all." E.J. smirked.

The 460's eight-inch barrel crashed across E.J.'s eye socket. Norty followed the blow with a backhand from the hand cannon across E.J.'s face. His nose erupted in blood.

Despite the crushing blow, E.J. launched himself forward, throwing his knee upwards. His thigh reached his strapped right hand. He'd touched the pistol a thousand times yet never tried to fire it through his pocket. His thumb snapped the safety, and his finger stabbed the trigger through the denim.

Percussion stomped his ears. An intense burn streaked down his thigh. The hydrostatic hollow point mushroomed through Norty's chest. Then ricocheted off the heater, igniting the gas into a flame.

Norty's fire-covered body flew forward over E.J. The force flung E.J. backwards in the chair, landing on his back.

THE END

EPILOGUE

A FIELD OF BLUEBONNETS POPULATED THE LANDSCAPE.
All over Texas, people made pilgrimages to take photos,
yet it never occurred to him the flowers would grow in the
desert and mountainous region near Big Bend National
Park as well.

A palette of greys and browns in the distance
contrasting the carpet of blue and yellow flowers didn't
seem to agree with Sunshine. The mount kicked out,
making a little pitch to the left. Sharla swung the horse
into a tight turn before patting his neck.

E.J. didn't need to ride his rented sorrel to her.
Whatever had spooked Sunshine, Sharla calmed him.

The commotion made Shasta's horse turn around. Hall
said, "Horses know they're in a different world, but not
sure the girls have figured it out. I know they don't know
how to get back to the stables."

"You'd think our girls could do a little detective work,"
E.J. said.

Hall spoke just above a whisper. "They're gonna offer Widow Welchel twenty to do for all of it. I was trying to find the right time to tell you. Seemed light to me. Prosecutor is tickled with it, considering he has little evidence of the murders, and she was too smart to tie herself to Norty. Says at her age it's a death sentence."

E.J. turned in the saddle to face Hall. "Crime pays."

"Always been a growth industry, brother. But we both know if she'd have had any credibility after Norty tried to kill you, some of us might be singing Yankee Doodle Dandy in Angola."

"I don't know all the words." E.J. let Sharla and Shasta get a little further away to make certain they were out of hearing. "You been looking out for me for a long time. I want to tell you I appreciate it. I don't know why you stick your neck out, but I appreciate it," said E.J.

"Told you, could have been Shasta," said Hall.

"Seems like more," said E.J.

"*Tenaha, Timpson, Bobo, and Blair.*"

"The Tex Ritter song? I didn't know anybody remembered it. That's my grandad's era," said E.J.

"More than a song. Kind of slang term for a section of Highway Fifty-Nine where a lot of folks got stopped with drugs and relieved of a lot of unnecessary cash and vehicles when you worked on the road."

"I remember those days. Roadside waivers were still legal," said E.J.

"At the bureau, we took the complaints, and we knew who was dirty even when we couldn't catch them," said Hall.

"I swear—"

"Point is, we also knew who the good guys were who

ended things when they came upon them. I knew you before we ever met. The longer I hold this job, the more I realize there's no black and white. It's the shades of grey we see that make good police. You're good police, and I don't need anybody to tell me that."

"I like to believe I call balls and strikes," said E.J.

"Don't we all," said Hall.

E.J. slid his spurs back, and the horse took off.

ABOUT ATMOSPHERE PRESS

ATMOSPHERE PRESS is an independent, full-service publisher for excellent books in all genres and for all audiences. Learn more about what we do at atmospherepress.com.

We encourage you to check out some of Atmosphere's latest releases, which are available at Amazon.com and via order from your local bookstore:

Where No Man Pursueth, a novel by Micheal E. Jimerson

Shadows of Robyst, a novel by K. E. Maroudas

Dying to Live, a novel by Barbara Macpherson Reyelts

Looking for Lawson, a novel by Mark Kirby

Surrogate Colony, a novel by Boshra Rasti

Á Deux, a novel by Alexey L. Kovalev

What If It Were True, a novel by Eileen Wesel

Sunflowers Beneath the Snow, a novel by Teri M. Brown

Solitario: The Lonely One, a novel by John Manuel

The Fourth Wall, a novel by Scott Petty

Rx, a novel by Garin Cycholl

Knights of the Air: Book 1: Rage!, a novel by Iain Stewart

Heartheaded, a novel by Constantina Pappas

ABOUT THE AUTHOR

MICHEAL E. JIMERSON lives with his wife, Mona, and son, David, on the family farm where he was raised in East Texas. Mona runs Simply Southern, a catering business. David keeps both his parents on the baseball field most of the year.

Micheal graduated from the Baylor University School of Law in 1993. Thereafter, he entered private practice. He concentrated on personal injury, civil litigation, and criminal defense. *Pro Bono* work for the local women's center led him to be elected office as County and District Attorney.

The privilege to serve as an elected prosecutor has led to many jury trials, accolades, and documentaries, but more important it has provided an opportunity to witness the timeless values, faith, and courage of ordinary people facing down exceptional evil every day.